D0439182

THE MASTER
MAGICIAN

ALSO BY CHARLIE N. HOLMBERG

The Paper Magician
The Glass Magician

Followed by Frost

THE MASTER MAGICIAN

CHARLIE N. HOLMBERG

47NORTH

Text copyright © 2015 Charlie N. Holmberg
All rights reserved.

Published by 47North, Seattle

www.apub.com

Amazon, the Amazon logo, and 47North are trademarks of Amazon.com, Inc., or its affiliates.

ISBN-13: 9781477828694
ISBN-10: 1477828699

Cover design by Megan Haggerty

Library of Congress Control Number: 2014956168

Printed in the United States of America

To the person who works all materials:
Phil Nicholes, my dad. Thanks for teaching me the
importance of hard work.

CHAPTER 1

CEONY, WEARING HER RED apprentice's apron over a ruffled blouse and plain brown skirt, stood on her tiptoes on a three-legged stool and stuck a square of white paper against the east wall of the Holloways' living room, right where the wall met the ceiling. The family was celebrating Mr. Holloway's awarding of the Africa General Service Medal, and had submitted a request to hire the local Folder—Magician Emery Thane—to fashion the party decorations.

Of course Emery had passed the "frivolous task" on to his apprentice.

Ceony stepped down from the stool and backed up to the center of the room to survey her work. The large living space already had most of its furniture removed for the sake of the elaborate decorations. Thus far, Ceony had adhered twenty-four bearing squares to the wall and plopped large sheets of plain white paper around the room, cut according to the measurements Mrs. Holloway had sent via telegram.

After ensuring her bearing squares aligned correctly, she said, "Affix."

Twenty-four long sheets of paper leapt up from their looping coils on the ground like hares darting through a field, each surging toward its appointed bearing square and latching to it. The heavy sheets sagged from their bearing squares until Ceony called out, "Flatten," and the sheets adhered to the walls like wallpaper, evenly coating the room in white. Minus the stairs on the north wall, of course.

Mrs. Holloway had requested a jungle theme to reflect her husband's brief campaign in Africa, and so Ceony—after referencing several books on the subject—had written the requisite spells on the backs of the large paper sheets and Folded the tips of their corners accordingly. Now she only had to test her design.

"Portray," she ordered, and to her relief each sheet darkened into hues of green and brown, coloring and morphing the same way a paper doll would. Dark swathes of hunter green cast shadows against the walls, and brighter mints and chartreuses gave the appearance of light pouring unevenly through leafy canopies threaded with vines. Wisps of olive formed patches of long, wild grass amid shades of umber and mahogany in the uneven soil near the floorboards, and the song of a red-throated loon called between fluttering bug wings in the distance. At least, Ceony's best rendition of a red-throated loon. She had never actually heard one before, only guessed on the sound based on what bizarre African birds she had been able to find in the zoo.

Ceony circled the room with small steps, taking in her massive illusion, a live mural created from the magic of her own hands. Every thirty seconds a long-eared mouse skittered between two trees, and every fifteen seconds leaves and vines rustled in a gentle breeze. Despite not holding paper, her fingers tingled with it. Spells like these never ceased to amaze her.

She let out a long breath. No mistakes—good. If she couldn't perform illusions like this one flawlessly now, she'd never pull them off when she tested for her magicianship next month. She planned to take the test within a week of her two-year anniversary as Emery Thane's second-and-a-half apprentice.

Retreating to the front door, Ceony crouched over her large tote bag of spells and pulled out a wooden case filled with starlights, which Langston, Emery's first apprentice, had taught her to Fold so long ago. The small pillow-like stars were no larger than a farthing, and all had been Folded using amber-colored paper, although the merchant who sold the paper to Ceony had listed the color as "goldenrod." Ceony had Folded dozens of the stars over three days' time, until her fingers cramped and she feared early arthritis. She had then affixed a small zigzag of paper to the back of each star, also amber.

She dumped the starlights onto the darkly polished floorboards and commanded, "Float."

The starlights all turned zigzag side up and glided like bubbles to the ceiling. Ceony ordered them, "Glow," and the starlights burned with a soft internal fire. Once the Holloways extinguished the electric lights, the room would take on an eerie and somewhat romantic radiance.

Ceony animated small paper butterflies that would flutter about the room, as well as triangular confetti across the floor that would shift around guests' feet, giving the illusion of blowing wind. She had even Folded and enchanted paper napkins for the dinner, which would glow turquoise and read "Congratulations, Alton Holloway" when the guests unfurled them. She had considered including the occasional ghostly story illusion of an elephant or lion, but she would need to stay during the party in order to read the spells. That, and she feared some of the older guests might react poorly. Just a few months ago she'd read an article in the paper about a grandmother who'd had a heart attack after seeing a mirror illusion of an oncoming train by the theatre, an ill-advised advertisement for the new American play being performed there. It would surely ruin the party if a guest attempted to shoot a paper lion.

As Ceony released animated songbirds with the instructions to only fly close to the ceiling, Mrs. Holloway came down the stairs and let out a startled cry, which was fortunately followed by a wide, tooth-filled smile.

"Oh, it's astounding! Just magnificent!" she cried, hands pressed to her heavily powdered cheeks. "Worth every pound! And you're just an apprentice."

"I hope to test for my magicianship next month," Ceony said, though she beamed under the compliment.

Mrs. Holloway clapped her hands twice. "If you need a recommendation, dear, I will give you one. Oh, Alton will be so surprised!" She turned to the stairs. "Martha! Martha, leave the laundry a moment and come see!"

Ceony grabbed her bag—much lighter now—and bowed out of the home before her customer's excitement could grow too out of hand. The decorations needed no further maintenance, and Mrs. Holloway had prepaid by check earlier that week. Emery would no doubt let her keep the entire sum—a considerable sum—though apprentices usually had to work for free, minus a monthly stipend. She would send most of the money to her parents, who had finally moved out of the Mill Squats and taken up a flat in Poplar. Her mother, especially, hated receiving "charity," but Ceony could be just as stubborn.

Crouching on the walk outside, Ceony pulled out a sheet of paper and created a small glider with oblong wings, then wrote in its center the address for the intersection at the end of the street. Bringing it to life with the command "Breathe," she whispered coordinates to it and released it to the wind. The little glider flipped a loop and took off southward.

Slipping her bag over her shoulder, Ceony started down the walk, her simple brown skirt swishing about her ankles, her two-inch heels clicking like shoed horse hooves against the ground. This was a ritzy suburb of London, with a great deal of green space between its houses, half of which were guarded by elaborate stonework or wrought-iron fences. A few were adorned with Smelter-worked ornamentation, such as elinvar pickets that rotated in response to passersby and brass gate locks that unlatched themselves when an expected visitor drew near. The year had matured enough to erase all lingering signs of winter, and May flowers bustled up in tidy gardens beyond the fences. A few had even managed to grow in cracks where the walk met the cobblestones, in utter disregard of the precise order of the neighborhood. A breeze tousled a few stray hairs from the French twist holding back Ceony's pumpkin-colored mane. She tucked them behind her ear.

A few minutes after Ceony reached the corner of Holland and Addison, a buggy pulled off the road and up to the curb. Ceony bent down to peer through the glassless passenger window.

"Hello, Frank," she said. "I haven't ridden with you in a good while."

The middle-aged man grinned and tipped his bowler hat toward her, the small glider she had Folded pinched between his index and middle fingers. "Always a pleasure, Miss Twill. Heading toward Beckenham again?"

"Yes, please, to the cottage," she said, moving to the back door. "No need to get up," she added as Frank reached for the driver door's latch to help her in. She slid into the backseat quickly and patted the seat before her to signal she was settled. Frank waited a moment for traffic to pass before pulling out onto Addison Avenue.

Ceony leaned against the backrest as the buggy made the forty-five-minute trip back to Emery's cottage. She watched the city flash by her window, the houses gradually moving closer together and shrinking in square footage, the streets and walks filling with more and more civilians carving through another day. She saw a baker airing smoke out of his small shop, boys playing marbles in a narrow alley space, and a mother pushing a stroller while a young boy held on to the pocket in her skirt. This last sight made Ceony think of one of the first spells she had ever learned, a fortune-telling spell called a "fortuity box." She would never forget what she'd once seen in one—a warm, blessed image of herself standing on a flowering hilltop with two children, presumably her own. The man standing beside her in that vision had been none other than her assigned tutor. There was a stigma attached to the very idea of a romance with her mentor, of course, which was why Ceony had confided her secret concerning the paper magician to no one save her mother, who had only met Magician Emery Thane once.

Eventually the city died away, and Frank drove the buggy up the familiar dirt path toward the cottage, dotted with spring-green trees along the way. Ceony averted her gaze from the river beyond it. A small river, but one that unnerved her still. Twenty months ago Ceony had worried that she and Emery would have to leave the quaint, country-esque cottage behind for the sake of safety, but with their enemies either dead, jailed, or in a perpetual state of being frozen, danger had decided to leave them alone. It was a relief, if for no other reason than that Ceony surely wouldn't be ready to test for her magicianship if she had to battle for her life every ninety days.

Reaching into the purse nestled in the corner of the tote bag, Ceony slid her fingers over the round surface of a makeup compact, tracing the engraved Celtic knot on its surface. She shouldn't make light of her past . . . adventures . . . even in fanciful thoughts. The cost had been steep. She swallowed a bitter taste of shame.

The buggy pulled up to the cottage, which from the road looked like a dilapidated, towering mansion infested with poltergeists, complete with self-made wind and cawing crows. The "haunted house" was Emery's favorite illusion to put about his home, more so than the barren plot or the quaking graveyard he had tried out last March. Ceony's protests had made him take it down after two weeks. Or perhaps it was the milkman's heart arrhythmia that had ultimately convinced him.

The illusions were Folded about the fence, so their spells vanished as soon as Ceony stepped past the gate, revealing the house as it was: yellow-bricked with a porch Ceony and Emery had painted russet two weeks ago. A short stone walk bordered a garden of paper daffodils, and a flesh-and-blood starling clung to the ivy hanging over the office window, shrieking at the small paper dog sniffing too close to its nest.

"Fennel!" Ceony called, and the paper dog lifted his head to seek her out with his eyeless face. He barked twice, a wispy, papery sound, and bounded down the path toward Ceony, leaving prints in the dirt between the tiles. A few months ago, he would have barely left a mark, but Ceony had given him plastic bones back in February. It had taken months of study to learn how to form the bones and joints so that they'd move with Fennel, though the Polymaking spell that held them together had been simple enough to master. She had done the magic in secret, of course. These were studies best kept quiet.

The dog jumped at Ceony's feet and propped his front paws on her shoes, wagging his plastic-reinforced paper tail wildly from side to side. Ceony stooped down to scratch him under the chin.

"Come on," she said, and Fennel ran ahead of her to the front door, where he waited with a whipping tail, his nose buried in the doorjamb. When Ceony opened the door, Fennel ran to the end of the hall and back, then dived into the perfect clutter of the front room, where he immediately began chewing on a wad of stuffing protruding from the sofa's most threadbare cushion.

Ceony headed first to Emery's office, a rectangular room filled with shelves bearing stacks of paper of varying thicknesses, colors, and sizes. The ivy over the window gave the room a dark-aquamarine light, almost as if the cottage were submerged beneath the ocean. Emery's desk sat across from the door. Heaps of paper, a wire note holder, glue and scissors, half-read books, a jar of pens, and a vial of ink littered the desk's surface, though *littered* may not have been the best word to describe it. Every item fit into its neighboring items like pieces of a puzzle, and nothing was askew. Only a fraction of elbow room to work in, but the desk, like everything in the cottage, looked as immaculate as a mess could look. In all her twenty-one years, Ceony had never met a hoarder so tidy. At present, the room was empty.

Behind the desk hung a wood-framed corkboard, upon which Ceony and Emery both pinned work orders, receipts, telegrams, and memos, all neatly spaced from one another, fitting together like brickwork. Emery's doing, of course. Ceony pulled Mrs. Holloway's decoration request from its brass tack and took it to the dustbin, but first commanded it, "Shred."

The work order tore itself into a dozen long pieces and fluttered into the dustbin like snow.

After leaving the office, Ceony closed the door behind her so Fennel wouldn't make a mess and passed through the kitchen and dining room to the stairs leading to the second floor, where the bedrooms, lavatory, and library were situated. Her room was the first door on the left, and she stepped inside to drop off her tote bag.

The room looked much different now than it had when she arrived two years ago. She'd moved the bed to the far corner near the closet and set her desk by the window, since she spent most of her time in her room there, either Folding or writing the occasional paper when Emery went on an academic whim. She'd stained the floorboards a deep cherry during a bout of boredom last winter, and her own paper creations adorned the walls and ceiling, much the way Emery's decorated the wainscoting of the kitchen and dining room. Tiny paper dancers dressed in elaborate ballerina skirts seemed to dance down one wall, and an assortment of premade chain spells hung from the other. Paper carnations with spiraling petals, alternating red and blue, framed her window; fringed paper garlands in the same colors bordered her closet door. Paper star ornaments with twelve or eighteen spikes hung on string from the ceiling, varying in size from half a fist to a dinner plate. Paper feathers cut from women's magazines, a mobile of animated sea horses, and starlights ringed her nightstand, upon which sat a vase of red paper roses Emery had created for her twentieth birthday. A four-foot-tall paper cutout of London occupied the wall space at the head of her bed like a giant snowflake—a gift Emery had made for her two Christmases ago. Paper clouds hovered near the door, and baby-pink paper pom-poms sat upon a two-shelved bookcase where Ceony stored her textbooks.

All of the décor had accumulated over one year and eleven months' time; it wasn't until Ceony's baby sister—Margo—visited in April that Ceony realized she had created something of a wonderland.

A crinkled envelope rested on her pillow. Abandoning the tote bag, Ceony approached it and felt its contents: the rubber buttons she had ordered from the *Magicians Today* catalog. She stashed the small package in the bottom drawer of her desk, where the book *Precise Calculations of Fire Conjuring* was hidden, along with certain other materials she preferred to keep out of sight, and trotted to Emery's room.

She knocked, opened the door, but found the space empty. The library as well.

She heard a thump overhead.

"Working on the big spells again," she murmured to herself, opening the door to the set of stairs that led to the home's third story, which made up in height what it lacked in floor space. Emery didn't work on his "big spells" often, but when he did Ceony could count on him being absent for entire twenty-four-hour periods.

He'd finished his seven-foot-long paper-puff-shooting "elephant" gun in March, which he donated to the boys' orphanage in Sheffield. She wondered what absurd idea he'd put his hands to now.

In the farthest corner of the third floor, Jonto—Emery's skeletal paper butler—hung by a noose from a nail in the ceiling, hovering over a mess of rolled paper tubes, tape, and symmetrical cuts of paper. Emery, wearing his newest coat, a maroon-colored one, stood on a stool beside him, affixing a six-foot-long *bat wing* to Jonto's spine.

Ceony blinked, taking in the sight. She really shouldn't be surprised.

"I thought I had a few more years before I saw the angel of death," she said, folding her arms under her breasts. "Even just half of him."

Emery teetered on the stool and glanced over his shoulders, both hands holding up the stiff paper that would form the end of Jonto's left wing. His raven hair danced about his jaw as he did so, and his vivid green eyes gleamed like afternoon sunlight.

Even now, Ceony could lose herself in those eyes.

"Ceony!" he exclaimed, turning back to his project and finishing his work with the wing. "I wasn't expecting you back for another hour!"

"Her requests weren't as complicated as we feared," Ceony said, a smile teasing her lips. "Care to explain why you're making a dragon of Jonto?"

Emery stepped down from the stool and rolled his shoulders. "I had a peddler today."

"A peddler?"

"Selling shoe polish," he said. He rubbed the stubble at the base of his chin. "Decently priced, I must say."

Ceony nodded. "And so Jonto needs wings."

He smirked. "I haven't had a peddler since I moved here," he explained. He brushed bits of paper from his coat and pants and crossed the room, passing by the second version of his giant paper glider, as Ceony had lost the first one. "Apparently the place's facade isn't nearly as menacing as it used to be. I blame Joseph Conrad's popularity for that. And since we've decided against the graveyard, I thought I'd have Jonto, or the 'angel of death,' as you so aptly put it, terrorize further inquisitors away."

Ceony laughed. "You're going to keep him outside? What if it rains?"

"Hmm," Emery said, stroking one of his long sideburns. "I'll have to make the wings detachable. I think it's a viable option, though."

He smiled, more in his eyes than in his mouth—the most genuine of smiles—clasped Ceony's shoulders, and chastely kissed her on the mouth.

"Now," he said, tucking that stray piece of hair back behind Ceony's ear, "what do I have to do to convince you to make kidney pie for dinner?"

"Kidney pie?" Ceony repeated, brow raised. "Do we even have kidneys?"

"As of this morning," he replied.

Ceony covered her mouth in feigned shock. "No. He didn't buy groceries *by himself*, did he?"

"I had to meet with the Praff board. For apprentices," he said with a shrug. "The boy I paid to pick up everything did a fine job."

Ceony rolled her eyes, but her smile stayed. "All right, but I'll have to start on it now. And I'm not gone yet, mind you."

Emery squeezed her shoulders before releasing her. "They do like to stay ahead of things. Graduations have been a mess since Patrice left."

Ceony nodded. Mg. Aviosky had resigned from the Tagis Praff School for the Magically Inclined a year and a half ago, after being offered a position on the Magicians' Cabinet, Department of Education.

Excusing herself, Ceony headed back to the first floor, where an anxious Fennel sat by the stair door, waiting to be let up. The kidneys had been wrapped in paper and tucked into the kitchen icebox, which had a cold confetti spell cast over it. Ceony brushed off pieces of round confetti from the package and set to work. She rinsed the kidneys until the water ran clear, then fried them in a saucepan with bay leaf, thyme, and onion. She diced and mashed tomatoes while they cooked, but had to substitute a bit of vinegar for the mustard, since they were out.

With nothing urgent in her study roster, Ceony decided to break some eggs and whip up a crème brûlée for dessert; one of Mrs.

Holloway's maids had mentioned the dish was being served at the party, and now Ceony had a hankering for it. She beat the cream, egg yolks, and sugar until her arm ached, then poured the pudding into two ramekins, which she set in the oven next to the kidney pie.

When both dishes had finished baking, Ceony pulled them out and set the table. Listening for Emery's footsteps and hearing none, she opened the cupboard where she kept her cookbooks and, from the binding of *French Cuisine*, retrieved a small matchbox, which contained a few matches and a ball of phosphorus. Palming it in her left hand, Ceony grabbed a wooden spoon with her right and said, "Material made by earth, your handler summons you. Unlink to me as I link through you, unto this very day."

It was not the first time Ceony had severed her supposedly unbreakable bond to paper, nor was it the second. She set the spoon down, pressed her hand to her chest, and said, "Material made by man, I summon you. Link to me as I link to you, unto this very day."

Finally, she lit a match and murmured, "Material made by man, your creator summons you. Link to me as I link to you through my years, until the day I die and become earth."

She then grit her teeth and stuck her fingers into the flame. To her relief, it didn't burn her, which meant she had bonded to it. Pyres were immune to fire they created themselves—a nice perk to the magic, needless to say.

Her skin tingled from the flames, a surprisingly pleasant sensation, until the match died out. She stuck the matchbox into her apron pocket. She'd need the ball of phosphorus to break her bond to fire, once she finished using it.

Opening the oven door, Ceony coaxed forward a spark with the command "Arise," then pulled forth a small flame at the tip of her index finger with "Flare."

Pyre magic was the last materials magic Ceony had tested for herself, for one slip could injure her or burn down the house. She had tried out her first spell with her feet submerged in the bathtub. Fortunately, she had only suffered a rather nasty blister. Now she confined herself to small, novice spells.

She used the tiny flame to caramelize the tops of her crème brûlée. Hearing Emery's steps on the stairs, she blew out the fire rather than commanding it "Cease."

"Smells wonderful," Emery said, stepping into the dining room. "Ah, I got lost in myself. I should have set the table," he added when he saw she had already done just that.

"I needed something to do while I browned this pastry," Ceony said, grabbing a towel and carrying the kidney pie to the table.

Emery stroked her neck with the back of his fingers, sending cool shivers down her shoulders. "Thank you," he said.

She smiled, feeling the slightest pink prickle her cheeks. Emery pulled out her chair and she sat, tugging off her apron and slinging it across the back.

Absent-mindedly, Ceony stuck her hand in her pocket and ran her fingers over the matchbox. She'd need to restore her bond to paper as soon as dinner concluded. Surely Emery wouldn't give her a surprise test midmeal, not after she'd handled the Holloways' party for him.

She stabbed a slice of kidney pie with her fork. In a way, the magic—the bond breaking—felt like cheating.

The man she had learned it from would probably agree, were he still alive.

CHAPTER 2

AFTER DINNER EMERY washed the dishes and Ceony hurried upstairs to her room, phosphorus in hand, to break her bond to fire. She resealed herself to paper while stroking Fennel's hairless body, then took out her rubber buttons for examination. She wanted to use them to create sturdy padding for Fennel's paws. They were close to the right size, so hopefully she wouldn't have to manipulate the material too much. She could hardly ask for Emery's assistance in such a task.

She paused, rubber in hand. Did she really have time to be doing this?

After learning the secrets of bond breaking in Mg. Aviosky's home nearly two years ago—a secret only she knew—Ceony had awoken in a hospital bed. Her body, which had been sliced open like a Christmas turkey, was intact, having been healed by an Excisioner. The magician who'd saved her life was legally sanctioned to work with his material, but the idea of anyone using blood magic on her was horrifying, particularly at that time, only moments after she'd watched an Excisioner murder her dear friend.

She had awoken as a Gaffer—a glass magician—having changed her material to save her life. After rebonding herself to paper, she had forced herself to forget Grath's bizarre magic for two months.

But hers was a mind that couldn't forget. She remembered everything, down to the most minute detail: her first spelling test in the fifth grade, the recipe for kidney pie, even the shoe buckles Mg. Aviosky wore the first time Ceony met her on September 18, 1901.

She remembered the way Mg. Aviosky's body had hung from the rafters of her house, her wrists swollen and her head lolling to one side. She remembered every piece of glass that had cut through her own skin—she felt them slicing through her now and shivered, rubbing the gooseflesh away. And she remembered the terrified look in her friend Delilah's eyes well enough that, had she any skill in drawing, she could sketch it blindfolded.

So she knew exactly how Grath Cobalt had broken and resealed his bonds to become an Excisioner.

She had told Emery about her new ability in the hospital—proved it, even—without sharing the details. He had never asked for them. What little knowledge he possessed about her ability to shift materials had not sat comfortably. Understandable—Ceony had more or less achieved the equivalent of breaking gravity. She hadn't shared her desire to delve into the other magics, what with their newfound relationship being as precarious as it was.

Initially, she'd planned to never test her new, unwanted knowledge, and she'd allowed him to think she still felt that way. While she didn't think he would judge her, she couldn't stomach the thought of disappointing him.

So a secret it had stayed.

At first she set strict rules for herself: no studies in other materials magics until her Folding studies had been completed, along with all her other duties as an apprentice. She'd only broken her rule a few times, for spells too alluring and interesting to pass up, like enchanting bullets or altering her image in a mirror's reflection.

But now, with the test for her magicianship only a month away, could she really spare time to adhere rubber to her paper pup's paws?

She closed her fingers around the rubber buttons. A part of her knew she was ready. She knew how to mold and animate creatures made of dozens of pieces of paper. She knew how to create the most abstruse paper illusions, how to construct fifty-four different paper chains, and how to make paper vibrate so quickly it exploded. She could probably teach her own apprentice!

But still . . . Ceony didn't know *what* she would be tested on, or how. Emery claimed he could not reveal any details about the testing process. For that reason alone, Ceony knew she should study harder. Study *Folding*, study every possible angle of paper magic. Any articles or essays that might be new to her, even if the content wasn't.

With a sigh, she set down the rubber buttons. She still had leisure time. There would be the opportunity to upgrade Fennel then.

Glancing up, Ceony peered out her window, which was half-concealed by the branches of an alder tree. A brilliant pink highlighted the tree's leaves, and the sky beyond looked lavender.

Tucking back that stray piece of hair, Ceony walked to the library, where the window was broader and un-skewed.

The view was beautiful.

Ceony had never appreciated sunsets until becoming a Folding apprentice. Her home in the Mill Squats had been surrounded by tall buildings, which blocked out the horizon and most of the sky. At Tagis Praff, despite having a room on the sixth floor of the student tower, she'd always been too focused on her endless mounds of homework to give heed to the palette of the setting sun.

Here at the cottage, where city met country, where no other people or architecture could obstruct her vision, Ceony had discovered the allure of sunsets.

Tonight several chunky clouds haloed the sun, acting as canvas to its dying light. They glowed a bright apricot where they were closest to the cap of gold descending beyond the hills, turning salmon and violet farther out, until they met the deepening azure of the evening sky. The clouds looked like ethereal creatures, sky-fish swimming across the blue expanse, following the sun to the other side of the world.

A hand settled on her shoulder, just at the base of her neck, pulling Ceony from the mural beyond the glass.

"How hopelessly romantic," Emery said, the corner of his lip tugging upward almost enough to make a dimple. His eyes took on a more olive hue in the window's light. His fingers felt cold from the dishwater.

"Just like the novels," Ceony agreed, stepping back into his arm and leaning against him. "The same thought occurred to me. I was rather hoping we could re-create a scene from *Jane Eyre*."

"I admit I'm ignorant on that one."

"Quite good," she said. "In a sad way, but it ends well."

Emery turned toward her and lifted his hand to her jaw. "As long as it ends well," he said. He ran his thumb along her cheek and studied her for a moment, his gem-like eyes gliding over her mouth, her cheekbones, her eyes. Ceony loved it when he looked at her like that. It made her feel . . . *present*.

She stood on her toes, and Emery closed the rest of the space between them, touching his lips to hers.

Despite her keen memory, Ceony couldn't recall how many times she'd kissed Emery Thane since that day outside the train station nearly two years ago. Many times, yet the feel of his mouth still filled her with childish delight, still made her blood course faster.

Perhaps too fast.

Her fingers danced up his neck and over his earlobes, traced the length of his sideburns and the day's worth of stubble that bordered them. The smells of him—brown sugar, stationery, charcoal—filled her lungs as she broke for a breath. Then she kissed him the way a lady should never kiss a man to whom she was not wed.

The tip of his tongue slid over her bottom lip, but he wouldn't oblige for long. Sometimes Ceony wished he would forget she was a lady. He certainly never forgot he was a gentleman, no matter how hard Ceony tried to coax the rogue out of him.

Her back met a bookshelf. She curled a lock of Emery's hair around her pinky, enticing him further. It worked for a moment, a second, really, before the kiss began to slow, Emery reining himself in as always. Kisses like these could lead to other things, especially in a house where the only possible interruption came in the form of a paper dog. But Emery—noble Emery—would not do other things with Ceony outside the bond of matrimony, and he wouldn't marry her so long as she held the title of "apprentice." He had said so himself, twice.

All the more reason for her to test for her magicianship as soon as possible.

They broke apart, their breaths spanning the short distance between them.

Ceony opened her eyes. "Yes, just like in the novels," she whispered.

Emery chuckled, then kissed her forehead. "These books you're reading . . . I question your taste, Miss Twill."

She straightened the collar of his maroon coat. "I'll read what I please, Mr. Thane."

"I have a suggestion," he said with a wry smile, stepping away and glancing back at the sunset, which had already grown ruddier. "I have a dissertation on eighteenth-century Folding basics on interlibrary loan. It's wonderfully dry and has all its nouns capitalized. I think you'll enjoy it."

Ceony frowned. "You want me to study primitive Folding techniques?"

"Only subprimitive," he said, a smirk playing on his lips. "It never hurts to go back to basics, even if you think you know them."

"I do know them."

"Are you sure?"

Ceony paused. "Is this a hint for my test?"

Emery stuck his hands in his trouser pockets. "I am not allowed to give you any hints, Ceony. I wouldn't dare jeopardize your passing."

His tone grew a little more serious on that last sentence. Stepping over to the table against the west wall, he patted his hand on a worn book as thick as Ceony's wrist. Her shoulders slumped. Surely this tome wouldn't help her win her magicianship.

But she was not any more willing to risk her chances of passing than Emery was. Sighing—louder than necessary—Ceony grasped the heavy volume in both hands and heaved it onto her hip.

The telegraph on the table began tapping.

Emery raised an eyebrow. Ceony held still and listened intently, translating the Morse code in her head. *An interesting query. I acce*—

"Study hard," Emery said with a hand on her back. He pushed her toward the hallway.

"But what about—"

His eyes brightened. "It's a secret, dearest." And with that, he shut the library door.

Ceony frowned, then pressed her ear to the wood, trying to make out the sound of the telegraph. Two seconds later Emery pounded against the door. He had already learned all her eavesdropping tactics during their time together.

Frowning, Ceony retreated into her bedroom and cracked open the dissertation, waving away the dust that spun up from its thick cover.

"Chapter One: The Half-Point Fold."

It was going to be a long night.

The clouds thickened after the sunset, veiling the night stars. By the time Ceony turned off her lamp to go to sleep, rain had begun to fall. It came first as a sprinkle, then a shower. A gale picked up and woke Ceony as it whistled through the eaves, ripping bits of paper illusion spells from the walls and fence. No amount of waterproofing could save the spells from a squall like this one.

As the night grew colder, rain turned to hail. It clacked against the roof and window like a thousand telegraphed messages. Covering her head with her pillow, Ceony returned to her slumber . . .

Rain surrounded her in her bedroom, pouring down through a vanished roof, pelting the furniture and peeling paper art from the walls. Ceony stood in the middle of the room in a black skirt and white button-up shirt with a gray ascot around her neck—her student uniform from the Tagis Praff School for the Magically Inclined. She stood over a drain in the floor, but something was clogging it. Rainwater puddled about her feet, and she smashed her shoe into the drain over and over, trying to force the water down.

The obstruction wouldn't budge.

She turned but couldn't find the door to the room. The furniture had vanished as well, leaving her with only wood and rain. Raindrops grew in size, falling now like long quilting needles, splashing against her skin, dribbling from her uniform into the growing lake churning around her legs. The cold water climbed up her knees, her thighs.

Ceony's heart seized. She frantically waded through the dark water, searching for something to stand on, but found nothing. No desk, no bed, no ladder or stool. No doors anywhere. Even the windowsill had vanished beneath the beating storm.

"Help!" she cried, but her voice couldn't pierce the racket of the percussing rain. It beat into her harder and harder, prodding her like shards of glass. Water surged over her hips, her navel.

She couldn't swim. She tried to float, tried to push her pelvis toward the sky as Emery had instructed her the one time he tried to teach her, but she only sank.

Her head went below the water. She flailed, kicked off the floor to come back up.

Breaking through the water's surface, she heard someone cry, "Ceony!"

She turned toward the voice, splashing in the water, desperately trying to keep air in her lungs. And there she was. Delilah. Sitting atop a bookshelf floating on its side, reaching her hand out toward Ceony. In her other hand, she clutched the compact mirror she'd given Ceony for her twentieth birthday, its embellished Celtic knot pressed into her palm.

"Swim!" Delilah shouted.

"I can't!" Ceony cried. Water lapped into her mouth and she coughed. Her toes sought the floorboards, but they had vanished. Everything had vanished but the water and the rain. She was drowning in an endless ocean, no land in sight.

Delilah reached her hand out farther. "Hurry!" she cried.

Ceony kicked and paddled, reaching once, twice for Delilah's fingers. On the third attempt, she caught Delilah's wrist.

But Delilah frowned. Her brown eyes rolled back into her head, and Ceony stared in horror as Delilah's arm fragmented from her body in uneven pieces, drizzling blood into the water. Ceony screamed as the rest of her friend disassembled like a broken mannequin, until the only tangible trace of her was a scarlet mess atop a sinking bookshelf—

Ceony gasped and sat up in bed, her pillow toppling to the floor. She blinked several times, taking in her dry room, listening to the patter of rain against her window. The hail had stopped.

Dragging the back of her hand across her forehead, Ceony took a deep breath, listening to the thrumming of her pulse in her ears. Her neck pounded with blood.

Blood.

She threw back her blankets, searching beneath them for something, anything. She scanned the room, empty save for where Fennel slept on the desk chair.

Another deep breath, and another, but still her pulse hammered. She stood and paced to the other side of her room and back, running her hands over her messy braid.

She hadn't had a nightmare like that for months. She hated it when they felt so . . . real.

Tears threatened her eyes, so Ceony looked up at the ceiling and blinked rapidly, urging them away.

She hadn't made it to Delilah's funeral, being unconscious in a hospital bed, but Clemson, the Pyre apprentice she'd met at the factory tour, later told her it had rained.

Light flashed outside her window, followed by thunder almost as loud as the beating of her heart. Ceony stared at the mess of her bed, then at Fennel.

She swallowed, stood. Waited. Stared.

She picked up her pillow and padded to her door, cracking it open. Peered down the dark hallway. The dimmest candlelight shone from behind the farthest door on the right. Emery never had invested in magicked lamps.

Chewing on her bottom lip, Ceony moved toward it. She adjusted her nightgown and knocked, as softly as her trembling fingers could manage. She didn't want to wake him if he had already—

"Yes?" his voice said through the door. How late was it, for him to still be awake?

She cracked the door open. Emery lay in his bed, covers up to his hips, reading, but he reached over and set the book down on his nightstand. His candle only had a half inch of wax left to burn. She had caught him just in time.

His eyes met hers, and his forehead wrinkled. "Are you all right, Ceony?"

She flushed, feeling like a child. "I . . . I'm sorry. I just . . . Can I sleep on your floor?"

His expression didn't change. He sat up. "Are you ill?" he asked, ready to stand.

"I just . . . I'm not sleeping well. Again," she admitted. "I'll be quiet. I just . . . I don't want to sleep alone, not tonight. Please?"

His lips pressed together. He knew about her nightmares. They had been awful after Delilah died. After her . . . murder. Ceony had slept with a light on for three weeks. They came infrequently now, but when they did come, Ceony dreamed with a vengeance.

He gestured for her to come, and Ceony stepped into the room. "I'm sorry, I—"

"Ceony," he said softly, "don't apologize."

He pulled back his covers and scooted over, making room for one more.

She hesitated—she had never slept in Emery's *bed* before—but she yearned for company. Yearned for him. A paper chain she could neither see nor touch pulled her toward him, and the spell to stop it was the only one she didn't know.

She plopped her pillow down beside his and crawled onto the mattress. Emery snuffed the candle with his thumb and lay down on his side, looping one arm around Ceony's waist, holding her against his chest.

So warm. Ceony relaxed into the embrace, listened to Emery's familiar heartbeat, his calm breathing. Matched her breaths to his.

Gradually the images of her nightmare faded from her mind, and Ceony fell into a safe and dreamless sleep.

CHAPTER 3

CEONY AWOKE WITH a sore right shoulder and a numb right ear, the right side of her face still burrowed into her pillow. She blinked at the steady sunlight streaming in through the uncovered window opposite the bed. It looked to be around seven thirty, perhaps eight. It took her a moment to identify that the cluttered nightstand and window were not her own. The blankets were definitely Emery's.

She sat up, blood running back into her ear, and scanned the bed. Empty, and made up on one side. She rubbed her eyes and pulled the tie from her messy braid, running her fingers through the long, wavy locks.

Her chest flushed, just a little, more in temperature than in color. She wasn't as embarrassed as perhaps she should be . . . *She* had requested the floor, after all. Not that she minded the invitation. Had Ceony been in a better state of mind, she might have taken advantage of it.

She smiled, picturing what Mg. Aviosky's face would look like if the Gaffer ever got wind of last night's arrangement. She'd be furious.

Mg. Aviosky knew about their special relationship, of course. At least, Ceony felt certain she knew. She'd confessed her feelings for Emery to her once mentor, but nothing more. Still, the way Mg. Aviosky's eyes narrowed when she saw Ceony and Emery together, that distinct hum she made in her throat, told Ceony the Gaffer assumed more. Hopefully no one else did . . . at least not yet.

The door opened then, and Emery entered back-first, carrying a small wooden tray in his hands. Fennel scurried in between his feet and barked, sniffing about the bed and wagging his tail. The mattress was too tall for him to leap upon it.

Emery, already dressed, set the tray on the bed. It held two pieces of buttered toast and a seven-minute egg.

"Oh, Emery, you didn't have to do this," Ceony said.

Emery shrugged. "I suppose I didn't," he replied. He sat on the opposite corner of the bed, the mattress's edge, so as not to disturb the tray. "Are you feeling all right?"

"Mm," she said, mouth full of toast. She swallowed and added, "Thank you."

He merely smiled. Fennel, giving up on Ceony's side of the bed, scampered over to Emery's feet and began tugging at his pant leg.

"Emery," Ceony said, pausing her breakfast, "what was that telegram about yesterday?"

"Hm?" he asked, shaking Fennel free. For a moment, Ceony imagined equipping the paper dog with more substantial teeth— plastic, or perhaps steel. The latter would likely weigh his head down. And what did Ceony need a dog with steel teeth for?

"I suppose it's well for you to know now," Emery said, combing back his hair with his fingers. "You see, I won't be the one testing you for your magicianship."

Ceony's hand hovered over her breakfast tray. She processed the words. "Pardon?"

"I won't be the one initiating your test," he repeated.

An uneasiness filled her, like a boat tipping back and forth inside her chest. Ceony moved the tray aside and scooted forward on the bed. "But . . . are you joking? The apprentice manual states clearly in the preface that the apprentice's mentor is the one who gives the test for magicianship."

"So it does," Emery said, his expression a little softer now, but not teasing. He stood from the bed and walked to his closet, grabbing his indigo coat from its hanger and slipping it on. "It's something that's been on my mind for months now—surely it's crossed yours."

He paused again at the foot of the bed and looked her over, smiling with his eyes. His lips, however, bore the slightest frown. "I'm worried anyone who suspects our relationship will believe you were tested with a bias."

Trying to hide her own frown, Ceony nodded. "I did consider that, once or twice. But I haven't told—"

"Sometimes, darling, you don't have to say it out loud," Emery interjected. "I've made other arrangements for you. You're a wildly talented Folder, Ceony. Almost as much as myself," he added with a pompous grin. "I would hate to have anyone cast doubts on your abilities, now or in the future."

Ceony felt herself droop a little—she couldn't help it. Without Emery as her tester, she was faced with yet another unknown in this process. She knew even less of what to expect now than she had this morning. And, if she didn't pass the test the first time, she'd have to wait another six months. If she failed three times, her name would be crossed out from the books forever, unredeemable. Any subsequent attempt at magic would send her to a jail cell.

What if she didn't pass?

She sucked in a deep breath. "Very well. I trust you in this. May I ask *who* will be handling my test in your stead?"

"Ah yes," Emery said, clapping his hands together. "I got his consent in that telegram. You, Ceony Twill, will test for your magicianship under the scrutiny of Magician Pritwin Bailey. Actually, you'll be staying with him and his apprentice for a couple weeks prior to testing, as per tradition."

Ceony's lips parted, and a moment later she asked, "A couple weeks?"

"Two or three."

"Magician Bailey?" she asked, twisting a lock of hair around her index finger. The name wasn't familiar, but—

She paused, her memory itching at her. Something about it . . .

For a moment Ceony found herself reeled back into the halls of Granger Academy, the secondary school both she and Emery had attended. The memory was not hers, but his—something she had spied when she traveled through his heart two years ago in an attempt to rescue it from a horrid Excisioner named Lira, who also happened to be Emery's ex-wife. She recalled Emery and two other boys picking on a gangly, aspiring Folder. A Folder named Prit.

"Prit?" she asked. "The boy you bullied in school?"

Emery scratched the back of his head. "'Bullied' sounds so juvenile . . ."

"But it's him, isn't it?" Ceony pushed. "Pritwin Bailey? He became a Folder after all?"

Emery nodded. "We graduated from Praff together, actually. But yes, he's the same."

Ceony relaxed somewhat. "So you two are on good terms, then?"

The paper magician barked a laugh. "Oh, heavens no. We haven't spoken to each other since Praff, save for this telegram. He quite loathes me, actually."

Ceony's eyes bugged. "And you're sending me to test with him?"

Emery smiled. "Of course, in a few days. What better way to prove you had no bias than to place your career aspirations in the hands of Pritwin Bailey?"

Ceony stared at him a long moment. "I've been shot to hell, haven't I?"

"Language, love."

She pressed a palm to her forehead. "I have more studying to do than I thought. I'm doomed. I . . . I need to get dressed."

She rose from the bed and hurried out into the hallway, palm still pressed to her forehead, Fennel following at her heels.

"You haven't touched your egg!"

But Ceony had far larger concerns on her plate than breakfast.

Ceony read through another eight chapters in the Folding dissertation Emery had given her, occasionally pinching herself to keep her mind alert and attentive as she read each long-winded, dry-as-toast paragraph about spells she already knew. Regardless, she refused to skim, and she studied the diagrams as though she had never heard of a full-point Fold. At least the artistic style in which the dissertation had been illustrated was new to her.

She later assigned herself complex animation for practice, picking an animal she had never before created: a turkey. With a few pictures for reference, she carefully Folded tail feathers and crimped paper to form a spherical body. She used three square pages for the neck, another for the head, and carefully cut and morphed a beak and snood. It took her the better part of the day to create and animate the fowl. The next day she Folded a larger turkey using more paper, carefully interlocking each piece to ensure safe mobility. After two days of working on that, she worried her knees would permanently indent with the lines of the floorboards she'd knelt on for hours.

Knowing the importance of her test, Emery seemed content enough to keep to himself, but he did pop in on occasion to offer advice, persuade Ceony to take a break, or, oh, maybe cook something. Ceony could only smile at the veiled requests.

By the end of the week, however, Ceony had thoroughly burned herself out on dissertations and animation, so she retreated to her closet to study up on Siping, the magical manipulation of rubber.

She crafted the rubber buttons into paw pads, though she had to discard the first two after cutting them wrong, then used affixing spells to adhere the pads to the bottom of Fennel's feet. This way his paws wouldn't wear out as often, and if he stepped in a very shallow puddle, his paws wouldn't crumple into soggy wads. After studying her finished work for a moment, she nodded to herself, satisfied that Fennel's feet could pass as a mere craft project—nothing that would make a magician look twice.

Utterly tired of all things magic, Ceony went to bed early that Friday night, only to be woken a few minutes past midnight. Not by a nightmare, thank goodness, but by the faintest *click click* sound heard through the wall, just loud and familiar enough to pull Ceony from the space between dreams.

She lifted her head from her pillow, holding her breath to be sure she had heard right. The noise continued: *click click click, click, click*. The telegraph.

She sat up in bed, careful not to rouse Fennel, who dozed on her mattress tonight, curled up near her feet. She rubbed her eyes and put her bare feet to the floor. Who would be sending a telegram this late at night? The weather was clear; why not send a paper bird instead? Was Prit as opposed to normal rest as Emery was? Was this a message to cancel their arrangement? Ceony wouldn't mind if it were.

She stepped out of her room. The cracks around Emery's door were dark, so she padded to the library and opened the door.

The telegraph clicked steadily from its place on the table. It stopped before Ceony took two steps into the dark room, leaving her alone in an eerie silence.

Ceony reached for the switch for the electric lights and flipped it. The bulbs hanging from the library ceiling flickered on for a moment before their light fizzled out, recasting the library in shadow. Blinking purple spots from her eyes, Ceony flipped the switch back and forth a few times to no avail. Had the power gone out again? Being so far from the main city, Emery's circuitry had a habit of turning sour.

She padded across the room, avoiding the loudest floorboards out of habit. She reached the table and tried the lamp, but it too stayed dark. She lit the candle beside it instead and picked up the curling telegram. The brief message seemed scrambled for a minute. She scanned the words, but they didn't stick in her head. She tried again, slower.

prendi escaped en route to portsmouth for execution stop thought you should know stop alfred stop

Her fingers went numb holding that slip of paper. It didn't tingle beneath her touch as it should. It felt dead, limp. Heavy.

Alfred. She hadn't seen Magician Hughes since her ordeal with Grath, which had finally brought her entwinement with Criminal Affairs to an end, or so she had believed.

Ceony's eyes fixated on the telegram's first word. *Prendi*. Saraj Prendi. Grath's dog. The Excisioner who had tried to kill her twice, all for the sake of convenience. The man who had threatened the lives of her family and her love.

And now he was loose.

CHAPTER 4

THE ELECTRIC LIGHTS came on, burning spots into Ceony's vision, temporarily blotting out the name Prendi in her hands.

The candle flickered. The door hinges creaked.

"Ceony?" Emery asked, punctuating her name with a yawn. "What are you . . . Telegram?"

Ceony didn't answer. Her thoughts danced around her family's home and down into the river that had swallowed a buggy and its driver whole, almost claiming Emery and Ceony, too. They zoomed east to Dartford, to the paper mill's newly rebuilt walls.

Emery's hand touched her shoulder. Handing him the telegram, she turned and walked away, the distance from the telegraph to her bedroom passing beneath her without notice. She flipped on the light. Fennel stirred. She crossed the room to her desk and pulled out a square sheet of white paper and a pencil. She wrote furiously, her words unaligned. She had just started her second sentence when Emery's soft voice asked, "What are you doing?"

"Warning my family."

"He doesn't know where they live now, Ceony," he said, gentle as a summer breeze. He entered the room slowly, his footsteps like a deer's on the forest floor. "And Alfred will make them a priority. He probably already has."

Ceony shook her head.

The paper magician's hand found her shoulder again, the fingers curling gently around her. "I'm so sorry," he whispered.

Ceony slammed the pencil onto the desktop, breaking off its point. She turned to Emery and felt tears sting the corners of her eyes. "Why haven't they executed him yet?" she asked, the question burning her tongue. "They've had two years. All the people he's hurt . . ."

Emery cupped either side of her face, wiped a thumb under one of her eyes to catch a tear. "They lost Grath and Lira. Saraj was the only means of obtaining information for the underground."

"It doesn't matter!"

"I'm not disagreeing with you," he said, voice faint. He pressed his forehead to hers.

Ceony dropped her eyes and pulled from his touch, but then leaned forward into his shoulder. His arms encircled her, his warmth providing some amount of comfort. "What if he's still after them . . . us?" she whispered.

"He won't get far. We'll leave it to the Cabinet. They'll take care of it."

"If we left everything to the Cabinet, we'd both be dead."

He stroked her hair. "Regardless, Saraj's primary concern will be to escape. He has no reason to chase you anymore, and I doubt he cares to torment me. He'll be heading for the coast in the hopes of crossing the channel. If Alfred has time to send word to us, we can assume it's because he already has men on Saraj's tail."

Ceony let out a long breath, trying to wrap Emery's reassurances around her like a warm blanket. She calmed a little, relaxed, but a ping of worry still warped her pulse. Nothing Saraj did was ever direct or predictable. What if her family still lay in his sights?

Grath's voice licked her thoughts as she heard him repeat her mother's and father's names. She shuddered.

At least Emery wouldn't be involved in this mess. He hadn't worked with Criminal Affairs since Saraj's arrest. With his ex-wife out of the picture for good, Emery no longer had a reason to deal with Excisioners, and the Cabinet had accepted that.

She stayed in Emery's arms a moment longer before pulling back. Emery kissed her softly.

"I can try to find out more in the morning if it will help," he offered. "The best thing we can do now is rest."

"And ward the house—"

"The house is warded." He managed a faint smile. "You are safe, Ceony, and so are they. I promise."

She nodded. Emery lingered a moment, then pressed his lips to her forehead and excused himself without words. She could stay with him again tonight. To hell with propriety. Still, she decided against asking. She trusted Emery, of course, and she didn't want him to think otherwise. But how could he really know where Saraj Prendi would go, what he would do?

Fennel lifted his head and offered a papery bark. Sighing, Ceony picked up her half-finished message and crumpled it in her hands, then tossed it into the dustbin with the command, "Shred."

She shut off the lights and climbed into bed, beckoning the paper dog to lie by her head. Yes, the best thing she could do now was sleep.

She didn't sleep well.

———

"Oh, bugger!" Ceony cried the following afternoon as sour smoke funneled up from the oven door. She waved a dish towel back and forth in a futile attempt to clear the air. Coughing, she pulled open the oven door. Smoke assaulted her and burned her eyes, but Ceony reached through it and pulled out a well-charred brisket, black down to its juice. Hacking, she set the smoking dish on the stove and retreated for the back door, yanking it open and savoring the clean, late-spring air. Tendrils of smoke wafted over her head, dissipating into the outdoors. The smell lingered between the cabinets.

Leaning against the door frame, Ceony took several deep breaths, hoping they would clear her head and calm her nerves. She hadn't burned brisket since she was eleven. At least Emery wasn't home to witness the catastrophe; he'd gone to Dartford that morning to inspect a new line of paper products designed especially for Folders, and he likely wouldn't be home until after dinner.

Ceony slid along the door frame until she crouched at the bottom. Fennel's dry paper tongue licked her knee, but when she didn't respond to him, he hopped outside after the smoke, padding about the lawn with his new rubber feet. They gave more spring to his step, letting him run a little faster, closer to the speed of a flesh-and-blood dog.

Ceony rubbed the bridge of her nose where the cartilage met her forehead. She'd been upstairs reviewing written spells—paper magic accomplished with a pen or pencil—all while writing down next week's grocery list when the burned brisket made itself known with the foul stench of dying food. Having formed a pact with herself that morning to keep busy, she'd barely allotted herself time to use the washroom, and she'd forgotten about the brisket, which she had cooked hours before dinner just to give herself something to do. Now, crouching in the smoke-laced air, her troubled thoughts caught up to her.

Emery had taken the telegram, but it didn't matter. Its blocky letters had already inscribed themselves into her mind. Saraj had loosed himself on the world, and though Ceony would like to believe he would flee England and be done with them, she did not trust it would happen that way. There was something broken inside Saraj, something crucial. That's what Emery had told her, not long after

Grath Cobalt's death. Emery didn't like talking about Excisioners, but Ceony had insisted.

A sigh escaped her mouth. Yes, the house was warded, but that hadn't stopped Lira from busting down the front door and ripping Emery's heart from his chest. Paper was a poor repellant to Excision. And if Lira was little more than an apprentice, what horrors could Saraj dole out?

Ceony stood, examining the empty house. Emery picked one hell of a day to leave town! It seemed he had restored the spells concealing the house, at least.

Snapping her fingers, Ceony beckoned Fennel inside and locked the door, then marched to the front of the house and checked the locks there as well. The windows next. Despite the heat, she locked her window and the library's, even secured the trapdoor to the roof.

As she stepped into her bedroom to resume her studies, her eyes settled on her empty desk chair, knocked askew from her flight to the kitchen. Her fears turned on her, transposing the quivering body of Delilah upon the chair, a gag in her mouth, ropes binding her down.

Ceony closed her eyes and rubbed circles over her temples in an attempt to stave off a growing headache. This wasn't fair. She'd never meant for Delilah to be hurt . . . At least Grath had been buried six feet under along with her, though Ceony would have preferred for his grave to be even deeper.

Lowering her hands, Ceony studied her palms, imagining the scars that would have marred them had a nameless Excisioner at the hospital not wished them away. She could feel the bite of the glass as it cut into her skin, the pressure in her hands as she stabbed the shard into Grath's torso and shouted, "*Shatter.*"

She didn't feel guilty for killing him. Perhaps she should, but she didn't. Her only remorse was not making it to Mg. Aviosky's home sooner. If she had arrived before Grath, there was a chance Delilah would still be alive.

"*Or you would be dead, too,*" Emery had said when she related the thought to him, his tone dark.

She returned her focus to the chair, only this time she saw her brother Marshall tied to it, not Delilah. Marshall, Zina, Margo, her parents. Emery. It could have been any one of them. It could *be* any one of them.

Ceony pressed her lips together. She hated being the victim. If Saraj did come back, she wouldn't be his. Not her, and not her loved ones. Not when there was a way to protect them—something she, alone, could do.

Leaving the door ajar, Ceony hurried down the stairs and made her way to Emery's study, where she took several lengths of smooth twine. She revisited the cookbook in the kitchen for her ball of phosphorus, then retreated to her room, shutting the door behind her despite being the only one home.

She sat at her desk and went to work.

She measured the twine around her neck and cut it accordingly, then began forming the charms, one by one. She started with the easiest—paper. She snatched up the closest piece of paper—an essay she had written about the history of paper animation. She sliced the top of it off with her Smelted scissors and Folded a thick starlight. The words "in 1744" graced the starlight's face. Using a pair of pliers, she looped a piece of wire from a paper clip through one of the starlight's points. Ceony wrapped more wire around a match, which contained both wood and phosphorus and would serve a dual purpose—allowing her to both break her bond to paper, as well as strike a flame to bond to fire.

Second, she cut a rectangle from one of her sturdier handkerchiefs and, with the supplies from a small sewing kit, stitched up its sides, using a bit of spare twine for an enclosure. She retrieved a jar of fine Gaffer's sand from the back of her bottom desk drawer and poured a tablespoon of the sand into the tiny bag and set it aside. She picked up her makeup compact—the one Delilah had given her—and held the handles of her pliers over it, but hesitated.

Several seconds passed. She set the compact aside and instead went downstairs, selecting a glass cup from the cupboards. Back in her room, she chipped a shard from its rim and wound it in wire. She wrapped up the phosphorus next, and strung three more matches together, ensuring she could loosen one at a moment's notice.

Ceony leaned back in her chair and rolled her head, hearing her neck crack too many times to count. After flexing and unflexing her fingers, she started on the more difficult charms.

She pierced wire through a spare rubber button, stole a bronze bead from a bracelet, and threaded twine through a small wing of melting plastic she had purchased in town at the beginning of the year, when she had studied Polymaking. She'd given up on the plastic-based magic after making Fennel's skeleton, however. Being the most recently discovered material magic, there were few spells Ceony could find that didn't require molds and plastic welding kits.

Siping with rubber and Polymaking with plastics had been her more recent studies merely because finding samples of their natural substance proved far trickier than the rest. She had done a great deal of research and dealt with a fair number of peddlers who didn't take her seriously, as she was neither a Siper nor a Polymaker most days, and she dared not claim otherwise. But enough prodding and investigation had paid off, and she had samples of the materials she needed for bonding.

She searched the house for half an hour, trying to find a vial smaller than the one half-filled with almond extract in the kitchen. Then she remembered the perfume samples her sister Zina had given her. She dumped the weakest-smelling one and rinsed out the tiny vial, then pulled a fist-sized jug of oil—only somewhat different from the substance that ran through the engine of an automobile—from the back of her bottom desk drawer. She carefully poured a few drops into the perfume vial, corked the vial tightly, and wound it up with wire.

Another item she had stashed in the drawer was liquid latex, which had come in a bottle small enough for her purposes. This had been the hardest natural substance for her to find, and explaining why she needed it had proven a chore. She wound it in wire, then retrieved a pure silver spoon from the same drawer. The spoon, albeit tarnished, was her magic wand for breaking the Smelting bond.

She took the tip of the spoon's handle in her pliers and bent it back and forth until the soft metal snapped. She wound the belled portion in wire and topped it with a hook.

She strung her handiwork along the twine, forming a haphazard necklace, memorizing the placement of each item. She secured the twine and slipped it over her head, careful not to scrape herself on the glass and broken silver.

Her back ached, but she felt accomplished. With this, she could be ready for anything. Saraj might have had power over flesh and blood, but she had power over everything else.

Ceony checked the clock. There was still time.

After hiding the necklace beneath her blouse, Ceony packed a small bag and snatched her bicycle, ready to make the long ride into town.

It was time to visit Mg. Aviosky.

CHAPTER 5

CEONY PEDALED INTO London, cutting through Parliament Square and passing St. Alban's Salmon Bistro, the place where she had first met Grath Cobalt and last lunched with Delilah. She tried not to dwell on the memories as she swung around Big Ben and crossed a narrow one-way street between slow-going automobiles, though it felt as if her dear friend's fairylike laughter followed her.

Glad that her self-made wind cooled her from the warming sun, Ceony rode her bicycle down Grange Road and through Lambeth. The loud, low whistle of a departing train from the Central London Railway echoed through the city, though the tracks didn't cross through this part of London.

Ceony slowed as she rounded a corner, passing quaint houses until she reached a sizeable house painted a deep sage green, though the heavy stonework across its face almost hid the color entirely. It had a small yard and a short wrought-iron fence, every other picket topped with enchanted Gaffer's bulbs that would light up once the sun went down. A security measure, Ceony imagined. Mg. Aviosky had never particularly cared for aesthetics.

Ceony dismounted her bike and combed her fingers through her hair before re-pinning it into its French twist. Mg. Aviosky had resided in this home for nearly two years, having moved after

Delilah's passing. The Gaffer must have suffered from her own bad memories, though she never spoke of them to Ceony.

She approached the front door, knocked, and for a moment she stood on the porch of another house, knocking on a door that no one answered because Grath had already tied them up in the attic . . .

Shaking her head, Ceony squeezed her eyes shut and tried to banish the memories from her mind.

If you had gotten here sooner, she'd still be alive, her own voice whispered from the black caves somewhere at the back of her skull. It had become an all-too-familiar refrain.

She rubbed her temples. *I'm always too late, aren't I?* she thought, her bones growing heavy. Had she made it but half an hour sooner to her dear friend Anise's home years ago, Ceony could have stopped the other girl from killing herself. Had she arrived at Mg. Aviosky's home in better time, she could have stopped Grath from murdering Delilah.

"Stop it," she whispered to herself. She rapped on the door, the sound of knuckles on wood shattering her redundant thoughts. Only then did she realize Mg. Aviosky might not be home, especially given the business of her career. Ceony frowned. As far as she knew, the Gaffer no longer kept an apprentice. She couldn't bring herself to, not after what happened to Delilah.

"At least I got exercise," Ceony murmured to herself. She knocked again for good measure, then rang the bell.

To her relief, she heard soft footsteps approach the door from inside. They paused for several seconds before the door opened.

"Miss Twill," Mg. Aviosky said, standing in the door frame and not sounding the least bit surprised. She must have spied Ceony with some spell or another. "I certainly didn't expect your company today."

"I suppose I should have telegraphed, or sent a bird," Ceony replied, clasping her hands behind her back. "I do hope you have a few moments to spare? I need to discuss some important . . . and private . . . matters with you."

Mg. Aviosky's thin lips frowned as they were wont to do, but the gesture lasted only a moment. She adjusted her glasses on her nose— a new pair, silver, and enchanted, judging by the faint etch marks on the upper-right-hand corners of each lens. If Ceony recalled correctly from her ancillary Gaffer studies, that enchantment could make the lenses magnify something to a near-microscopic level. "Of course," she said, stepping aside. "Come in."

Ceony stepped in and removed her shoes. Mg. Aviosky closed the door and gestured to the front room.

"Are you here because you're concerned about your test?" Mg. Aviosky asked, smoothing her skirt and sitting on a lavender chair near the fireplace. "You're not required to try for your magicianship after two years, Miss Twill. Or are you troubled that Magician Thane won't be the one testing you?"

Ceony blinked, sliding down onto the edge of the sofa patterned with large prints of maroon and navy lilies. "You know about that?"

"It's my business to know," Mg. Aviosky said, pointing her nose slightly closer to the ceiling. She relaxed her shoulders. "But truthfully, I feel an obligation to follow up with charges of mine from Tagis Praff, at least until they're settled into their careers."

Ceony nodded, then smiled. "I didn't take you for the sentimental type."

Mg. Aviosky raised an eyebrow.

"But no," she continued, clasping her hands over her knees. "I'm not here about my test. Or to speak about my studies at all. I came to you because of a telegram Em—Magician Thane received last night."

Stiffness seeped back into the glass magician's shoulders. "From Magician Hughes," she said. It didn't sound like a question, but Ceony nodded regardless. Mg. Aviosky must have received word of Saraj as well.

Releasing a sigh, Mg. Aviosky leaned back in her chair and pressed an index finger to her forehead, just above the nose guard of her glasses. "That man cannot keep his wits all in one jar," she said. "He might as well initiate Magician Thane into the Criminal Affairs department officially."

"Magician Thane is retired from that line of work," Ceony said with a little too much push. Fortunately, Mg. Aviosky didn't seem to notice. Or, at least, she did not respond.

The Gaffer took in a deep breath, dropped her hand, and leaned forward in her chair, placing her elbows on her knees—a very casual position for a woman Ceony had never before associated with that word. "I'm not part of Criminal Affairs," she said, meeting Ceony's eyes. "I only know wisps, perhaps nothing more than what you know already."

It wasn't an outright refusal; Ceony had been dealt enough of those in her life to know the difference. Mg. Aviosky had been more receptive to her ever since the incident with Grath. Perhaps that was why she'd stopped investigating Ceony's relationship with Emery.

"What I know would fit in a single telegram," Ceony said, her voice growing quiet, despite the lack of eavesdropping ears. "Please tell me more. He threatened my family. He's"—she swallowed—"he's supposed to be dead."

"They did take their time, didn't they?" Mg. Aviosky quipped, almost more to herself than to Ceony. "I wonder, once this is all over, if the need to dig information out of the man will have been worth it. I'd hate to think—"

Her voice cut short. After clearing her throat, she finished with, "Of the people who he'll hurt."

Ceony bit her lip. For a moment, the ghost of Delilah stood in the hallway outside the front room, laughing at some unheard joke. But she was gone, her laughter only heard in memory.

Another sigh passed from Mg. Aviosky's lips, as if the same

thought had occurred to her. "He escaped en route to Portsmouth prison, where he was scheduled for execution."

"From Haslar."

"Mm," Mg. Aviosky agreed. She shifted in her chair. "Somewhere near Gosport, I believe, between cities. I didn't press Magician Hughes for details."

"But how?" Ceony pleaded. "I researched the imprisonment of Excisioners. Straitjackets, constant guard, solitary confinement. They even put bits in their mouth to keep them from drawing blood from their own tongue and cheeks!"

Ceony felt her neck warm.

"No need to school me, Miss Twill," the Gaffer said. "I'm quite aware. I believe he head-butted his guard and blew out his sinuses hard enough to give himself a nosebleed. I've heard Excision spells cast using the magician's own blood are far weaker, but it was enough. He managed to collapse the side of the carriage and get away."

Ceony thought of the spell Lira had once used to break down Emery's front door. "No one pursued him?"

"I don't know," Mg. Aviosky said with a tilt of her chin and the faintest air of exasperation. "I imagine there was a chase. No sane person would think to transport Saraj Prendi without a great number of guards, especially of the magician type. But it's not under my jurisdiction. I simply don't know."

But where? Would Saraj try to flee England, as Emery suspected? Portsmouth and Haslar were on the southern coast, weren't they? An easy escape. Saraj would be a fool not to take it.

Still, the contents of her stomach churned.

Ceony kept the thoughts to herself, shoving them down deep enough in her brain that they tickled the back of her neck. She cleared her throat, trying not to react noticeably to the news, and asked, "What did Saraj do prior to the paper mill?"

Mg. Aviosky tapped her chin, then readjusted her glasses once more. Instead of offering another excuse about how she wasn't involved in Criminal Affairs, she managed to say, "I believe he was involved in some ordeal in Scotland, along with Grath Cobalt and Lira Hoppson. I'm not sure of the details. But Miss Twill," she said, scooting forward on her chair, "you must believe that you and your kin will be safe. It's not in Saraj Prendi's criminal profile to pursue them any further."

The words offered little comfort. "I thought you weren't part of Criminal Affairs," Ceony said. "How would you know?"

The Gaffer frowned. "Saraj Prendi has a reputation extending far beyond English law enforcement. That is a naïve question."

Ceony sighed. "You are right, of course."

She wrung her skirt in her hands but stopped short of wrinkling it. Her thoughts felt like muffin batter. Smoothing out her skirt, Ceony closed her eyes just long enough to gather her senses. Then she reached into her bag and grabbed a rectangular piece of gray paper. She tore it in half down the middle and instructed it, "Mimic."

Mg. Aviosky raised an eyebrow.

Ceony handed half of the paper to her. "Think of it as mirror-to-mirror communication," Ceony explained. Indeed, a mirror spell would be much more prudent than this Folder's spell, but Mg. Aviosky didn't know about Ceony's exercises in bond breaking, and Ceony was not ready to share the information. Once a secret spread to too many minds and mouths, anyone could learn it—including an Excisioner.

Ceony continued. "Anything you write on your half will appear on mine. Please, if you hear any more news, or if you need to contact me for whatever reason, use this. It's quicker and more . . . private . . . than a telegram."

The glass magician glanced over the half sheet of paper. To Ceony's relief, she nodded and folded it into quarters before slipping it inside her tailored jacket. "Very well," she said. "I'll keep it on hand."

Ceony's shoulders relaxed, which was how she realized they had tensed. "Thank you for your help. I'm just trying to . . . ease some concerns."

Gosport, she thought. *Haslar to Portsmouth. I need to know for certain that he fled, that he won't come after us. I have to know there won't be any more Delilahs, Anises.*

Ceony stood, holding her bag to her. Mg. Aviosky stood as well.

"Would you like some tea?" she asked, lips twisting with what could have been worry. "Do you have a buggy waiting?"

"No, thank you, and I'll get home fine," Ceony said, punctuating her reassurances with a smile. "And I should be getting home. I have more studying to do before my test."

Mg. Aviosky seemed pleased with that statement. "Agreed. Take care, Ceony."

The Gaffer showed Ceony to the door. Ceony took up her bike and walked it across the yard and down the walk, watching Mg. Aviosky's front door through the corner of her eye.

She turned the next corner and seated herself on the bike. She rode farther into the city, toward Parliament Square, where she heard Big Ben chime the second hour.

This time she didn't cut through the square to return to Emery's cottage. She parked her bicycle outside St. Alban's Salmon Bistro, which was, ironically, the place where she had lost the last one.

Smoothing her skirt and fixing her hair, Ceony began to walk toward the Parliament building itself. It was more public than she would have liked given her purpose, but she knew the mirror was of good quality, ensuring a certain measure of safety. Besides, there wasn't time to find anything better. The lavatory door locked, at least.

As she neared the building, a familiar laugh caught her attention. Passing Fine Seams, a tailoring shop, Ceony peered around a corner and searched the various shoppers and pedestrians filling the narrow road leading away from the square. She spied her sister

Zina leaning against the brick side of Fine Seams in a dress that was almost indecently short. She was with two men: one who was barely old enough to be called a man and another who looked to be Zina's age. He held a cigar in one hand and leaned one elbow against the brick wall.

"Zina!" Ceony called, jogging down the street. A surprise to see her sister here—her family had moved to Poplar, which was too far away for a comfortable journey to Parliament Square.

Zina glanced over. She didn't seem enthused by the chance meeting, which made Ceony slow down.

Ceony nodded to the two men before asking, "What are you doing here? Mom and Dad . . . are they here, too?" *Prancing around the heart of London, just waiting for a certain Excisioner to put them on the menu?*

Zina rolled her eyes. "I'm nineteen, Ceony. I don't need an escort."

"I didn't say you did. I was just wondering—"

"Can you 'wonder' over there?" Zina asked, gesturing down the road. "I'm a bit preoccupied."

Ceony glanced to the older man. "Excuse me, just a moment," she said. He did not so much as step back. To Zina, she said, "What's wrong? Why are you acting like this? I haven't seen you in two months and suddenly I'm a pest?"

Zina buzzed her lips to imitate a fly. The two men chuckled.

Ceony swallowed a grumble and straightened her shoulders. Leaning toward Zina, she said, "Listen, you should probably go home. There are . . . things afoot right now, and I'm worried about the family. Would you—"

"Ceony!" Zina snapped, "Are you deaf? You, of all people, have no right to tell me about propriety."

A few passersby glanced over at Zina's outburst.

"I'm not talking about propriety! I'm talking about your safety!" Ceony countered. Her mother had mentioned Zina's new habits—the late nights and unruly friends—but had her sister really grown so hard?

Zina pushed off of the brick wall and straightened, standing about an inch taller than Ceony did. "I know about you and Magician Thane, you know," she said, a little too loudly for comfort.

Ceony flushed. "What about me and Magician Thane?"

"I heard our parents talking, that's what," she said. "Criminy, Ceony, it's like shagging the principal. Isn't he a divorcé, too?"

Scalding heat permeated Ceony's skin, reddening her like a tomato. Voices muttering *What did she say?* and *That girl?* echoed around her. She could feel time slowing, and the passersby slowed along with it, clearly eager to overhear more gossip.

Zina folded her arms.

Ceony's pulse drummed in her ears. She felt sick in her chest. "I'm not," she whispered, "doing that, Zina. With anyone."

She thought her ears would light with fire, her cheeks burn to ash, but the moment passed, as even the worst moments do.

"Whatever you say, sis." Zina waved a hand carelessly and walked away without a backward glance. The man with the cigar grinned at Ceony and even dared to waggle his eyebrows at her before following.

Feeling stark naked and an inch tall, Ceony spun back for the main road, walking briskly on marionette legs. To her horror, she spied none other than Mrs. Holloway, who leaned toward an older companion as she stage-whispered, "I know him. Magician Thane, that is. The girl so young, and him without a wife. All alone . . . It's a wonder what they get up to."

God save me, Ceony prayed, clutching her bag to her body. *I've done nothing wrong.*

She continued walking, the exercise moving her blood away from her face, and with it any outward show of humiliation. Her mind whirled. True, she and her sister had grown apart in recent years, but they had been the best of friends before Ceony started secondary school. *What's wrong with you, Zina?*

The Parliament building loomed ahead. Ceony's memory flashed back to her conversation with Mg. Aviosky, and she clung to it with all ten nails. Saraj. She needed to focus on Saraj, not on Zina. Not even on Emery.

She let herself inside.

Two guards glanced at her as she passed, but just about anyone was allowed to traverse the first floor of the building so long as they didn't look suspicious. And a young woman of Ceony's stature never *looked* suspicious. Not with her skin more or less returned to its normal hue.

She walked with her eyes straight ahead, smiling at anyone who passed, nodding at a businessman who first nodded to her. When she reached the women's lavatory on the left, she kept her pace and stepped inside, listening for the sounds of others before locking the door.

She took a moment to gather her wits and catch her breath. *Saraj. Focus on him.*

In the powdering space between the door and the toilets hung a large mirror against a wallpapered wall, just over a polished dresser beside a cushioned chair. Ceony remembered this mirror well; Delilah had used it to take her to and from her temporary flat.

Ceony squared her shoulders and pulled the chair around to the front of the dresser so she could stand on it and reach the mirror. Ceony slipped her hand under the collar of her blouse, pulled free her charm necklace, and pinched the wood charm in her fingers, muttering the words that would break her bond to paper.

She resealed herself to glass, then touched the edges of the mirror the way her friend had done so long ago.

And she searched.

She pushed her consciousness into the mirror, probing for an unknown signature, feeling her spirit pull like taffy as she explored farther and farther from the lavatory, past the mirrors in Parliament and its square, past the mirrors in London and Croydon and Farnborough. She stretched, her consciousness spinning into threads. It drained her—she had never tried this spell at so great a distance. But it would work. She had tried the spell before, in the confines of her bedroom, albeit with a much smaller mirror.

There, she thought, *this feels close enough.*

Holding on to her search spell, Ceony traced her hand around the mirror clockwise, counterclockwise, and clockwise again. She murmured, "Transport, pass through."

The mirror rippled into silvery liquid, waiting to swallow her.

Holding her breath, Ceony stepped through it.

CHAPTER 6

THE LIQUID GLASS draped over Ceony like a curtain of ice water, seeping through clothes and skin without leaving a trace of wetness. Her mind flashed to the memory of her buggy hitting the surface of a dark river, cold water creeping up her body as Saraj watched from the bank. That very sensation was one of three reasons Ceony didn't mirror-transport often; it reminded her of drowning.

The second reason was the fear of getting caught.

The third was the danger of getting stuck within a damaged mirror . . .

Which was exactly what happened. Despite stepping into a clean mirror, Ceony found herself in a limbo filled with gray matter—sharp stalagmites and stalactites jutting below and above her, charcoal gems hanging midair, silvery webs floating like clouds or crawling as fog.

She inched forward, scanning each obstacle, each danger. This mirror she had found had been treated poorly, dirtied, and split, resulting in the dangerous obstacle field ahead of her. Far to her left, the ground shifted down as it might in an earthquake—the manifestation of a crack.

Chewing on her lip, Ceony slid one foot forward, then the other, searching for a clear path. If she found none, she'd go back—her small investigation wasn't worth losing her life in this glassy prison. But it was worth a try.

She stepped over a stalagmite, sidestepped until she could move around a web—the manifestation of a scratch—which was seemingly constructed of razor blades. It looped around itself like matted hair pulled from a hairbrush and reached to her midthigh. Ceony ducked under another web and got her skirt caught on a third. A quick tug freed it with minimal damage.

The floor bowed slightly past the wiry clouds, but beyond that she saw the glimmering veil of her destination mirror: a rather large one. She treaded carefully over the ice-slick, concave floor until she reached it, bracing herself for another cold wash.

When she emerged, she found herself in some sort of storage room, thankfully empty. The mirror she had stepped through hung frameless on the wall, about six feet high and four feet across, its surface marred with stains and scratches. Another, narrower mirror leaned against the opposite wall, supported on either side by bolts of unorganized fabrics.

Ceony blinked a few times, adjusting to the dimness of the room—savoring the momentary solitude. Two bare dress mannequins, one in disrepair, greeted her, and beyond them rested an old wooden shelf filled with poorly folded scraps of fabric, everything from satin to cotton to flannel. A box full of bits and cuts of fabric, too small to be of use to anyone, blocked her way to the door. Ceony heaved it aside—moving slowly, so as not to stir up too much noise—and stepped through the doorway into a cramped hall.

A dress shop.

Ceony spied down the hallway to a front area displaying premade gowns and coats, as well as fabric bolts propped on slim shelves against the wall for purchase by the yard. A large, middle-aged woman shuffled about the cash register, but she kept her back to Ceony. Ceony tiptoed in from the back and made it to the shelf of fabric bolts before the woman turned around.

She gasped. "Oh, heavens! You startled me." Her hazel eyes glanced to the door and the chime hanging against it. "I didn't hear you come in."

"Oh, sorry," Ceony said, forcing a light laugh. "I wanted to see if you had something for . . . a polka dot pattern I saw in a magazine. This is close"—she gestured to a pale-orange fabric with peachy speckles—"but not quite what I'm looking for."

"Polka dot?" the woman repeated. She tapped her chin. "I do have a booklet you can look at if you'd like to special order something."

Ceony gripped the straps of her purse in her fingers. "Oh, I may. There's one more place I'd like to look, but I think I'll come back."

"Oh. All right, then. Take care."

Ceony nodded and headed toward the door, but before its chime could ring she asked, "I just came in from the train—what part of Portsmouth am I in?"

The woman played with a lint brush on the counter beside her. "Portsmouth is eight miles south, dear. Not far. This is Waterlooville. Did you not see the sign?"

"Thank you," Ceony replied. She stepped outside and counted the pounds in her purse, wondering if she should hire a buggy or make another attempt at mirror travel.

She pinched a few bills between thumb and forefinger. "A buggy would be safer," she murmured to herself. The journey through the mirror in the dress shop had left her with a bit of a headache, besides.

She called the next buggy that passed and offered some weak instructions concerning Gosport—could she be dropped off somewhere in the middle?—and rode silently in the backseat. She spied signs for Portchester Castle on the way, and the great behemoth of a fortress hulked in the distance beyond her window. She wondered if Emery would be interested in touring something like that. She'd have to ask, but carefully. She didn't want him to wonder how she'd come up with the idea.

I just need to know, she thought, fingering the clasp of her purse. *If he's left England, that will be that. If not . . . I'll tell someone. Investigate further.*

Her palms sweated.

Ceony watched the sea loom closer and closer to the buggy, its body filled with checkered rows of ships, often two or three docks between each ship. Most of the boats stationed there now were small, but a few larger ones sat farther out on the water, too distant to be menacing.

A naval yard—and between two prisons, so the location made sense. But it also made Ceony's muscles itch. She might not get far, surrounded by military.

She instructed her driver inland, a comfortable distance from both the naval yard and the ocean itself. She tipped him well when they finally stopped, and waited for the automobile to turn around and start for Waterlooville before venturing off.

Studying the road before her—it was barely large enough to fit two buggies—Ceony wondered if this very path had been taken by Saraj and his entourage, or if she had missed the mark entirely. Surely the law would have taken him by way of ferry between Haslar and Portsmouth, unless they feared him traversing open water, bound or not.

A cool, salt-laced breeze caressed Ceony's ears, pulling her thoughts toward the ocean. She remembered standing on Foulness Island with Lira two years ago. The Excisioner—little more than an apprentice herself—had dropped blood in the water to send a wave crashing into Ceony's backside, ruining most of Ceony's paper spells. What could Saraj Prendi do with the sea if he had enough blood at his disposal?

She shook herself, glanced at the sun. This was no time to dawdle.

Leaving the road and journeying closer to town than to the military post, Ceony pinched her paper starlight marked "in 1744" and rebonded herself to paper. Finding a small clearing not too overrun with tall grass and briars, she knelt down and started Folding. Emery had a silly rule about Folding in one's lap, but she could hardly drag a board all the way down here with her. Folding on her thighs did require more concentration, however.

She formed several paper songbirds, a simple spell she had learned at the beginning of her apprenticeship. She made four: two white, one yellow, one red.

"Breathe," she said.

The paper creatures came to life in her hands, as if her one word had instilled them with souls. She pinched the bases of their bodies to keep them from flitting away.

"We're searching for some specific things," she said to their beaks. "Search the area, a few miles' worth if you can. Look for broken pieces of carriages, skid marks, perhaps signs of a fight. Wide-spaced footprints. Blood on the street or in the soil. A thin Indian man with a narrow face."

She paused, considering. "And any mirrors or other glass surfaces that are outdoors, away from the naval base." If luck was with her and she could find a mirror with a wide view of the area, she might be able to dig into its past and see Saraj for herself. "Fly back to me if you see any of these things."

The birds flapped their pointed wings, and Ceony released them, letting a second breeze glide them into the air. One of the white spells and the red spell flew toward town together; the other two split up, one gliding toward the coast, the other back up the road on which Ceony had arrived.

Any passersby would think them mail birds. And if Saraj spotted one, hopefully it would spot *him*. A double-edged sword was more useful than no weapon at all.

In the meantime, Ceony walked.

She stayed on the road for a while, keeping note of the passing time. Perhaps Emery would stay late in Dartford and she wouldn't have to worry about punctuality, but she doubted it. The paper magician wasn't overly fond of business trips, whatever their purpose.

The thought of Emery sent Ceony's mind back to the ugly scene in Parliament Square. *Overheard them talking,* she wondered as she walked. What had her parents been discussing, and so loudly that Zina could overhear? Then again, Zina's knack for snooping rivaled Ceony's own. She was angry with her sister . . . Of course she was, but her primary concern was for her family's safety. Did Saraj know what all of them looked like? But even if Saraj hadn't fled the country, he couldn't have made it to London already, not on foot. And why would he go somewhere so populated? Unless he had a specific purpose in traveling to the capital . . . but Ceony couldn't imagine what that would be, outside of finding her.

Too risky, even for him, isn't it? she thought. *Surely he's fled. I shouldn't even be trying to prove otherwise.*

Both Emery and Mg. Aviosky, people she trusted implicitly, had assured her that her family would be safe, so perhaps she should leave Criminal Affairs' affairs be.

Still, if she had worried *more* about Delilah, perhaps things would have turned out differently. She had to know for sure.

Soon Ceony ventured off road, scanning the uncultivated lengths between the naval base and the town, searching for the things she'd tasked the birds with finding. She came across a patch of flattened grass about an hour in and, after bonding to glass, took a rubber-lined circle of the material from her purse and commanded it, "Magnify." The glass, little larger than the front of a picture frame, immediately turned into a looking glass, enlarging the crushed grass at her feet. She found nothing unusual.

"*Criminy, Ceony, it's like shagging the principal*," her sister's voice intruded on her thoughts. "*Isn't he a divorcé?*"

Zina had said it so *loudly*. And in such crude language!

She swatted the thoughts away. "Focus on Saraj," she chided herself. "He's the bigger problem."

Another half hour later, her feet growing weary, one of the white birds returned, fluttering tired wings. Ceony rebonded to paper and beckoned it down.

"What did you find, little one?" she asked, chills pricking her sun-heated shoulders. The paper songbird bounced in her hands thrice before flying westward, keeping low to the ground. Ceony hurried after it, grabbing her long skirt in her hands as she went.

The bird flew quite a distance, heading away from the road. By the time it landed on a dirt path overgrown with weeds, not far from the town line and an exposed sewer pipe, Ceony's face had flushed red, and perspiration clung to her hairline and camisole. Ceony knew the spell for a fan that would cool her quickly, but in her excitement, she settled for waving both hands before her face.

She looked about her. Some of the weeds and wild grasses here looked trod upon and torn, as though a brawl had occurred. Something shiny caught her eye—squatting, Ceony picked up a spent bullet, smashed. It must have struck something hard—perhaps the carriage itself? But Ceony saw no wheel tracks. The bullet was etched with a targeting spell, she noticed, meaning that at least one Smelter had been on duty. Unless, of course, the bit of metal was from the naval base. Ceony doubted it.

The white bird, its wings starting to bend backward from the brisk wind, perched on a skinny vine of sunburned morning glory, half rooted from the ground. Ceony dropped to her knees and pushed aside weeds and dirt. The summer sun glinted off a brown piece of glass barely larger than her thumbnail, perhaps from a beer bottle left behind by an off-duty naval officer. She wiped a thin layer of dust from it and saw her reflection on its smooth side—the inside of the bottle. Not a spotless reflection but adequate for her current needs.

"Good birdie," Ceony wheezed, wiping the back of her hand over her forehead. "Cease."

The proud bird toppled onto the ground, immobile.

Ceony held out the brown glass in her palm. She'd never attempted a mirror-based spell on something that wasn't a mirror . . . but Gaffer spells could work on substances other than Gaffer's glass, so it was worth a shot.

Ceony's fingers fiddled with her charm necklace. She broke her bond with paper and became a glass magician once more.

Staring at her tinted reflection, she said, "Reflect, past."

Her image contorted left, then right, then swirled. Her face vanished from the shard, and instead she saw strands of grass and a peep of sky laced with a single, stretched-out cloud.

Pressing her lips together, Ceony searched her memory of the Gaffer books she had read for pertinent manipulations to this spell. "Backward reflect," she commanded it.

The reflection of the cloud slowly crawled off the glass.

"Tenth increase," she said, and the reflection on the brown bottle reversed itself ten times as fast. The light darkened. A star appeared. Sunrise. The grass wavered in the wind.

"Tenth increase, tenth increase," Ceony instructed, and the shard's memories rewound faster and faster. This spell, something a Gaffer apprentice would likely learn in his or her first year, already felt far more complicated than nearly all the Folding spells Ceony knew. Perhaps another reason why paper magic had become so unpopular in England.

Day, night, day, night. Rain. The broken piece of bottle sped through its memories beneath Ceony's scrutiny. It likely wouldn't reveal anything useful—

"Hold," Ceony instructed, catching sight of shadows, but they proved to be the silhouettes of two little boys, their indecipherable banter playing on the glass in tandem with their images.

She commanded the glass to continue back through its memories. A larger shadow appeared after another two days. "Hold," she said, her voice almost a whisper.

The image played at normal speed. The mirror was masked by shadow at first; then something shifted and the sun highlighted tight curls on a head of hair. The head looked back, and in the distance, Ceony heard a whistle, someone yelling. Police officers.

The shadowy man disappeared from the reflection a moment later. The police officers never entered it.

"Saraj," Ceony whispered, lowering her spyglass as it shifted back to a view of the swaying grass and summer sky. It had to be him. She had seen his darkened silhouette before and could summon the memory as easily as she could recall what she ate for breakfast. And in this location, with those sounds . . . she felt almost positive.

Her gaze fell back to the shard in her palm. One thing she knew for certain—the shadowy figure that grazed its surface had headed *north*, toward town. Not south, east, or west, all of which would eventually lead him to the ocean. To potential escape.

If her calculations were correct, Saraj had bunkered down in England, not fled it.

She let a curse roll off her tongue and savored the sharpness of it. Her heart palpitated inside a rib cage made of needles. She fisted the glass shard until its edges threatened to split her skin.

He's not coming for you; he's not coming for you. Something else. Perhaps he went that way because the police were in pursuit from the south . . . or he wanted to avoid the naval base, that's all. And just because he headed north doesn't mean he continued *north.*

Why couldn't the logic soothe her? But the answer to that question was apparent enough. She knew neither where Saraj Prendi was nor his intentions. He'd left her—and the rest of Criminal Affairs—in the dark, again.

Ceony stood, brushing dirt off her knees, and slid the shard into her purse.

A yellow paper songbird glided overhead.

Pinching her necklace and uttering the words, Ceony returned to paper magic and beckoned the bird down. It swayed on the breeze and almost missed her hand. Its crinkled body looked weary. Ceony smoothed a bent wing.

This one had traveled far.

"What did you find?" she asked it, wishing the spell could talk. Would the paper bird be strong enough to make the trip back? Would Ceony be able to follow if the distance was as great as she feared?

She pressed her lips together and hummed. Scanning the sky, she saw no sign of her other two birds. Cradling the yellow bird in one hand, Ceony headed toward Gosport and, after a few attempts, found a buggy.

After the driver pulled over, she stepped up to his window and showed him the paper bird hopping on her palm. "I'm a Folder," she said, for that morsel of information would make the rest of her request sound less foolish. "I need you to follow this yellow bird best you can, and I'll compensate you when we reach our destination."

The man eyed her and rubbed one eyebrow, then the other. "How . . . far? Will it keep to the roads? I'm not savvy with Folding, miss."

"Not too far," Ceony assured him, though she hadn't a clue. "As for roads . . . well, he's yellow. Hopefully that will make him easy to follow, regardless. I have absolute faith in your abilities, as far as traffic laws permit them to extend, of course."

The driver inhaled deeply, held the breath in his cheeks a moment, then blew it out like he would cigar smoke. "I hope magicians tip well," he said under his breath, but loud enough for Ceony to hear. "Er . . . set the thing down on the hood, I guess. Do you need help in?"

"I can open my own door," Ceony said, and she did, taking the seat right behind the driver. "Show me what you found!" she called to the bird.

The songbird beat its rumpled wings and flew a few feet ahead of the buggy. The driver took after it at a slow speed, but picked up his pace once the bird made its first illegal turn. The driver mumbled what could only be foul language not meant for a woman's ears, while Ceony pretended not to notice. He wound west through Gosport, then north, honking on occasion at stopped carriages or pedestrians who seemed to be considering crossing the street. Ceony only lost sight of the bird once, when it dove behind a bank of grass, but it reappeared a moment later.

Meanwhile, Ceony quickly Folded a new bird, constructing it differently from the others. There were Folds one could place into a spell that enabled non-Folders to use it, else paper magicians would have a difficult time making any money. She incorporated these Folds now to disguise the fact that the bird had come from a Folder. Mail birds were common; this one would blend in with the rest, no more obscure than a purchased envelope and stamp.

Muddling her handwriting, Ceony wrote into the bird's body, *Saraj headed north after his escape. Please follow. Do not attempt to contact me; I wish to remain anonymous.*

After animating the creature and whispering to it the address for the Magicians' Cabinet's central building, Ceony let the bird fly out the buggy window and out of sight.

The buggy followed road after road for just over a half hour. The streets had become mostly residential, with a small shop set on approximately every other corner.

The yellow bird swung back around to Ceony's glassless window and into her hands. So this was it.

"Cease," she told the bird. To the driver she said, "Take this road slowly, if you would. I need to look around."

The driver did as asked without so much as a grumble. Ceony pressed her back into the seat, keeping herself out of direct sight. As the buggy crept past the line of houses and buildings, she scanned them, noting the arc of the sun. She needed to return to the dressmaker's shop soon if she hoped to make it home before Emery.

What caught Ceony's attention first wasn't what she saw, but what she heard and smelled. Beautiful music—almost festive, yet eerie in its own right. It was like nothing she'd ever heard. The melody played on the lips of flutes and the twanging of . . . well, Ceony couldn't be sure.

She smelled meat, lamb perhaps, and spices. She picked out marjoram and curry, but the rest of the nuances eluded her.

Then she spied what the bird must have seen amid a cluster of squat homes: an Indian man.

Not Saraj: that much was clear. He wore an eggshell-white turban on his head and loose clothing that wasn't quite a robe. A thick beard hid half his face. He carried several planks of wood on his shoulder and waved ahead to an Indian woman who was about Ceony's age. The woman glanced in Ceony's direction, but her eyes didn't linger.

The music grew louder, then fainter as Ceony passed more homes. There were Indians of all ages, children playing with stones on porches and old women with long gray braids. She spied into a larger home and saw an enormous table set with shallow metal dishes full of foods Ceony had never seen in any English cookbook. People on the walk called to one another in a language she presumed to be Hindi.

An Indian neighborhood, an enclave—that's what the bird had found. She knew of a much larger Chinese settlement east of London. She had given her paper spell specific characteristics to find, and it had found them.

But Saraj wouldn't be here, would he? Surely he didn't have family in England . . . at least, not family who would harbor him. The police force would have investigated that route without delay, and besides, the enclave was too close to the location of Saraj's escape for him to feel safe. At least, were Ceony in his position, she wouldn't feel safe.

I'll find you, Saraj, she thought, chewing her lip nearly hard enough to pierce it. *And if you're still in England, I'll stop you. For them.*

She made a mental note of the area but didn't feel confident it carried any sort of useful clue. She certainly wouldn't go barging into these strangers' homes searching for an Excisioner!

She rubbed her thumb over the paper bird's back.

"Miss?" the driver asked. They had reached the end of the road.

"Oh. Turn right, please," Ceony said, relaxing into her seat. "Thank you, that was all. But if you could be so kind as to take me to a dressmaker's shop in Waterlooville, I'll make it worth your while."

She'd have to pay him the rest of the money from the Holloway job, likely, but she was used to not having spending money. The cottage had everything she needed, besides.

The cottage. The clock was ticking.

"Push the speed limit, if you would," she added. The driver peeked over his shoulder at her. Ceony offered a small smile.

She got to the dress shop just before it closed and set up a special order, though she snuck away to the back room while the clerk looked up the item number in a catalog. She transported back to Parliament through the mirror maze, only to find the door to the lavatory unlocked—someone had called in a locksmith, then. She could have transported clear to the lavatory mirror in Emery's cottage were it not for the bike.

Hurrying out to her bike, Ceony pedaled back to the cottage on legs somewhat unwilling to put forth the effort.

The front door to the cottage was unlocked. She let herself in, taking a breath to call Emery's name and see if he was home, but it caught in her throat as she stepped into the hallway.

Emery stood there with his arms folded tightly across his chest, his green eyes blazing with a fire that could only be meant for her.

CHAPTER 7

CEONY RUSHED THROUGH a mental checklist of her appearance: Her hair was a little windblown from the bike ride, her cheeks rosy, but when were they not rosy? Her blouse, dress, and shoes were acceptably clean. It wasn't unusual for her to carry a purse, so that wouldn't be a source of suspicion.

She glanced at her fingernails. Not too bad.

"Emery!" she said, missing only a heartbeat. She grinned. "I didn't expect you home so soon."

"I didn't expect you home so late," he countered, his eyes narrowing without losing any of their brilliance. "Did you take the scenic route from Patrice's house?"

A flush inched up Ceony's neck. "I did visit her today," she said, adjusting her purse strap on her shoulder. She pressed her thumb into her collar as she did so, ensuring that it hid her new charm necklace. "How did you know? Did you run into her?" Ceony swallowed. "Did she . . . send you a telegram?"

Emery chuckled, but it wasn't a happy laugh. "Oh no. Why use the telegraph when a certain nosy apprentice might be around to swipe the message? She found me through the lavatory mirror. And I believe it's been approximately six hours since you stopped by her home to ask her about Saraj Prendi."

The creeping flush chilled white and sunk back into Ceony's spine. *Aviosky! You couldn't keep a secret if your life depended on it!*

But of course Mg. Aviosky had told Emery. Ceony was only an apprentice; Mg. Thane was technically her guardian.

"I went shopping," she said, wincing as the poor lie escaped her lips. She had no bags, no receipts. Nothing to prove it, and Emery knew her well enough to know she couldn't tolerate window-shopping for six hours.

She swallowed a sigh and straightened, but her five-foot-three frame had nothing on Emery's. "I didn't do anything wrong," she said, moving down the hallway. She tried to pass him, but he caught her elbow.

"By all means, enlighten me on what you did do," he said.

Ceony felt her own fire pulse outward from her chest. "I'm not dabbling with Excisioners, if that's what you're worried about," she snapped, pulling her arm free.

The reference to Lira—Emery's ex-wife—was too hard of a blow, but Ceony stomped into the kitchen before she could glimpse his face. Fennel jumped up from where he lay by the dining room table, but Ceony ignored him and fled up the stairs to her bedroom. She dropped her purse on the floor—kicking it under the bed—and yanked the clip from her hair. Uneven orange curls tumbled over her shoulders. She shook them out before placing both hands on her hips, then sucked in one deep breath. Another.

She didn't even hear the paper magician's footsteps approach her door, just his voice. "Ceony."

"I went to Gosport," she said, not turning around.

"Gosport and back in six hours?"

"You're not the only one with a glider," she lied, hoping he wouldn't call her out on it. "Magician Aviosky couldn't tell me much, so I went to Gosport to look around. I didn't find much, but I thought I'd make the effort. I've gotten weary of letting our enemies find me first."

The door frame creaked as Emery leaned against it. "I thought you were over this—running off and taking matters into your own hands. I thought we talked about this. On several occasions."

She turned around. The fire had left his eyes, but his face remained mirthless. "You talked *at* me about it, maybe." She sighed. "I'm not jumping through mirrors hunting down an Excisioner with a gun again." Half lie. "Saraj wasn't anywhere near Gosport." Hopefully a lie.

"But he could have been."

"He could also be in my closet," she quipped. "Or hiding in the ivy." She gestured to the window. "Or having tea with the butcher, biding his time until one of us needs a pound of pork. You yourself said that Saraj has no reason to come after us." *Or does he?* North. Why did he go north?

"Then you have no reason to go after him," he replied. He stood straight and ran a hand back through his hair, making the waves fall unevenly about his face. "It makes me sick to think about it, Ceony. Lira, Grath . . . It's like you have a checklist for dangerous criminals tucked into your pocket, and you won't be satisfied until you've had a personal encounter with each."

Ceony folded her arms, more for comfort than out of anger. "I just want to know my family is safe."

"Are they?"

It wasn't a mocking question, just a prod into what Ceony had found. She debated telling him, but she didn't want Emery dwelling on her unnatural use of magic. She'd kept the secret for too long to tell him now.

"I don't think he left England," she replied, softer. "And if that's true, I want to know why. Did you know he escaped near a naval base? Even he wouldn't risk crossing the water near so many soldiers.

What if he's trying to lose himself among the common folk, all the while harvesting them as he plans his great escape, or worse?"

Emery stepped into the room, a long breath passing through his nostrils. He set a heavy hand on either of Ceony's shoulders. "I messaged Alfred today, but he had little information to share. I will contact him again and ask to be kept informed," he offered. "Will that be enough?"

Would it? Ceony didn't know. "So long as he doesn't involve you in the case," she said.

"Or you," Emery added. His grip lightened, as did his tone. "Promise me you won't try to go after this man."

Ceony frowned. "I'll promise if you will."

A slight smile touched Emery's lips and eyes. "Promise."

"Promise."

He kissed her lightly on the lips. "Let's find something for dinner," he said. "And pack your bags. I'm to introduce you to Magician Pritwin Bailey tomorrow morning."

———

Nerves roused Ceony early the next morning, but she took her time getting ready, humming old lullabies to herself as she dressed and pinned her hair in an effort to keep herself calm. She chose a rose-colored dress from her closet—she'd obtained a few rather nice pieces of clothing during her apprenticeship—and summoned Jonto to help her with its buttons. She looped a light-red ascot around her neck and, despite the warm weather, the dark-olive jacket that had come with the dress. She left the matching hat on her bed while she had a boiled egg for breakfast. It would be impossible to stomach more than that.

Today is the start of the finishing, she thought as she broke into the shell of her small meal. *A couple weeks with Prit—no, Magician Bailey—and I'll take my test. I'll become a magician.*

Emery entered the kitchen, covering a yawn with his knuckles.

Ceony slid the spoon into the egg's flesh. *I won't be Emery's apprentice anymore. No more secrets. No more gossip. No more waiting.*

She smiled to herself and chewed on the bit of egg. It grew bland in her mouth. *Unless I fail.*

She could take the test again, eventually. But Ceony suspected that the humiliation of failure would carry a greater weight than the failure itself.

"Should I be jealous?" Emery asked as he pulled a half loaf of bread out of the cupboard—cheese-and-herb bread Ceony had made two days ago.

Ceony glanced up from her egg. "Hmm?"

"I don't think you've worn that since Patrice's luncheon. Magician Bailey will be impressed."

Ceony rolled her eyes. "I want to make a good impression."

Emery chuckled to himself and buttered two slices of bread. "The buggy should be here soon. Do you have your suitcase packed?"

"So eager to get rid of me?"

"Eager?" he repeated, rolling back the sleeves of his favorite indigo coat. "My kitchen will be empty in two days and I'll be forced to purchase my own groceries. How could I be eager for that?"

Ceony smiled and scooped out more egg. "You could always have Jonto cook your meals."

In fact, Emery once *had* tried to get Jonto to cook his meals. It had taken the paper magician two days to reconstruct the right hand and arm of the paper skeleton, which had burned off after Jonto attempted to light the coals in the oven.

"I'll be sure to stock up on sandwich supplies," Emery murmured.

"And all you'll miss is the food, hm?"

His eyes glimmered. "I may miss the mid-night companionship."

Ceony flushed. "Emery Thane!" *That was* one *time.*

Emery just chuckled, the cursed man. Peeling the shell off her breakfast, Ceony asked, "When was the last time you saw Magician Bailey?"

"Saw him?" Emery repeated between bites. "I suppose at that fund-raising banquet. The one where a certain hot-tempered young waitress dumped a pitcher of wine on a guest's lap." He smiled. "Spoke to him, though . . . My graduation from Praff, unless you count the recent telegrams and mail birds."

"You really don't like each other, then."

"He doesn't like *me*," Emery corrected. "And I can't blame him. But he's not the most remarkable fellow himself."

"Emery!"

The paper magician smiled, the expression all in his bright-green eyes, like he knew something Ceony didn't. Ceony sighed. She would miss those eyes. But her test had been scheduled for three weeks from today. Compared with how long she'd already waited, three weeks was next to nothing.

The buggy arrived. A violet paper butterfly rested on the seat beside the driver, bearing the cottage's address on its right wing in Emery's handwriting. Emery loaded Ceony's suitcase into the automobile's trunk before taking a seat beside her. The buggy turned around and headed back into London.

"Relax," Emery whispered after a few minutes on the road. He placed a hand over Ceony's, which had been twisting a pleat in her skirt between thumb and middle finger. "You'll be fine."

"Would I pass your test?" she asked back, keeping her words low. "If you tested me, would I pass?"

"It's all the same test. There are certain regulations."

"Maybe the answer keys are all the same," Ceony began, "but that doesn't make it all the same test."

Emery hummed an agreement. He said nothing more, only took Ceony's hand between his own. The warmth of his skin buzzed up her arm like fireflies.

The buggy drove through London, hitting a bit of horse traffic near Newington. Ceony focused on her pleats as the buggy passed over the River Thames. They drove by Parliament Square and headed west out of the main city, toward Shepherd's Bush, where Mg. Bailey lived.

Shepherd's Bush was a mostly rural and residential area spotted with farmland. Ceony watched the houses scroll by, their yards and walls growing with each passing mile. She soon found herself staring at homes bigger than the cottage, then bigger than Mg. Aviosky's house, then bigger yet. The space between the houses grew, too, and the street became narrower.

She glanced at Emery, but he seemed just as curious as she. Of course he had never been to Mg. Bailey's home.

After a few more miles, the buggy reached the end of a long dirt road with a row of grass growing in the middle of it. The vehicle turned about in a wide circle, pulling up to a thick and well-pruned wall of bushes that acted as a fence around a property that seemed larger than the entire Mill Squats. The trim grounds had no flowers, only decorative shrubbery of all shapes and sizes.

Ceony stepped out of the buggy, her movements sluggish, her mouth agape. The house itself stood a dozen times larger than the cottage, built of brick that looked like sandstone in the sun and mauve in the shade. Three chimneys rose from the tightly shingled roof, and every window held three glass panes trimmed with white. Ivy covered half the house, including a smaller section on the left that looked to be servants' quarters but seemed unoccupied.

The mansion dwarfed Ceony the way Big Ben might dwarf an ant. She had thought Mg. Aviosky's house excessively large, but Ceony's entire family, her cousins included, couldn't possibly use all the space inside this manor.

But perhaps the starkest difference was the lack of paper. Emery's home was covered in paper wards and paper décor. Even the gardens sported paper plants. But not a shred of magic touched this house. It looked positively normal, if expensive.

She glanced to Emery. "This *can't* be the right place."

"Oh, I have a feeling it is," he commented, circling the buggy to pull Ceony's suitcase from the trunk. "The textbook industry must be doing remarkably well."

"Textbooks?"

"Last I heard, that was Prit's specialty. Enchanted textbooks that rewrite themselves depending on the student's reading level, diagrams that pop off the page, and the like. Very popular in America. Did you not have them at Praff?"

She frowned. "No, but wouldn't that have been remarkable? Perhaps I wouldn't have dragged my feet about Folding so much had my donor provided them."

Emery chuckled.

Ceony scanned the bushes until she found an arched gateway several paces to her left. She took a few steps toward it before turning back to Emery and asking, "Do we . . . let ourselves in?"

Emery opened his mouth to respond, then spied over the bushes and answered, "Seems help is on the way."

Ceony followed his gaze and stood on her toes. She spied a cobbled walkway leading from the mansion's central door and a flash of sunny-blond hair bobbing along it—hair that made Ceony think of Delilah. Moments later the gate unbolted and a man Ceony's age stepped through.

Though it had been two years, Ceony recognized him immediately. "Bennet Cooper?" she asked. He had graduated with Ceony from Tagis Praff, having placed third in class. Ceony had placed first.

Bennet offered a sheepish smile. Sunlight glinted off his straight, equally sunny hair. He wore simple tan slacks and a simple, white, collared shirt without pockets under his red apprentice's vest. Ceony wondered if she should have worn her apprentice's apron as well.

"Hi, Ceony," he said. He then stiffened like a soldier and added, "Magician Thane, it's a pleasure to meet you finally."

Bennet took a few long strides and offered his hand to the paper magician, who stood taller in height by several inches. Emery shook the apprentice's hand with an amused twinkle in his eye. Bennet continued. "I've heard a great many things about you."

"And you still shook my hand?" Emery asked. "Your mother raised you well."

Bennet blinked wide eyes. "Sir?"

Emery patted Bennet's shoulder and strolled up to the gate. "I'm sure Magician Bailey has chattered quite a bit about me in the last few days . . . Ah, here he comes now."

Bennet glanced in Ceony's direction and finnicked with the elbows of his shirt before hurrying to the gate. He pushed it open and held it for several seconds before a tall man emerged.

Ceony recognized him from the memory of Emery's secondary-school experience, though Pritwin Bailey had certainly grown these last fifteen years. He stood straight and narrow, wearing simple clothes as Bennet did, though they had been well tailored and made of fine materials. His pale skin looked as if it had never seen the light of day, and his dark hair only made his complexion appear more washed out. He had a long, slim face free of any facial hair and a pair of thin, gold spectacles perched on his nose.

But what struck Ceony foremost about his appearance was the lack of a smile on his face—or any sign of goodwill whatsoever.

"Thane," he said, clasping his hands behind his back. There would be no handshake, then. "You seem unchanged."

"I do try," Emery replied. His lip quirked almost as if to smile, and Pritwin's mood seemed to grow ever grimmer.

Bennet cleared his throat. "Magician Bailey, this is Ceony Twill, Magician Thane's apprentice."

"I know who she is," Mg. Bailey said, and though his response was bland, Ceony didn't detect malice in his tone. Good—the man had no reason to hold qualms against her, save by association. Mg. Bailey adjusted his spectacles and looked down at Ceony. "I hope you've come prepared. I have no intention of postponing your test for lack of study."

Ceony chewed and swallowed a frown before it could touch her lips. "I assure you, I'm quite prepared."

Emery said, "Miss Twill could take the test tonight and pass. I have every confidence in her abilities."

"Hmm," Mg. Bailey said. "And that confidence is the reason you're leaving her with me, is it?"

"I'm sure there's something you can teach her that's slipped my mind. Something somewhere in this enormous house of yours. How are the acoustics, if I may ask?"

Mg. Bailey's face took on the puckered look of someone who has tasted a bad lemon. Bennet began playing with his sleeve elbows again.

"I'm sure the acoustics are grand," Ceony said, turning to Emery for her suitcase. She gave him a warning glare, but he pretended not to see it.

"Oh, here, allow me," Bennet chimed, hurrying forward to take the suitcase before Ceony could get a grip on it.

"Well," Emery said after a few seconds of silence between himself and the other Folder, "I suppose I should be on my way. You're in well-practiced hands, Miss Twill. You may be a Folder the next time I see you."

Ceony paused at that, meeting Emery's gaze, wondering if he noticed her surprise. *I hope it's not that long*, she thought, urging him to read her mind. He smiled at her enigmatically.

"She may be," Mg. Bailey agreed, though he seemed to emphasize *may* without actually emphasizing it at all. Perhaps Ceony had imagined it.

She wanted to say good-bye to Emery, to embrace him, to kiss the line of his jaw, but she certainly couldn't with two witnesses—three if she counted the buggy driver, who had worked his way through half a fag while still seated in his automobile.

Emery nodded to the other paper magician and to Bennet before telling Ceony, "Good luck. You know how to reach me in case you need anything."

Ceony nodded, feeling an unseen band of rubber stretch between her and Emery as he turned to go.

"Good day, Magician Thane!" Bennet yelled after him. Emery waved politely before getting in the car. The driver dropped his burning cigarette out the window and turned back onto the road.

Ceony frowned as the buggy drew away. Three weeks suddenly seemed a very long time.

"Bennet, fetch that," Mg. Bailey said, and Bennet—suitcase still in hand—rushed over to the fallen cigarette and stomped it out with his heel, then picked it up and pocketed it.

Mg. Bailey headed back through the gates and into the house without further ado. Ceony hesitated, wondering if she should follow, but fortunately Bennet reappeared at her side and gestured toward the cobbled path. "This way, Ceony. It's all right to call you that, isn't it?"

"It is my name," Ceony said, letting herself relax. "You called me that at Praff, and I'm not a magician yet, besides."

Bennet smiled. "Neither am I. Obviously." He cleared his throat. "Um, this is the front of the house; that window up there, in the corner on the third floor, is yours. Gets a little warm in the early afternoon if you don't pull the shades."

Ceony nodded, taking in the grounds of the mansion. They seemed even larger now that she could see beyond the bushy perimeter. "It's all very . . . impressive," she said.

"Isn't it?" Bennet asked. "Unless you've lost something. It's a pain to find things in there."

"Is it just you and Magician Bailey?"

He nodded. "A maid comes by three times a week, if that counts for anything."

"Pets?"

"No . . . Magician Bailey doesn't like animals," he answered, looking ahead at his tutor, whose quick strides had already pulled him to the front door. The Folder didn't wait for either apprentice before letting himself in.

"He's a little standoffish," Ceony said.

At the same moment, Bennet asked, "Does Magician Thane keep pets?"

"He's allergic, but I do have a paper dog," she said. She smiled. "His name is Fennel. He's folded up in that case, actually."

"Oh, interesting! But no Bizzy, I take it," he said, referring to the Jack Russell terrier Ceony had kept in her dorm at Tagis Praff.

"No Bizzy. She's back with my family now."

"I'm sure Fennel will be a treat. Just"—he paused—"keep him away from Magician Bailey. Just in case. I mean, Magician Bailey is great and all, but it's better to be safe."

They reached the door, which Bennet opened for Ceony. A broad hallway, painted white with dark-stained oak floorboards underfoot, greeted them. An oriental rug of burgundy and navy covered most of the floor. At the end of the hall spiraled a set of white-banistered stairs. The left side of the hall opened onto a grand sitting room, complete with a fainting sofa and a pianoforte. A five-tiered crystal chandelier hung above a crystal table in the center of the room, upon which sat a tray of unused teacups. It looked very much the opposite of Emery's front room—surfaces were uncluttered, or they only sported one or two pieces of show, such as a vase or music box. It all looked rather immaculate.

The right side of the hallway opened onto a smaller room. It had a small table with four chairs and a granite fireplace but didn't appear to be meant for dining. Perhaps snacking? Ceony wasn't sure what sort of rooms could fill a house this size, particularly one that was only home to two people.

She tore her eyes away, trying not to stare. "So you signed up for paper?"

Bennet laughed an awkward, airy laugh. "Not really. I was assigned it by Magician Aviosky. She didn't give me much room for negotiation."

"She didn't give me any, either," Ceony agreed. Bennet seemed pleased to hear that he was not alone in his experience.

She wanted to add, *But I'm glad it turned out this way*, but Bennet interrupted the thought with, "Well, I'll start the tour here. Down this way is the leisure library and the guest lavatory, as well as Magician Bailey's office, but don't go in there unless invited, and if the door's closed, don't knock. He doesn't like being disturbed when he's working."

"Working on what?" Ceony asked, followed by, "Where *is* Magician Bailey?" Shouldn't *he* be giving her the tour?

"Um," Bennet said, glancing up and down the hallways on either end of the spiral stairs. "I think he's in his office. He was in there before you came; he's getting ready for your testing. There are preparation materials of some kind. He couldn't really tell me what."

Ceony nodded slowly. It made sense, at least. But so far Pritwin Bailey's reclusiveness made Emery look like a socialite.

"Down here"—Bennet gestured to the left—"is the kitchen, the casual dining hall, and the formal dining hall. You can tell the difference by the table size and the lighting. The formal dining hall has color-shifting glass and a longer table."

"Oh," Ceony said. *Color-shifting glass?* That was a spell she didn't know. She'd have to look it up and learn how to cast it. Her youngest sister, Margo, would faint to have such a spell in her bedroom!

"The chef will be here in about an hour," he added. "Past the stairs—"

"Chef?" Ceony asked.

"Yes, ma'am," Bennet said. He smiled and brushed hair off his forehead with his free hand. He certainly was a handsome man. "Magician Bailey has one come in every weekday, and on weekends we fend for ourselves."

"I can cook," Ceony offered as Bennet moved to the base of the spiral stairs. "I don't mind. I enjoy it."

"Really?" Bennet asked. He glanced from her face to her feet and back again. "This weekend, maybe? Magician Bailey won't cancel his cook . . . Besides, I'm sure you'll be busy. With your preparations for the test and all."

Ceony nodded.

"Past the stairs is the sunroom, and through there the greenhouse, though I only have a few plants thriving at the moment. Magician Bailey hasn't tried to grow anything for a while. It's a lot of work. And there"—he pointed to a back corner of the house with his suitcase hand—"is a storage room and the hallway to the servants' quarters, which we don't use."

Ceony committed the layout to memory, though the last bit proved difficult, as she hadn't seen the rooms herself. The house was so large she wondered if even her quick memory would be able to master it.

Bennet continued the tour through the second and third floors, pointing out the music room, the technical library (where all his study materials lay, along with two very large maps), a few guest bedrooms, his bedroom, a drawing room, trophy room, deck, and study. Farther in, he indicated another drawing room, two "dressing rooms," a materials room for magic crafting, a private sitting room, a study just for apprentices, and an assortment of different-sized lavatories. A small one resided just outside Ceony's bedroom. If the sheer, needless vastness of the mansion didn't make Ceony's head spin, the idea of having her own bathing room did. Even at Tagis Praff she'd never had that luxury.

Bennet opened the door to her room, which had indeed been overwarmed by the afternoon sun. It had a long off-white rug running perpendicular to the dark oak floorboards, which readily creaked under their footsteps. A rather large bed with rose-colored blankets sat in the middle of the room, extending out from the length of wall between two westward-facing windows. A dainty glass table and two white chairs for private breakfasting were arranged in one corner. Against the wall with the door rested a large wardrobe, and across the corner from it, a tall dresser.

It was one of the smaller bedrooms Ceony had seen in the mansion, but it was easily two and a half times the size of her room at the cottage.

The cottage. Ceony missed it already.

Bennet set her suitcase down on one of the chairs. "I'll give you a chance to settle in, and I'll call you down to dinner, unless you'd like to eat alone in your room."

"No, no, I'll come down," she said, feeling a little lost in the wide space.

"Do you like it? I could move you," Bennet offered. "I made sure to dust it this morning, and the sheets are clean. Is it too hot? Oh, I forgot the pitcher and basin."

Ceony smiled. "It's lovely, and I don't need a pitcher with a lavatory right next door," she said. "Thank you. It's just different, that's all."

Bennet nodded, seeming pleased. "All right. My window is just below yours, so if you want to send a paper messenger to me for anything, please do."

"Perfect," Ceony said.

Bennet hesitated a moment, then nodded and excused himself. Ceony took the time to hang up her clothes and organize her personal items until dinner, which Mg. Bailey took in his office. Afterward, Ceony arranged her study materials in her dresser drawers. She could use one of the desks in the apprentices' study tomorrow. She slid her charm necklace around her neck and under her blouse, then reanimated Fennel, who sniffed about his new surroundings with a papery vigor.

Letting out a sigh, Ceony leaned against the mattress of the bed, surprised at how soft it felt. The sun had just begun to set, but perhaps she would turn in early and get a fresh start tomorrow. She did have a lot of work ahead of her.

A faint tapping on the rightmost window caught her attention. Lifting its curtains, she spied a turquoise paper butterfly hovering outside the glass. A message from Bennet?

It took a few heaves to open the seldom-used windowpane. Once she did, the butterfly fluttered in and gracefully landed on the glass table.

"Cease," she said, stilling its wings. She turned it over and unfolded it, recognizing the handwriting hidden inside its body immediately. Bennet hadn't sent this spell.

Emery had.

CHAPTER 8

CEONY CAREFULLY UNFOLDED the rest of the butterfly. The message had been scripted in pen—the copper-toned one Emery kept on his nightstand. The beautiful, flawless curves of each stroke made her smile before her mind even sorted out the words.

I hope this finds your room and not the housemaid's. There's nothing like jam and cold bread to make a man appreciate a woman.

Setting the butterfly down, Ceony retrieved a few pieces of paper she had packed into her bag—it was always smart for a Folder to carry a personal supply—and wrote out her response in the center of a white square.

You wouldn't be in poor company if you hired a cook. Prit does! I need to write a letter to Mg. Aviosky and thank her for assigning me to you and not him. I don't know how Bennet has kept such a stiff upper lip, working with him so long.

She paused, wondering if she should be careful with names. Shrugging, she Folded the square into a crane, slipping a farthing into its belly to give it some weight, should a nightly wind try to interrupt its course. She then Folded a link to a chain spell—only one, for the crane was small—out of a portion of the butterfly Emery had sent.

"Lock," she said, and the link tightened around the crane's torso without interfering with its wings. The spell would ensure that only the man whose handwriting was on the chain would be able to unfold the crane. Anyone else would destroy it trying.

Uttering instructions to the bird, Ceony sent it out her window and watched it fly off through the last tendrils of sunlight.

Fennel whined at her ankles—an unsurprising complaint, for she had neglected him most of the day. If nothing else, he would provide some entertainment while Ceony waited for her paper charm to fly across London.

Lighting a few extra candles—the mansion didn't have electric lights in most of the guestrooms—Ceony threw a knotted stocking back and forth for the paper dog for several minutes before slipping into the lavatory to wash her face and change into her night things. She tied a robe around herself even though she had no intention of leaving her room—one could never be too careful about avoiding Peeping Toms in a new place.

Fennel huffed at her, and in the spaces between his enchanted breaths, Ceony noticed how silent the large house really was. Someone could drop a fork in the kitchen two floors down and she'd hear it from up here.

She rubbed gooseflesh from her arms. With his room directly beneath hers, Bennet had the benefit of hearing her floorboards squeak.

Ceony's eyelids were growing heavy by the time a second, gray butterfly flew through her cracked window and landed gracefully on the breakfast table. Like she'd done with her crane, Emery had fastened a privacy link about the spell's body. His managed to look much more refined than her own, despite sporting all the same Folds.

She unfolded the butterfly and read:

It will do wonders for your patience. Don't let him postpone your test, Ceony. You're ready. I have every confidence in you.

And I do hope you're not focusing too strongly on young Bennet's upper lip.

Ceony smiled as she reread the message, rubbing her thumb over the coppery mark where Emery had smudged the word *young*.

Abandoning the table, Ceony pulled her pink lipstick from its place in the set of drawers and carefully smoothed it on, then pressed her lips to the center of another square of paper.

She penned *Only yours* on the sheet before Folding it into a bird and whispering, "Breathe."

It appeared that Mg. Bailey's hired chef did not report for breakfast, so early the next morning Ceony acquainted herself with the kitchen. The room was enormous, of course, with two ovens and three enchanted iceboxes, a bar with stools, a wine cabinet, and a long, casual table built to hug the far corner. The cupboards all matched the dark wood stain of the floor, and the counters even boasted a small preparation sink in addition to the normal one.

Ceony had started eggs and hollandaise sauce when Bennet, hair still wet from a bath and with newspaper in hand, came in. "I see you've situated yourself well," he said, stifling a yawn with his first two knuckles. He pulled over a stool and sat, spreading the Social News section before him. "What, um, are you making?"

Ceony held up an egg. "Would you like some?"

Bennet's shoulders sagged as he let out a long sigh. "Yes, please. I'm starving and I love hollandaise."

So does Emery, Ceony almost said, but she bit back the comment quickly enough. She substituted, "I'll try not to burn it. Should I make enough for Magician Bailey?"

"Magician Bailey already ate," sounded a third voice from the hall. Pritwin Bailey walked into the kitchen, well groomed and looking just as pale as he had yesterday, a piece of paper rolled like a scroll in his right hand. His tone was chiding.

"Good morning," Ceony offered, trying to be pleasant. She needed to make a good impression on the Folder, even if he seemed uninterested in impressing her. "I apologize for not being up earlier."

Mg. Bailey scoffed. "Does Thane use you as a maid, then? Cooking his meals, cleaning his windows, folding his laundry?"

Ceony almost swallowed her tongue to withhold the retort that tried to slip out. Then, to her dismay, the faintest blush betrayed her—she *did* do all those things, actually. But that didn't make her maidly.

"I just wanted to bestow the gesture," she said. Her voice sounded sweet enough.

"Hmm," Mg. Bailey replied. He set the rolled-up paper beside the stove. "I'm not one to waste time, Miss Twill. Here is a list of projects you'll need to complete before I will test you."

Ceony dared to stop stirring the sauce long enough to unfurl the paper. A cold shock struck her chest. "There has to be fifty or sixty items on this!" she exclaimed, reading over the bizarre requests. *#1. Something to open a door. #2. Something that breathes. #14. Something to hide the truth.*

"Fifty-eight, specifically," Mg. Bailey said, his face as stiff as his thin frame. "Standard. I suggest you get started when you're finished with your . . . gesture."

Ceony set the list down and stirred her hollandaise before it could stick to the bottom of its pan. "I need to Fold something for each number?"

"It is a Folder's test, Miss Twill," Mg. Bailey said while raising his eyebrow. To Bennet, he said, "Your report on chapters fifteen through twenty-one is due at noon."

"I'll have it to you," Bennet said.

"And your lesson at one."

"Of course."

Mg. Bailey nodded and turned from the room, not allowing Ceony another second of his time.

Ceony released a grumble and took the saucepan off the stove. *Intolerable! I almost don't blame Emery for picking on him at school.*

"Is it done?" Bennet asked excitedly. At least Mg. Bailey's sharpness didn't penetrate his apprentice's good humor.

As Ceony lifted her head from the sauce, however, she glimpsed an article title in the lower-left-hand corner of Bennet's newspaper: "Magicians' Cabinet to Rule on Opposite-Sex Apprenticeships."

"I . . ." she trailed, turning her head to try and read the script, but the letters were too small. "Done enough," she said. "Could I see that paper for a moment?"

"Uh, sure."

Abandoning the saucepan, Ceony scooped up the page in question and skimmed the article, pausing on one paragraph in particular:

"It is, in part, a means of decency," said Mg. Long. "We've had several complaints in regards to mixed sexes working together, from apprentices to magicians to even family members. When the ruling is approved, and I believe it will be, any apprenticeships not involving same-sex pairings will be split and reassigned. In today's England, such measures must be taken before scandal erupts."

Several complaints? Ceony thought. Surely not about her and Emery. Surely! So few knew. Mg. Aviosky wouldn't have reported anything, would she have? And Ceony knew her mother would never have said a word. She had seemed rather taken with the idea of having a daughter in romantic league with a magician.

She thought of Zina and felt her stomach sink. Surely Zina wouldn't have filed a complaint with the Cabinet . . . and wouldn't it take more than one complaint to make a ruling, besides? Ceony *had* to believe the best of her sister or go insane imagining the what-ifs. If nothing else, Ceony could take comfort in knowing Zina would likely be too lazy to fill out a report.

How strange it all felt. She and Zina had never been at odds before, not like this.

"What is it?" asked Bennet.

Reassigned. Ceony frowned. If she didn't pass her magician's test in three weeks, she might not be able to continue her tutelage under Emery. Perhaps she wouldn't even be able to stay in London. There was only one female Folder of whom Ceony knew, and rumor had it she'd moved to the United States.

"Ceony?"

"Oh, sorry." She handed back the newspaper and passed Bennet a plate so he could serve himself. Bennet inspected the newspaper, probably trying to determine what article had so grasped Ceony's attention. To avoid conversation, Ceony examined the list Mg. Bailey had given her. After scanning to number fifty-eight, she refocused on the first item: *Something to open a door.*

Open a door? she wondered. As in a paper spell to open a door? But who would craft a spell to turn a handle when it could so easily be done without magic?

I have to pass this test, she chided herself. The stakes were higher now than ever.

She tapped the corner of the list against her lips. Jonto was capable of opening a door. Not that she had time to construct a paper butler, but it gave her an idea.

#2. Something that breathes. Any animation would do. She could Fold that in her sleep.

#3. Something to tell a tale. Story illusion.

#4. Something that sticks.

"Sticks?" she repeated. Something sticky, or something to stick to something else? A throwing star might serve a purpose there . . . but it would be best to come up with multiple solutions. Better to overprepare than be caught off guard. She had a feeling Mg. Bailey wouldn't give her any clues.

"Hm?" Bennet asked, swallowing a mouthful of egg. He eyed her list. "I don't think I'm supposed to know anything about that."

Chewing on her lip, Ceony rolled up the list and stuck it in her skirt pocket. "Let us assume that I'll be very, very busy while I'm here," she said.

She eyed the newspaper and wondered if Emery had seen the article, too.

Ceony took the cushioned chair in the corner of the apprentices' study while Mg. Bailey instructed Bennet in his next Folding lesson. The study was about the size of Emery's library, which meant it was relatively small for the enormous home. It had a short bookcase half-filled with books, a narrow shelf that appeared to be filled with homework assignments and notebooks, and a row of six desks—far more than necessary—taking up the east wall. A giant, multipaned window comprised the entire north wall, and the west held cubbies stacked with various lengths and thicknesses of paper. Two simple chandeliers hung from the ceiling, both made of glass bulbs filled with Pyre-enchanted fire, much like the streetlamps in downtown London. They would light when the room grew dark, and didn't require new glass or matches, though a Pyre would need to come twice a year to rejuvenate their glow. Ceony had learned that from her readings on fire magic.

Her attention wasn't focused on the lights, however, but on number fourteen on her list of tasks: *Something to hide the truth.* A blind box could work perfectly for that, unless Mg. Bailey expected her to use a nullification spell on a fortuity box. That didn't require much in the way of preparation, however. Ceony would merely need to command the fortuity box "UnFold" while the fortune-teller used it, and she doubted the test could be that easy.

"It will destroy the paper with random tears," Mg. Bailey said to Bennet from one side of a cherrywood table. Bennet occupied the other side. They both sat with rigid backs. The "Shred" lesson seemed overly formal, in Ceony's opinion.

"Observe," he said, holding up a piece of unused paper. Such a waste.

"Shred," Mg. Bailey commanded, and the paper tore itself into over a dozen uneven portions. Bennet collected the pieces into a neat pile on the table surface. Once he had finished, Mg. Bailey continued. "It works on various sizes of paper, and on active paper spells—"

Ceony twirled a strand of hair around her finger. *#53. A means of escape.* Emery's glider immediately came to mind—could she use something that large on her test? She couldn't see why not, though she had a feeling the items on this list would need to be brought to and used in the test itself, and a glider large enough to carry her would be difficult to transport, especially if she didn't want it damaged during the trip. Unless she rode in on it . . .

Concealing confetti, she thought. A trick parlor magicians loved to purchase from Folders—paper confetti that could be thrown in the air to teleport a person a very short distance, so long as it wasn't through a wall. She'd first encountered the spell in Belgium, when Emery had used it to circumvent Grath. Perhaps that would work.

Too bad I can't just mirror teleport, Ceony thought. She fingered the charm necklace hidden beneath the collar of her shirt.

"Miss Twill."

Mg. Bailey's sharp use of her name drew Ceony from her thoughts. She lifted her head and dropped her hand from the necklace.

The Folder frowned. "Did you not bring a ledger?"

She blinked. "A ledger?"

"For notes."

Ceony cast a glance at Bennet, who rubbed the back of his head and avoided eye contact. "Notes on this lesson?"

Mg. Bailey sighed. "Yes, Miss Twill."

"I know the 'Shred' spell, Magician Bailey," Ceony said.

"And would a review not be beneficial to your magician's test?"

Ceony felt as though her ribs had turned into vipers and were in the midst of attacking one another. She tried to smooth her eyebrows, which had skewed significantly in response to the Folder's questions. "I . . . no. I'm quite familiar with the spell and have used it multiple times successfully. Taking notes would be . . . redundant."

"And what of other spells I may teach today, or tomorrow, hm?" Mg. Bailey asked, his face looking even longer. The corners of his lips drooped into his chin. "Do you feel too experienced to benefit from them?"

A blush threatened to creep into Ceony's cheeks—or perhaps it was a flush of anger. "I mean no disrespect."

"Answer the question."

"Magician Bailey . . ." Bennet whispered, but if the Folder heard his name, he ignored it.

Ceony sat up as straight as her spine would allow. "If I did not feel confident in my knowledge of Folding, I would not be making the preparations for my magician's test. No, I don't believe I need a ledger. If by some means you teach something that Magician Thane has failed to instruct me on in *his* lessons, I will pay rapt attention, I assure you."

Mg. Bailey snorted. "If Magician Thane believes he can cover every aspect of Folding in two years, he's deluded."

The flush made it to Ceony's face this time. "You'll have to take that up with the Cabinet, then, Magician Bailey," she said, each word sticking to her teeth like saltwater taffy. "The education board is the department that deduced a person could earn their magicianship in two years. I'm sure Patrice Aviosky would love to hear your explanation as to why the department is in error."

Mg. Bailey narrowed his eyes. A few long seconds passed before he said, "You're dismissed, Miss Twill."

Gladly, Ceony thought, but she dared not push her luck with more words. Rising from her chair, she smoothed her skirt and walked to the door with the paper list in hand, fighting her desire to run, stomp, and curse the bloody man's name.

"Deluded," she mumbled to herself. She pinched her lips together, hoping the word didn't carry through the vast emptiness of the ridiculous house, if the man could hear *anyone* speak with that ego pressing against his eardrums. "No wonder this place is so empty," she added with a scowl. "Who on earth would want to live with *him*?"

She fidgeted with her necklace and daydreamed of going back into the study and turning Pyre right then and there. How she would love to hurl a ball of flames right at Mg. Bailey's head!

She found Fennel scratching at the door in her room, his rubber paw pads thumbing against the doorjamb. She picked the pup up in her arms and scratched his neck.

"Sorry, boy," she said. "I'm sure Magician Bailey would love to de-spell you if you wandered into his line of sight."

Fennel huffed and wagged his tail, jerking toward the window. Another butterfly rested on its pane, a brief letter from Emery hidden in its Folds. He recounted the dullness of his day and an invitation to a ball being thrown for new Tagis Praff graduates. He had likely been invited since he might soon be free to take on a new apprentice. So they both hoped, anyway, at least if the position opened for the right reason, and not because Ceony was forced to relocate and live with a female mentor. Of course, he claimed he didn't plan to attend.

Oh, how she missed Emery. And the thought of how Mg. Bailey had insulted him, not to mention *her*, set her bones blazing once more. She lowered Fennel to the floor and punched her mattress. That man was *trying* to be impossible.

Ceony pulled free her list of items to Fold for her test and set it on the breakfast table, which was slowly transforming into a desk. It would be best if she started now. The sooner she passed her test and left the Bailey prison, the better.

CHAPTER 9

THAT NIGHT, HOVERING over the breakfast table beside two thick candles, Ceony rubbed the sprout of a headache from her right temple. A ledger sat open under one wrist, while the list from Mg. Bailey was sprawled beneath the other.

#24. Something to cross a river.

She chewed on the end of her pencil. Surely she wouldn't have to physically cross a river! As far as she knew, the magician's test wasn't mobile . . . but then again, she knew never to expect the expected when it came to magicians, especially Folders. Emery had taught her that, and on her very first day as his apprentice, no less.

Something to cross a river. A shiver coursed up one arm, across her shoulders, and down the other. Would they make her demonstrate the device? Either way, she couldn't let her hydrophobia thwart her chances of winning her certificate. She just couldn't.

Sighing, Ceony scanned down the list to numbers thirty-two and thirty-three. *Something to cause a storm* and *Something to repel the rain.* All three items were water-related. The storm wasn't specific, though. Perhaps she could create the illusion of a storm, or Fold dozens of water-droplet-shaped spells that could fall from the ceiling like paper snowflakes.

As for repelling the rain—*real* rain, she assumed—Ceony's mind warped back to the night she and Emery had fallen into the river in their buggy, and the "Conceal" spell Emery had used. It had taken a bowed shape, similar to an umbrella. Such a spell, modified, could potentially repel rain for a short time.

Saraj.

Ceony shook her head. He, of course, had caused the accident, but she couldn't worry about him now. She had a test to focus on—a test that Mg. Bailey apparently didn't believe she could pass.

He's still in England, a voice in her head insisted.

Ceony set her pencil down and rubbed the base of her hands into her eyes. *Focus!*

A knock sounded at her door.

Ceony lowered her hands as Fennel's tail shot straight into the air in excitement. He yipped his whispery bark and hurried for the door.

Ceony almost stopped the paper dog, but surely Mg. Bailey wouldn't come all this way to speak to her. And about what? Certainly not to apologize.

"Come in," she said.

The door creaked open and Bennet poked his head in. His blue-eyed gaze jumped to Fennel almost instantly. "Oh my!" he said, crouching down and prodding the dog's ears. When he realized they wouldn't fall off or crumple under his touch, he let himself get a bit rougher. "This is the dog!"

"Fennel," Ceony said with a smile. "He's been aching for company."

Fennel yipped and put his front paws on Bennet's knees, licking his hands with that paper tongue. Ceony hoped it didn't leave any paper cuts in its wake, as it had been known to do.

After a moment Bennet stood. "Do you mind?"

Ceony waved him forward.

Bennet shut the door to prevent Fennel's escape, glanced around for a moment, then took the chair opposite Ceony, though there wasn't an inch of free space on the breakfast table. "I wanted to come by and apologize for Magician Bailey."

"He can't apologize for himself?"

"He's just got some chipped shoulders, if you know what I mean."

Fennel sniffed about the newcomer's shoes for a moment before occupying himself with something on the other side of the bed.

"I have a vague idea," Ceony said. She knew the man had been picked on in school—Emery being one of his tormenters—but that had been years ago. Surely he hadn't held on to such old grievances for so long! "But it gives him no excuse. If nothing else, I'm a lady."

"He's just . . . different, I guess," Bennet said. "I had a hard time adjusting, too, but after a month or so I started to understand him. We get on well now."

Ceony shut her ledger. "He treats you like a butler."

"No," Bennet said, "not really. I mean . . . *please* and *thank you* aren't foremost in his vocabulary, but he means them. Implies them. If he asks you to do a small task, there's no harm in doing it, and he'll be more pleasant afterward. That's one rule I've learned."

Despite being a "lady," Ceony snorted and leaned back in her chair. "*Rule?* What other *rules* should I be aware of?"

"Well . . ." Bennet paused, thinking. "It's best not to bother him in the morning if you need something . . . and requests are best made through paper mail. You know, sending a crane to his office."

"But we're in the *same house!*"

"A big house, but it takes the edge off," Bennet explained. "You know, lets him mull it over before answering. He doesn't like to be surprised, and he's more positive when given a chance to mull."

Ceony resisted the urge to roll her eyes.

"Really, though"—Bennet clasped his hands in his lap—"it takes him a long time to get used to people, and he just likes to keep to himself. Sometimes it's nice not to have to report every little thing, you know? As long as I keep up with my lessons and get my homework done on time, we get along. And he doesn't care what I do with my free time. There's lots of space to stretch out."

A long sigh passed through Ceony's lips. "I suppose he and I are just very different," she said.

Bennet straightened, eyes wide and hopeful.

"And," Ceony continued, "it's only for a few weeks. I can follow these . . . rules . . . for a few weeks."

Bennet grinned. "I'm happy to help, always. If you need anything. I know you're more advanced and all—"

"You'll be testing soon, won't you?" she asked.

Bennet shrugged. "Maybe in a year. I don't know. I don't think I'm ready."

Ceony frowned. "With a different teacher, you might be."

He smiled. "I appreciate your confidence. And when you need a break . . . there's a really lovely park not far from here. Magician Bailey has his own Mercedes, and sometimes he lets me take it out. There's a duck pond, and it's a nice place for a picnic."

Ceony, who had taken to bending the corner of her test list back and forth, slowed her fingers. She kept her shoulders lax, but her chest began to warm. Surely Bennet wasn't insinuating a date . . . Was he?

"Oh?" she asked. Prodded.

"Just say the word."

Ceony glanced to one of the paper butterflies beside her window. *I guess I just won't give the word*, she thought. *No harm done.*

"Thank you for the offer," she said. "Hopefully I won't *need* a break." She sighed and lifted the list from the table. "I have so much to do. I'll have to get to Folding tomorrow."

"Well, I won't keep you," Bennet said, rising from the table. Fennel ran over to meet him, perhaps hoping the visitor would play. Bennet laughed and rubbed the top of the paper dog's head. "So expertly made," he said. "I'm really impressed. Would you consider letting me take him apart to see how he works? I don't recognize some of these Folds."

Ceony stiffened. Her extra enchantments on Fennel aside, she couldn't bear the thought of someone taking him apart. Not when Emery's hands had so expertly crafted him, twice.

"I'd . . . prefer to keep him intact," she said.

Fortunately, Bennet didn't push the matter. "All right, but I wouldn't mind getting a lesson from you in advanced animation," he said, apparently assuming Ceony the pup's creator. "Have a good night."

She smiled. "You, too. And thank you."

Bennet left the room, shutting the door quietly behind him. Ignoring her work, Ceony penned Emery a note and Folded it into a crane.

She didn't mention Bennet's invitation.

———

Mg. Pritwin Bailey paced back and forth in the apprentices' study, turning just before reaching either curtain covering the large window. Morning sunlight gleamed off his spectacles whenever he passed in front of a certain ray of light, and he clasped his hands behind his back.

"Recite the steps for a 'Stiffen' spell," he commanded Bennet, who sat dutifully in a chair at the table.

Ceony, as before, had taken up residence in the corner of the room. She held her ledger on her lap, though the writing on the current page grew more lax and sloppy with each passing line. The words morphed from thoughts on her magician's test to unsorted notes regarding Saraj Prendi.

He wouldn't be in that community, Ceony thought, thinking of her personal investigation in Gosport. *But could I send in spies? No, if there were anything to find there, Criminal Affairs would have found it. They'd catch me, and besides, paper spells aren't complex enough to hold the orders I would need to give them. It's a dead end.*

Criminal Affairs had more information than she did. Mg. Hughes had been impressed with her before; perhaps he'd share something with her.

But Emery had already spoken with him. If he didn't relay any information to Emery, he certainly wouldn't let Ceony know his secrets. She frowned.

"—doesn't work with complex Folds," Bennet said from his seat. The "Stiffen" spell—a spell that would temporarily harden paper—was one Ceony had learned on her 211th day as an apprentice. It sounded like Bennet had learned it recently, written an essay about it, and was now being given a verbal quiz.

If I've heard nothing new about Saraj, he's probably not a threat, she chided herself. A moment passed before a speculative thought arrived: *But that also means he hasn't been caught.*

She adjusted herself on the chair. *I haven't been in contact with Magician Aviosky. And Emery . . . If Magician Hughes did update him, would he be willing to share bad news?*

She turned back one page in her ledger, where a creased magenta paper poked out from the ledger's binding, having once held the form of a butterfly.

Thinking of you. Study hard, and don't let them get to you.

She wondered if "them" included Bennet, or if Emery had been referring to the entire education board. Ceony wasn't sure how many of its members would be present for her actual test.

Letting out a long breath, Ceony flipped the page back over and examined her notes, which included drawings of stars with rounded corners attached to V-shaped bird wings. *#44. Something to guide your way through the dark.* She had decided to make starlights that would fly a step ahead of her when she moved. She had them half-Folded back in her room but had taken a break from her work after receiving a paper bat from Mg. Bailey, requesting her presence at Bennet's morning lesson.

She tuned in to the review for a few seconds. Pointless. Perhaps Mg. Bailey intended to waste her time so she wouldn't have a chance to finish her test preparation.

Bennet glanced in her direction, but Ceony averted her gaze to the window. After spending half a minute staring at the roof to the unused servants' quarters, Ceony kept her visage fixed on her ledger for the rest of the lesson.

She reread Emery's note. It made her chest hurt.

"Miss Twill."

She glanced up. Mg. Bailey stood at the end of the table where Bennet had sat perched moments before—Bennet himself had left—and smoothed out a long, rectangular piece of white paper across it. He then stood erect, folded his forearms behind his back, and gestured to the table with his narrow chin.

"Let's have a test of our own, shall we?" he said.

Ceony set her ledger down on the chair and stood. *We'll have a test of our own in two and a half weeks. Or have you forgotten?* She approached the table.

"Tell me," the Folder began, "how are your skills with paper illusions?"

"Were they not satisfactory, I wouldn't be here. Sir."

"Hmm. Show me." He gestured to the paper.

Ceony examined the paper before her, thinking of the party decorations she had done for Mrs. Holloway. So long ago . . . yet it wasn't. Did Mg. Bailey ever send Bennet on such errands? Ceony couldn't imagine the Folder taking time out of his schedule for that sort of work. Then again, she couldn't imagine anyone asking him for it. Textbooks, indeed.

"Did you want something in particular?" she asked.

Mg. Bailey walked around the table, taking up the same, slow march he had used during Bennet's lesson. "No," he said, "but try to impress me."

Ceony took a deep breath and held it in her lungs for several seconds. She stared at the paper. What would impress an arrogant man like Mg. Bailey? The illusion of a French dinner? A peek into a junglescape, like the design she'd created for Mrs. Holloway?

She thought of the park Bennet had mentioned, the one with the duck pond. She'd never done an illusion like that, and the prospect of trying it without testing it first made her nervous. But if she could turn the tabletop into fish-filled water and lily pads, it would undoubtedly be impressive. Emery would think so, anyway.

She moved to the far left side of the paper and picked up one corner but hesitated before Folding it. Mg. Bailey's eyes pinned her to the floor—she could feel his gaze on the back of her neck, but she ignored him.

The problem is that he can take a walk any time he wants and see a pond, she thought, chewing on her lower lip. *I need to do something different.*

She mulled, considering.

Mg. Bailey sighed. "To start, you should—"

"I'm merely giving my creativity a moment to work," Ceony interrupted, "but thank you for the willingness to assist."

After another moment, she began to Fold.

She started with the corners, pinching them, twisting one to add depth to the illusion. She grabbed a pencil from the desk so she could draw the spell's shapes, words, and other symbols that would contort the illusion into looking the way she wanted. She used a great deal of guessing in the appearance of the illusion—telescopes, enchanted or not, could only reveal so much—but hopefully that guessing would make the final result more "impressive."

Mg. Bailey watched her silently, thankfully withholding commentary. Ceony focused on her growing spell, trying not to wonder at what the Folder might be thinking.

A fan Fold, another symbol, and the long parchment darkened and speckled with spots of white. A mutted dog-ear Fold on the bottom corner made the specks rotate in slow motion. A whispered instruction added even more depth.

More words, more shapes hidden by blackness.

When Ceony stepped back, she and Mg. Bailey stared into a piece of the sky itself, beyond what the human eye could see.

Stars tumbled in different sizes and colors; a distant galaxy hovered in the upper-right corner; and a comet burned its way across the paper's surface. She included a rendition of the moon in the lower left, three-fourths of its cratered surface lit by the sun's light. Above it hovered Saturn, complete with a soft glow and dozens of tiny rings.

Ceony grinned; she had done well.

Mg. Bailey said nothing.

She looked at him, at the unreadable expression on his face. One forearm folded across his ribs; his other hand pinched his chin between thumb and forefinger as he studied her work. He didn't seem impressed. He didn't seem . . . anything.

Ceony wondered if she should ask for his evaluation or stay silent. She chose the latter.

A long minute passed before he said, "A decent illusion."

From Mg. Bailey, Ceony considered that high praise.

He continued. "I'm actually surprised at how quickly you finished it; twelve minutes and thirty-four seconds is fast for a page this size."

"You . . . timed me?"

He gestured weakly to the clock above the door. "A good time. Not the fastest, of course, but for an apprentice with only two years' experience, a good time. Hmm. Magician Thane must have finally gotten his wits about him and begun decent training, unless you had a second tutor."

Ceony's neck grew hot. She swallowed hard and said, "I did *not* have a second tutor."

He nodded, fingers still pinching his chin. "Wits it is, then. Good—I was worried the board would put him on probation after his illustrious failure with his last apprentice. I'm surprised they assigned a female apprentice to him."

Ceony's lips parted. Unseen spiders crawled up her back. For a moment she found herself speechless, but after a few seconds she found her voice. "How dare you," she said. "You know *nothing* about that."

Emery's second apprentice—Daniel. She had first learned of him during her journey through Emery's heart two years ago. Emery had transferred the apprentice after the situation with Lira, his ex-wife and a rising Excisioner, grew too heated. It had been for Daniel's own safety.

Mg. Bailey lowered his hand from his face. His eyes narrowed. "I'm stating a fact, Miss Twill. You'd do best to hold your tongue—"

"I will *not*," Ceony snapped. "I've been here three days, and already I've heard far too many jabs at Magician Thane. Regardless of any malice you two had in the past, he is a good man and a fantastic teacher, and I refuse to hear another word of this slander."

A flush burned a path across Mg. Bailey's pale skin. "How dare you speak to me in such a manner!"

"How dare you speak to *me* in such a manner!" Ceony shot back, feeling her own flush rise. "I did not come here to be insulted, or to listen to you affront my tutor!"

"Miss Twill—"

"You're just jealous that he's a better Folder than you," she spat.

Mg. Bailey's eyes went wide. Ceony snatched her ledger and marched for the door. She needed to get out of the room before she said more—this was the man who would be *testing* her, for heaven's sake! What fool thing had she done now?

Fortunately the Folder said nothing after her—nothing she could hear, anyway—and he didn't pursue her, not that Ceony turned around to check. Her footsteps echoed through the wide, empty halls, so lavish and cold. Her heels clomped in time with her pulse.

She made it to her bedroom and only just resisted the impulse to slam the door. Fennel, perched upon the bed, lifted his head, but even the paper dog sensed her foul mood and covered his muzzle with his rubber-lined paws.

Ceony pinched the phosphorus charm on her necklace. In less than a minute she could summon fireballs and literally burn this horrible mansion down to size. Let Mg. Bailey deal with *that*. Insufferable. How she pitied Bennet.

He'll toss me out, Ceony thought, pacing to the other end of the room. She pulled the pin from her hair and ran rigid fingers through the orange locks. *But what does it matter? I don't need him to be the one who tests me. Who cares if others question my abilities? I want Emery to administer my test.*

She thought of the newspaper article. *Scandal.* She harrumphed. *Who cares. Anything would be worth getting away from Pritwin Bailey!*

She dropped the hairpin onto her mattress and paced the length of the room two more times before pausing with her hands on her hips. She took a deep breath through her nose and released it slowly between tight lips.

"Study," she said aloud. Passing her test was her foremost goal now; she needed to be prepared regardless of who served as her tester.

Ceony jerked back one of the two chairs at the breakfast table, sat, and dropped her ledger on the table's glass surface. She opened it to the first page. Shut it. Opened it and turned to her notes on starlights. Flipped a few pages ahead and grabbed a pencil.

She held it over the paper, intending to pen a note to Emery, but she couldn't focus on that, either. What good would it do to write him a note in anger? Anyway, she knew he'd tell her to stay—if Pritwin would let her, at any rate.

Groaning, Ceony shut the ledger once more and leaned back in the chair. She would never pass at this rate. Mg. Bailey had utterly shattered her ability to concentrate.

Leaning back, Ceony stared at the ceiling and listened to her own breathing, waiting as it gradually slowed. Her neck hurt by the time she straightened.

She turned in response to a soft tapping at her bedroom window.

Ceony released a long breath, which contorted her lips into a smile. *Perfect timing*, she thought, rising from her seat. She couldn't run crying into Emery's arms, but his encouraging words always did wonders for her spirit.

She opened her window, expecting a small paper butterfly or glider, but the crumpled spell that fell over the windowsill had not been crafted by Emery's hands, but her own.

In her surprise, Ceony let the window fall shut. She scooped the red songbird into her palms. Rain had crinkled its pointed wings, and wind had bent and weakened its beak and tail. Dirt smudged the bright-crimson paper, making it look rusty.

Ceony smoothed the edges of the spell in an attempt to coax it to life, barely breathing as she did so. This songbird was one of four she had Folded in Gosport during her search for Saraj. How long had it spent scouring England for him? How long had it spent searching for *her*?

What had it found?

It was probably something inconsequential, like the enclave, but she had to know. "Can you show me where?" she asked the weakened spell.

The songbird hopped limply in her hands and toppled over against her fingers.

She pressed her lips together. The spell would never have the strength to fly to its destination, however near or far it might be. Ceony didn't think it could take to the air again at all, not with damage of this extent. She might not be able to follow it anyway. And she knew no way to transfer the knowledge of one spell to another—she couldn't Fold a second bird.

She chewed on the edge of her tongue for a long moment, then remembered the technical library.

Maps, she thought. Mg. Bailey had huge ones. It might be enough.

Holding her breath, Ceony dug out the mimic spell she'd shared with Mg. Aviosky. Perhaps the Gaffer had written back with news. If Criminal Affairs had a good lead on Saraj, there would be no need for her to follow up.

She found the spell. Blank.

Pinching the wings of the fatigued bird in her fingers, Ceony abandoned her studies and hurried to the technical library, trying her hardest not to run.

CHAPTER 10

MUTED LIGHT FROM the setting sun streamed into the library through its west-facing windows, making the book-lined walls look almost as rusty as the Folded songbird in Ceony's hands. Her footsteps sounded especially loud to her ears, and the creaking of the library doors as she closed them threatened to give her away.

Not give me away, she reminded herself. She hadn't done anything wrong.

Yet.

Her eyes scanned the tall set of drawers, which were bound to contain maps, but the ones hanging on the walls would be the true prize. On the left side of the library door hung a world map with several red pins marking cities in the eastern United States. The wall to the right of the doors displayed a large map of Great Britain, free of pins save for a yellow one marking Edinburgh, Scotland.

England stood almost as tall as Ceony herself. Perfect.

She cupped the red songbird in her hands and approached the map. "Can you tell me *where* you saw whatever it is you saw?" she asked.

The spell hopped weakly in her hands.

Pressing her lips together, Ceony eyed the map and the tacks that held it in place on the wall. The bird was too weak to float on its own for long. She set down the songbird on the drawers and grabbed one side of the map, freeing several tacks. She did the same on the other side until the wide, thick paper tumbled to the floor.

She laid it out flat and set the songbird atop it.

"Show me," she pressed.

The weak spell hopped once in place, then teetered onto one of its damaged wings. Ceony set it upright. It hopped down, moving toward London before it tumbled over a second time. Ceony righted it again.

The bird made its way to Reading in Berkshire and stopped.

Ceony scooped the spell into her cold hands and leaned in close to the map, pushing the tip of her right index finger into the circle marking Reading. "So close," she whispered. The words sent gooseflesh coursing down her arms. Her spine turned rigid.

But had the bird seen Saraj himself? Perhaps it had simply found another Indian community, or some foreigner matching Saraj's description. This might be another wild-goose chase. Of course, the bird could have located a different clue entirely.

"Thank you," she told the songbird as she drew back from the map. "Cease."

The animation flew out of the crinkled spell, putting the worn bird at rest.

She sat back on her heels, still cradling the bird. Reading. Could it be?

She had to know. She had to see for herself! A large part of her wished desperately that the bird was mistaken. That a simple paper spell couldn't have found anything of use.

Emery would tell me if there were any important updates, she thought. *And surely Magician Hughes would tell him . . .*

She glanced to the bird in her hands. Setting it down once more, Ceony used her necklace to become a Smelter, using "Target" and "Launch" commands on the tacks to return the map to its proper position on the wall. Returning to paper magic, she hurried from the library, winding her way back to her bedroom. The two rooms were spaced far enough apart that her lungs gasped for air by the time she reached her destination.

She set the songbird on the breakfast table and hurried to the window, checking its sill for further messages. Nothing. She opened the pane and stuck her head outside, searching the air and grounds in the dimming light. Seeing no sign of an incoming message, she sucked in a deep breath and stepped away from the window, leaving it open. She paced to the table and back.

So close, she thought, rubbing chills from her shoulders. She should send a message to her parents, alert them.

But she didn't know for sure. She couldn't until she went to Reading, explored it with her own eyes.

"You have no reason to go after him . . . Promise me you won't."

Ceony chewed her lower lip. "But I'm not going after him," she murmured to herself. "I'm only looking."

Her gut twisted, tight as a wrung rag, and her heart started to grow heavy. She glanced to the window again. Still nothing. She should write him.

And say what? she wondered, stretching back to relieve the twisting and weighing. Nothing that wouldn't get her into trouble, one way or another. And her nerves frayed too much for her to forge a cheery note.

She paced to the window and back, window and back, ignoring the way Fennel's eyeless face noiselessly followed her.

Reading. She could try and find a mirror . . . but the one in the lavatory next door was too small to fit through, and what if she missed the mark again and ended up somewhere outside Reading, alone and at night? Could she just transport from mirror to mirror until she got where she wanted, depending on luck to protect her from getting trapped in the purgatory between tarnished looking glasses?

She could summon a buggy at first light, but how much would it cost to hire a buggy to Reading? Would the train be faster? Would Mg. Bailey let her go? He might be happy to see the back of her, but she didn't want to antagonize him any more than she already had.

Ceony knit her fingers together and continued pacing. If she left now, she'd have the cover of darkness. Saraj would share that advantage, of course, but Ceony could handle that. Besides, if she were either a Gaffer or a Pyre, she could create light with the snap of her fingers. The cover of night would also help conceal her bond-breaking talent from others—bystanders, policemen, even Criminal Affairs itself. If others learned of it, they might not be as withholding with the information as Ceony was.

And what will you do if you find him, Ceony? she wondered. *Will you kill him?*

Her breath hitched. She worried her lip. She'd killed Grath, yes, and didn't regret doing so. He'd murdered Delilah. He would have killed her and Mg. Aviosky, too, if given the chance.

But did she really want to take a second life? Perhaps she could just maim Saraj, hurt him enough so he couldn't fight back . . . but no. She couldn't allow him another chance at escape. He had already been tried and convicted, besides. He was *supposed* to be dead.

Breathing in, Ceony filled her lungs until they threatened to burst, then let the air out all at once. *If* she found Saraj, *if* they had a confrontation . . . she wouldn't hold back. She couldn't afford to. He was undeserving of mercy.

But there was still the issue of getting to Reading. She could risk the mirrors again, but Ceony worried her luck with using non-Gaffered glass was wearing thin. A buggy might not come out this late, not without extra fees, and her next stipend payment was a week away. Still, it would be worth it, no? It would—

"Magician Bailey has his own Mercedes, and sometimes he lets me take it out."

"Bennet," she whispered. He could drive her to the train station *now*. She'd save on time, as well as a few pounds. And if she used the new enchanted Smelter rails installed at the Central London Railway, she could be in Reading before midnight.

Do you really want to involve another person in this? asked the voice in the back of her mind. Could Bennet end up traveling the same road as Anise and Delilah? Was she destined to leave a path of devastation behind her?

"I won't let him come with me," she told herself. "A drop-off at the train station, and that's it." *After that, I won't lean on Bennet for anything.* Perhaps a touch of flirtation would help convince him.

Seizing a gray square of paper, Ceony scribbled across its surface and Folded it into a simple glider, which she directed to the window below hers. She watched until Bennet's window opened and his hand guided the glider into his room.

The park will have to wait. Can you take me to the CLR? It's vitally important and would mean the world to me.

Best to leave Mg. Bailey to his rest. Secrets make friendships fonder, no?

Turning from the window, Ceony opened her ledger with her free hand and flipped to her notes on Saraj, despite having memorized the words verbatim. She'd written both Delilah's and Anise's names in the corner and traced them over and over again until the letters were so thick the names were barely legible. Her conversation with Mg. Aviosky played through her mind. She mulled over that piece of brown glass stowed away in her purse.

Ceony realized she had found a gold coin in the murky sewage of her situation with Mg. Bailey—a sort of freedom she would never have back at the cottage.

Emery wasn't here. She needn't worry about hiding secrets or bending promises so long as she resided in this empty mansion so far from her dear tutor, and no one, not even Mg. Bailey, supervised her time.

She cradled the red songbird against her chest. Yes. So long as she resided with the petulant Folder, she could—and would—continue her pursuit of Saraj.

Enchanted lamps and fire workings kept the CLR aglow as Bennet, his hands sweaty, white, and gripping the steering wheel of his tutor's car, pulled into the exact same parking spot Ceony had sat in nearly two years ago with Emery, before the paper magician had taken off to battle Saraj. Oddly, it was also the same place where he had first kissed her.

Ceony didn't mention this to her comrade, of course.

"I don't know what he'll do if I'm caught," Bennet wheezed, "but I don't think it will be good."

"You'll be fine," Ceony assured him. She squeezed his shoulder. "Thank you. I'll be back before too long. Don't wait up."

"Are you sure? I can come with you, help you with whatever it is that needs doing. You shouldn't go alone, Ceony. A woman out alone in the dark . . ."

I have to. No one else will get hurt if I'm alone. She smiled. "Unless someone robs the train, I'll be fine. You wouldn't be much good in a robbery like that anyway. Besides, you have Magician Bailey to worry about."

Bennet swallowed, looking sallow and ill. "What should I say if he asks?"

"Nothing," Ceony replied, slinging her bag over her shoulder. It pulled with the extra weight of her Tatham percussion-lock pistol, which she'd stowed in the very bottom, just in case. "I left an illusion in my room of me sleeping, if he bothers to check."

"He'll be able to tell."

"Only if he's looking closely," she countered. "Be safe."

Bennet nodded. "Best hurry. And then you can give me the details of why you need to be at the CLR so late at night. You can trust me, Ceony."

Ceony made no promises, merely let herself out of the vehicle and strode to the station, where she purchased a ticket and boarded the last train for Reading. Only three other people rode in the car with her.

Ceony fiddled with her charm necklace as the train sped west, its wide wheels practically floating over the Smelter-enchanted rails beneath it. How the metal-induced spell of speed worked, Ceony didn't know. None of her personal studies in Smelting came close to such a feat, which had only been built a few years back. She remembered glimpsing an article on it in the local paper, back when she'd still been a student at Tagis Praff.

———

Unease began to creep into Ceony's resolve when the train met its destination, blowing out smoke and steam as the engine relaxed onto its rails for a night's rest. She imagined it to be near midnight, and despite the glow of more magicked lamps in the Reading train station, Ceony couldn't help but focus on the dark spots in between them and beyond. She slipped her right hand into her bag as she walked, touching both Folded and un-Folded papers, fingering the handle of her pistol.

Emery would be furious.

Fortunately, Reading, like London, boasted a big enough population that most streets glowed with lamplight, all enchanted. In fact, Ceony couldn't find a single ordinary lamp. She supposed that was due to Reading being the host city of Magicians' English Enterprising, the largest material-magics engineering firm in all of Great Britain. It was the same company responsible for whatever hovering spell was boosting the railways' efficiency. They had given an address at Tagis Praff the week before Ceony's graduation, though it had turned into more of a hunt for future employees. As far as Ceony knew, the company didn't employ Folders.

The whistle of another train sounded through the illuminated city as Ceony strode down Broad Street, though this one came from another direction. At least three railways converged on Reading. Only one could take her back to London, however. Several people milled about despite the late hour—two businessmen absorbed in conversation, a scandalously dressed woman smoking a fag, three men exiting a different car on the train Ceony had taken, laughing hard enough to cry. Ceony left them all behind.

Stopping near a statue with the name "George Palmer" engraved on it, Ceony pulled three songbirds from her purse and commanded them, "Breathe." She whispered secrets to the birds, telling them how to detect Excision magic and find the elusive Saraj Prendi, and then released them into the air.

Staying on the lit streets, albeit out of the way, Ceony meandered by a noisy inn and peeked through a window unshielded by curtains, scanning the faces within, listening to the music a young balding man banged on a piano in the corner. She wished she had more to go on but also hoped she wouldn't find anything substantial. She'd considered bringing the paper bird that had alerted her of Reading, but the creature was so damaged it had ceased to hold its animation.

Stifling a yawn with the back of her hand, Ceony continued onward, taking one road and then another, avoiding dark alleys, using a Folded telescope to peer down lanes. She found no mirrors or bits of reflective glass to cast upon and eventually crossed the street to avoid a laughing, inebriated couple who stumbled over the pavement. Eventually Ceony followed a line of blue-lit lanterns toward the bank of the River Kennet, which wound down from the River Thames and sliced through the south side of Reading. She kept clear of the docks, wanting to keep a safe distance from the water at all times. She still hadn't learned how to swim, though Emery had mentioned wanting to teach her. Modesty, of course, was an issue, as was her unabated fear of drowning.

The flapping of paper reached her ears, and Ceony looked up to see one of her songbirds, Folded from black paper, descending to her. It hovered at eye level for a moment before backflipping in the air.

"You found something?" Ceony asked, voice low. How she wished these animated spells could talk! "Show me."

The bird flew over Ceony's shoulder and down a bend in the next street, winding closer to the river. Clasping the pistol inside her bag, Ceony hurried after it, not quite running. The dark spell disappeared between streetlamps, blending in with the night sky, but it didn't fly so fast that Ceony couldn't keep track of it.

It took her past a four-story building rowed with windows, a Victorian-esque structure waving a flag from its chimney, and a dark building that looked like a cross between a schoolhouse and a barn. A sign near its door read "Simond's Brewery." Only one of its windows— on the third floor—was dimly lit.

Canals branching from River Kennet looped through this part of Reading. Ceony grit her teeth as she hurried over a short bridge crossing the still water. Here the enchanted lamps, shorter than those in the other part of town, had Pyre-made flames that changed from lime to fuchsia, perhaps to draw attention to the waterline. Their reflections off the canal's surface looked like lily pads, but Ceony tried not to stare at the water too closely. She had more critical things to fear at the moment.

The black songbird landed on a sign that read "Kennet and Avon Canal, Authorized Vehicles Only." Ceony reached it, huffing to catch her breath. The little bird flew down into her hands, where she commanded it, "Cease," and tucked it into her bag.

She searched the area, noting a bench by the canal, as well as a drooping tree that had seen better days. Another bridge led to a dock behind her.

On the water she saw a small boat, little more than a canoe, carrying two people—one rowed; the other smoked a cigar. A lantern sat between them, casting a mustardy glow off their faces. The man with the cigar had an old face with a prominent nose and loose skin; the man rowing wore long, loose sleeves and had a dark complexion—

Ceony's breath caught in her throat, and a shiver ran down her spine. She stepped to the left to put the tree between herself and the boat, which steadily drew farther and farther from her. Saraj—could that man be Saraj? She thought so, but she had never gotten a clear look at the man in the light of day, only glimpses here and there. What was he doing? Where was he going, and who was helping him?

What exactly did Ceony plan to *do*? She had the upper hand of having found him first, but the water . . .

She swallowed. Her compact mirror was in her purse. She could use it to contact Mg. Aviosky or Mg. Hughes, alert them of what she'd seen. Perhaps they would believe she'd come across a Gaffer who'd agreed to help her with the spell. She'd have to explain herself . . . Word would reach Emery . . . Surely Mg. Aviosky wouldn't suspend her at the very end of her apprenticeship!

But so what if she *were* suspended? Wouldn't getting Saraj's neck in the hangman's noose be worth it? The well-being of her family was more important than any magician's certificate.

She released her pistol and fumbled through her bag for the mirror, glancing up to spy again at the distancing boat.

"You're like a kitten."

The honey-slick voice pricked at the back of Ceony's neck like cold needles, making her jump. She whirled around to see a tall, thin silhouette of a man standing at the edge of the bridge to the port.

Her hand snapped back to the pistol. "Excuse me?"

The man moved forward until the light of the nearest flashing lamp cast its green and purple beams on him. They glinted off the gold studs in his ears. An Indian man who stood a little too slender, matted curls jutting out from either side of his almost triangular head. He wore tattered clothes that needed washing. The clothing of a man on the run.

"A kitten," his accented words repeated. "Who wanders around and follows those who offer her milk. But I have no milk, kitten."

An icy tremor coursed down Ceony's back.

Saraj Prendi took one step closer. "So tell me, Ceony Maya Twill . . . Why have I found you wandering this city so late at night?"

He grinned a truly canine smile.

CHAPTER 11

CEONY'S THROAT CLOSED, and she took a step back from the Excisioner, her shoulder brushing a drooping branch of the tree. She dared to glance behind her, but the small boat and its oblivious passengers had sailed too far to hear her if she screamed. She couldn't see their lantern anymore.

"Curious," Saraj said, folding his long arms and taking a step toward her—once, twice. "Usually a kicked animal fears its abuser, cowers from him. Avoids him. But I have this strange"—he waved a hand in the air—"*inkling* that you've sought me out. Inkling, correct? I believe I'm using the word correctly. Yes. What a strange kitten you are, *kagaz*. Unless you have another purpose."

He paused, looking her up and down. His gaze felt like slime on Ceony's skin, but from what Ceony could see in the blinking lamplight, there was no lust in it. No, he looked at her as if she were a piece of furniture, an end table or chair. Something tossed on the street, and he couldn't decide if it was worth salvaging. "No," he said. "You're not dressed like a harlot."

"Of course I'm not," Ceony spat, her anger at the assumption giving her just enough fuel to speak. Still, she took another step back, her eyes searching Saraj's belt. Lira had kept glass vials of blood secured at her waist for spells, but there didn't appear to be any on

Saraj, unless they were under his shirt. Then again, an Excisioner wouldn't need blood to destroy her; just one touch would do.

Ceony's free hand moved to her necklace. She swallowed. "Why are you here, Saraj? Why not flee when you had the chance? I know about your prison break."

Saraj laughed. "I'm famous, it seems. If you must know, kitten, I have unfinished business to attend to. Things to collect. You are not my sun."

"Huh?" she murmured under her breath, barely moving her lips.

"My sun," Saraj repeated, relaxing his stance. He swirled an index finger around. "Orbits, rotations. My doings don't revolve around you. See?"

Ceony gave herself a few seconds before answering, her fingers playing across her necklace. "No, they revolve around Grath," she said, clearing her throat once to prevent a tremor in her voice. "He seemed confident about that. But he's not here."

Saraj frowned. "No," he agreed, but Ceony detected no remorse in the word, no regret, no loyalty.

He took another step forward. Ceony drew her pistol and pointed it at him.

Saraj grinned, his teeth not white enough to reflect the lamplight. He tilted his head to one side, staring at Ceony. Making her feel uncomfortable. Slipping a hand into his pocket, he began to chant words in a language no countryman knew—the language of the dark. She recognized this spell, its lilts and rhythm. A healing spell, not a spell meant to injure her. Not yet.

She let Saraj have his words and took the chance to whisper her own, hand on her necklace, hoping the darkness hid her lips.

"Is this about the rest of the litter?" Saraj asked, his chant finished. He held the spell in the hand embedded in his pocket, ready to use it should Ceony fire. Did he think she didn't know? "Your *parivāra*? The mum and pop and other kittens?"

Ceony's grip on her pistol tightened, her palm sweating. She kept it leveled at Saraj's chest.

Saraj pulled his hand free—a dark drop of blood dripped down from his thumb—and the skin of it glimmered gold. The healing spell. Well, Ceony doubted it could cure a bullet to the head.

She adjusted her aim for Saraj's forehead.

"Litter, kittens," Ceony repeated, "this is all just a game for you, isn't it? You didn't care about Lira, and I don't think you cared about Grath—"

"A game!" Saraj exclaimed, hand still aglow. "Oh, but they were poor players," he said, advancing with a long stride. "And your littermates make boring pieces. A favor for him before, but they're so dull, kitten."

Ceony's hand shifted on her necklace, skipping over the vial of oil, bag of sand, and starlight marked "in 1744." Her words were so quiet she may have only thought them. She couldn't let Saraj know her secret—Grath's secret—but even if he learned it, he couldn't share it if he were dead.

"I need money to get by, just like any dolly," he said, moving forward. Ceony moved back. "Got to collect. But that's not a game, is it? That's boring. But you . . . you're here, now. You've come to play. To show me what's inside you."

"I've come to put you down," Ceony growled.

Saraj laughed and clapped his hands, though the motion didn't disturb the glowing spell that awaited him on his right fingers.

"All a game," Saraj said, rooting his feet, stiffening. His grin grew lopsided, almost into a snarl. "And now kitten is on the board. I still need a heart, kitten. I suppose yours will do."

Cold sweat chilled Ceony from crown to knee. Saraj jerked forward.

Ceony flinched and fired.

The blast echoed between canal walls and off Simond's Brewery, surely loud enough to alert *someone*. Ceony couldn't see where she had hit Saraj until he lifted his glowing hand to his collar. The bullet had pierced just under it on the right. He coughed, wheezed, but the orange light of his spell quickly seeped into the wound and closed it up. He pulled his hand away seconds later and dropped the bullet onto the pavement.

"Checkmate," Saraj said.

"Wrong game, *friend*," Ceony countered, lowering her pistol. "I wasn't firing for the bullet."

No. She'd fired for the *spark*.

"Flare!" she cried, and the tiny spark she'd pulled from the pistol spit and grew, building a fire in her left palm. Giving her enough light to see Saraj's wide eyes.

"Combust!" she called, and she flung her left hand forward, sending a hailstorm of fire raining down on Saraj. With her eyes adjusted to the dark and her target so close, the fire's brightness seared her eyes, stealing her sight for a moment. Ceony staggered back, blinking away spots. Smoke assailed her nostrils. Coughing, Ceony backed up and croaked an "Arise" command, beckoning a spark back to her hand, preparing to finish off the Excisioner.

But as the hailstorm cleared, leaving scattered weeds and a board of the dock burning, Ceony's adjusting eyes couldn't pinpoint Saraj in the darkness. She whirled around once, twice, and commanded her little flame, "Flare!"

The fire grew in her palm, casting topaz light over the docks. Empty. Creaking.

Familiar shivers crept up her arms and back. She couldn't have incinerated the man! Where had he gone? Jumped into the river?

Her eyes focused on the black depths of the canal, the shivers growing ever colder. Had he teleported? Where was he? Watching her?

Ceony ran.

She ran hard and fast, her self-made wind snuffing out the flames still licking her fingers.

She ran down lit streets and around sharp corners until she heard the piano music still streaming from the inn. She grabbed the door handle and wrenched it open, dodging inside. The door slammed closed behind her.

A few patrons—only a dozen or so lingered in the foyer—glanced at her, but the music radiating from the corner of the room had apparently drowned out her arrival.

Ceony pressed her back against the door and slunk down to the floor, shrinking from the windows, breathing hard. She closed her eyes and beat the back of her head against the door's wood.

On the board now. Does that mean I've put myself in his path?

Smelt to hell, I showed him Pyre magic. If Grath ever confided in him . . . Saraj knows what I can do. A man like him would kill for that information. Stupid. Stupid.

Realizing she still held her pistol, Ceony stashed it in her bag before she alarmed anyone. She clasped her Folded songbird and pulled it free, pinching its narrow body in her fingers. She worried that by tracking Saraj down, she may have endangered Emery. Would the Excisioner go after him—after her family—for use as bait or persuasion, or would he head straight for her? She'd likely burned him badly; how easily could he heal himself? Could he come for her tonight?

Fumbling with her limbs, Ceony found her feet and hurried across the room as the piano man began a new tune. She approached a vested man behind a small bar and asked, "Please, is the owner awake?"

The man eyed her. "I'm he. What's wrong, lass?"

"Do you have a telegraph I could use? It's urgent."

Sweat trickled down her back.

"Got rid of it," he said, leaning his elbows on the bar. "Telephones are the new trend."

He gestured with a tilt of his head to the upright, black-lacquered telephone at the back of the bar.

"It uses an operator?"

The man nodded. "Go ahead and try it. Will you need a room?"

Ceony didn't answer but seized the phone and, with evident clumsiness, managed to connect to the local police.

"An Excisioner named Saraj Prendi is in Reading," she said into the telephone's mouthpiece. "He's dangerous, seen by the docks not fifteen minutes ago. Please tell the Magicians' Criminal Affairs."

She hung up without leaving her name.

After staying the night acutely awake in the inn lobby in Reading, Ceony used her return train ticket early in the morning, hoping to avoid the notice of watching eyes. She bribed a buggy driver to take her to Mg. Bailey's with some premade Folded spells, ones that could sell in the market for a decent price. With any luck, Saraj was holed up in Reading, licking his wounds.

Ceony managed to doze in the buggy, even dreamed that her fire spell had riled Saraj enough to scare him from England for good. But when the rough road leading to the Bailey residence woke her, she knew the idea to be *only* a dream. If anything, she had given Saraj a motive for revenge.

She wondered again if Grath had confided in Saraj about his desire to break his bond. If so, Saraj would know *exactly* what Ceony had done. No Folder could throw fire like that.

She dragged her heavy feet toward the mansion. Now there was a risk that the secret to bond breaking would fall into the hands of an Excisioner. Still, the Pyre spell had been her only way to escape. It had been that or her life . . . but if it came down to it, she'd die before revealing Grath's secrets to accessing all materials magics. She wouldn't let Saraj—or anyone else—use the knowledge for ill.

But I can't keep everything secret, she thought as she approached the front door. *I have to tell Emery the truth. Saraj will think I'm at the cottage. I can't risk Emery's life.*

She reached for the knob, but the door swung open before her fingers made contact.

Bennet stood on the other side, looking about as tired as she felt, his hair in disarray, his shirt half-tucked.

"Ceony!" he said, half-scolding and half-relieved. "Thank the Lord you made it back!"

Ceony stiffened. "Has Magician Bailey—"

Bennet shook his head. "He hasn't so much as mentioned your name. He's in his study doing . . . something."

The fellow apprentice stood aside to let Ceony in. "So where were you?"

Delilah's face flashed through Ceony's mind.

"A cousin of mine got into a bad lot," she lied. "Gambling . . . He wasn't specific. But he couldn't collect enough money and he wound up in a cell, even though he's only seventeen. Apparently he sent a letter to Magician Thane's home asking for help—he was too embarrassed to ask his father—and Magician Thane sent it to me in a bird."

Bennet rubbed the back of his neck. "That's awful. How much was it?"

"Not too much," Ceony said, pasting on a smile. "He was two pounds short."

Bennet frowned. "I'm sure Magician Bailey could reimburse you if you explained—"

"Oh no," Ceony said, dropping her voice. She glanced down the hall to ensure the Folder was nowhere in sight. "He's only told me. John, that is. My cousin. He made me promise not to breathe a word of it to anyone. His reputation, you see. He wants to be a journalist, and they can get picked apart. He needs a clean slate. I shouldn't have even told you."

"But to have a woman go out in the middle of the night—"

"I'm a magician," Ceony said with a wry grin. "Almost, at least. I can get out of tight spots, even if it's just with paper."

Bennet seemed to relax a bit. "I suppose that's true. But I would have gone with you."

"I appreciate it." She yawned. "I guess I need a bit of rest, though. It was a long trip, once you add everything up."

"Can I bring you breakfast?"

"I'm all right," she assured him. She offered a last smile before heading down the hall and up the two flights of stairs to her bedroom, where she'd left the window open. She searched the sill, the brick outside, and the rest of her room for a message from Emery, but found none.

Her ribs squeezed in. Since arriving at Mg. Bailey's home, Emery had sent her a message every day, even if just a brief note. Why hadn't he last night? Even a vengeful Excisioner couldn't have stopped yesterday evening's letter.

She rubbed sleep from her eyes and pinched phosphorus and glass on her necklace before heading into the lavatory next door. Now a Gaffer, Ceony traced the boundaries of the mirror there and sought out the mirror in the lavatory of Emery's home, which she had previously named "Cottage One." She used one spell to spy into the room, ensuring its vacancy, and a second spell to initiate a transport.

The glass rippled, a liquid portal, and Ceony passed through.

CHAPTER 12

IT FELT LIKE AGES since Ceony had left the cottage, though in truth less than a week had passed.

She stepped down into the sink and leapt onto the lavatory floor, then peered back into the mirror to adjust her blouse and hair. She'd tell Emery she'd come in through the front door after taking a buggy to the house—she still had the key.

Ceony made her way down the hall, peeking briefly into her room. The bed had been remade, and she smiled. Emery's odd knack for tidiness had him folding and tucking blanket corners as though crafting a spell, and while he had demonstrated to Ceony how to properly make a bed, she'd never taken the time to mimic the art. She often kept the door to her room closed just so Emery wouldn't be tempted to rearrange her things, but with her out of the house, there was nothing to stop him.

He must be bored.

She passed her room and stuck her head into the library, but the paper magician wasn't there. The table and telegraph had both been moved to the right of the window, however. Terribly bored, then.

Across the hall, she knocked softly on Emery's bedroom door. When she didn't get a response, she pushed it open. The room, cluttered yet neat, lay empty before her.

She stepped back into the hall and opened the door to the stairs that led to the third floor. "Emery?" she called. She listened for a response but received none. Nor did she hear any shuffling or footsteps.

Her heart beat a little quicker. "You're being paranoid," she murmured to herself. Ceony retreated down the hall and took the stairs to the first floor.

He wasn't in the dining room or kitchen, and Ceony noticed the distinct lack of noise in the cottage, like the building itself had settled into a deep, snoreless slumber.

Her fingers danced over her necklace as she moved to the front of the house, changing her material allegiance from glass to fire. Pyre magic was by far the most aggressive of the materials magics. Being armed with it—and matches from the stove to provide her with a flame whenever she needed one—made Ceony feel a little more powerful, a little safer.

She checked the office and the front room, the front yard and backyard, but Emery was in none of them. Even Jonto had been ceased. He'd left the house, then. He hadn't mentioned any plan to go away.

Uneasy, Ceony went back to the magician's bedroom and checked his closet. His magician's uniform hung there, so he hadn't left on any formal business. Perhaps he'd gone to the market for groceries, but Emery hated that chore and would hire a runner to do it for him if at all possible.

Ceony scanned his dresser, his nightstand, his bookshelves. She saw no sign of her Folded birds. She opened a few drawers and even glanced under the bed. Where did he keep them? Or had he thrown them away? But Emery wouldn't toss her notes to him, would he?

She frowned, but thoughts of Saraj pushed missish worries away. Could he have come for Emery?

She searched the rooms again, one by one, until she made it back to the front door. No signs of blood or struggle, no signs of a break-in. Becoming a Gaffer again, Ceony used a piece of glass from her purse to magnify the kitchen and dining room floor, searching for anything—a drop of missed blood, a piece of Saraj's hair, perhaps. Nothing. She even did a reflection spell on the lavatory mirror to see what had happened in that room over the past day—that is, until the mirror displayed Emery undressing. She broke the spell and left the lavatory with red cheeks.

She leaned against the hallway wall by her bedroom door. "He must be safe, then," she said. Hearing the words out loud gave her some small comfort.

Ceony waited several long minutes there, hoping she'd hear Emery unlock the front door, but the cottage remained silent. Peeling herself from the wall, Ceony went to the library and scrawled a note on a yellow square of paper there:

Patrice told me Saraj had been spotted near Berkshire. Please be careful.

Love you.

She Folded the paper into a songbird and left it on Emery's bedroom windowsill, making it look like she'd sent the bird from the mansion. Then she slipped back through the lavatory glass and into her room at Mg. Bailey's residence, where she finally managed to get a few hours of sleep.

———

Three days.

Three days of waiting for Saraj to make his move, of sending out birds to survey the area, of searching Mg. Bailey's daily newspapers for articles about Excisioners. Three days since her run-in with Saraj in Reading, and she hadn't heard one peep.

Not from him, and not from Emery.

Ceony still sent her birds—or moths, or bats—to Emery every evening as soon as twilight promised to hide their departure, but she hadn't received a response. That made four days without any contact with him, and she knew he'd returned to the cottage. She'd checked Cottage One through the glass in the lavatory and seen his wet towel hanging on the wall.

So why had Emery stopped responding to her?

She doodled water lilies in the margins of her ledger as this question plagued her. She sat at the table in the apprentices' study, across from Bennet, who labored over the links of an expansion chain. The command "Enlarge" would make the wearer of the chain appear larger to passersby. How large depended on the thickness of the paper. A rather complicated illusion spell, given the make of each link. It was one Ceony planned to use in her preparations for her magician's test: *#37. Something to defend against a tramp.*

But, once again, Ceony found she had a hard time concentrating on her studies.

Mg. Bailey had certainly given her space, though he still asked her to sit in on Bennet's evening lessons. He'd stopped ragging on Emery, but Ceony's relationship with the belligerent Folder had hardly become peaches and cream. In fact, Mg. Bailey's demeanor toward Ceony had soured further, if such a thing were possible. For days he'd looked at her with outright suspicion, treating her as the suspect to his detective. She could only guess that the man had noticed a scratch on his Mercedes and assumed Ceony to be the guilty party. And she was, more or less. Still, Ceony didn't care enough to ask Mg. Bailey if his breeches had grown too tight. She had enough men to worry about!

What if . . . she wondered, stilling her pen, *What if Emery's grown tired of me?*

Preposterous. Wasn't it? They got on splendidly, all the time. He loved her. They'd even discussed marriage! Ceony could laugh at the idea of him growing bored with her.

And yet she didn't. She blinked rapidly to hide a tear, then glanced at Bennet to see if he'd noticed, but his chain spell demanded all his attention. Taking a deep breath, Ceony finished her doodle.

What if he's using Magician Bailey as an excuse to distance us? she wondered. *What if all of this is meant to be some sort of cushion so he can break our relationship cleanly?*

Mg. Emery Thane had been married before, and it had ended very, very badly. Ceony had seen firsthand the damage that relationship had done to him, the jagged crack it had left in his heart. Surely that canyon had not yet been filled. And what if it never was? What if Emery couldn't handle the commitment once Ceony graduated from his tutelage and their romance became public?

What if Ceony was only ever meant to be a secret?

You'll kill yourself thinking like that, she chided herself, gripping her pen tighter. *Be reasonable. There must be an explanation.*

She wondered where Emery had gone the day she'd transported to his cottage and left that warning. He hadn't even replied to *that*.

"Do you remember Magician Whitmill?"

Ceony glanced up at Bennet's words. He held a completed chain link in his hands, and his blue eyes smiled at her. They made her think of a teddy bear.

Ceony blinked to clear her mind, to pull her thoughts away from Emery for long enough to search her memory for the name. It rang a bell, and her mind zoomed back nearly three years to her first semester at Tagis Praff. She sat in the auditorium of the school on the aisle, beside a classmate she didn't know, but whose face she recalled with perfect clarity, for all the good it would do her. In her mind's eye she looked ahead at the stage, at the portly Polymaker with gray-streaked hair and a gray-streaked mustache. She laughed.

Bennet smiled. "So you do?"

"He was recruiting for his textile company in Virginia," Ceony stated. "He brought in that huge pin board full of product and knocked it over with his hip when he bent down to pick up his handkerchief."

Bennet chuckled. "I shouldn't have laughed, but I did. I don't think anyone took him seriously for the rest of the lecture."

Letting her ledger close, Ceony asked, "What brought that up?"

He shrugged. "Just thinking, I guess. Folding makes for good thinking. I wanted to be a Polymaker, you know."

"I didn't."

"I only decided the month before graduation," Bennet admitted. "So much has yet to be discovered in Polymaking, and it would be interesting to find new spells for a new magic. Before that, I had thought rubber would be an interesting trade. Or, rather, my father did. He works facilities at a Siping factory."

"Is he a magician?"

"No. Just me. But I have a sister-in-law who's a Smelter."

He paused, turning his link over in his hand.

You can still be a Polymaker, Ceony thought. She touched the collar of her blouse, feeling the charm necklace hidden beneath it.

"You wanted to be a Smelter, didn't you?" Bennet asked.

She met his gaze. "I'm surprised you remember that." *When did I tell Bennet about Smelting?* Her memory spun. *Back at Tagis Praff, the Christmas dinner.*

"Are you . . ." He hesitated. "Are you disappointed? About Folding?"

"I was at first," she admitted, "but not anymore. I'm glad things worked out the way they did."

"Me, too, I think," Bennet replied. "I mean, I guess I can't really know without having a Polymaking apprenticeship for a comparison, you know?"

She nodded.

"I'm worried about leaving," he added, resting his chin in his palm.

Ceony wove her fingers together over her ledger. "You'll make a fine magician."

"Not that," he said. "I'm worried about leaving Magician Bailey. He . . . doesn't have many friends. Hard to believe, I know."

Ceony snorted.

"I'm sure he'll get another apprentice quickly, but he takes a long time to . . . acclimate. As you've witnessed. But deep down he means well. He's misunderstood. I think he's had it hard, you know?"

Ceony thought back to her journey through Emery's heart, where she'd first seen Mg. Bailey, or Prit. She wondered how many people had bullied him and for how long. Would she behave the same way if she'd suffered his fate?

"I know, a little," she said. "But you can't let that hold you back."

"I won't. It's just something I think about."

Ceony reopened her ledger. A paper slipped out from its back pages and onto her lap—a half-sheet of paper, roughly torn along one of its long edges. The second half of the mimic spell she'd left with Mg. Aviosky. Its face remained blank. She wondered if Mg. Aviosky knew about the anonymous tip on Saraj and suspected her. That was, of course, assuming anyone had bothered to relay the information to the Head of Education. Emery obviously hadn't fact-checked with Mg. Aviosky, or they'd both be pounding down Mg. Bailey's door.

Bennet clasped his hands together. "Ceony, I—"

"Could you excuse me?" she asked, standing from the table. "I need some of that 'thinking' time." She held up the ledger. "I have a lot more work to get done."

Bennet nodded. "Of course," he said, but he looked disappointed.

She offered the man a smile before exiting the study. It had not been her intent to cut him off—the words had already been in her throat—but she was grateful for it. Bennet was a wonderful friend and, admittedly, a wonderful specimen of a man, but she worried over his friendliness. At that moment, her name had sounded especially friendly on his lips.

"I'm awful," she mumbled to herself, letting her feet carry her a ways down the hall before slipping the mimic spell onto the cover of her ledger. Leaning it against her left palm, she wrote, *Have you heard anything?* to Mg. Aviosky. She didn't need to explain what she meant.

She leaned back against the wall, holding the mimic spell in front of her, waiting for Mg. Aviosky's scrawl to appear below hers. Seconds passed. A minute, two minutes, but the half page stubbornly remained blank. Of course, the mimic spell had no chimes or lights to alert its holder when writing appeared on it; Ceony would have to wait until Mg. Aviosky looked at her half of the spell. Her only hope for hearing word faster was to use a telegraph. She assumed Mg. Bailey owned one, as he owned a ridiculous number of things, but finding one and asking permission to use it didn't rank high on the list of things she was eager to accomplish.

She let out a long, slow breath and slipped the mimic spell back into her ledger. Outside, a cloud shifted in the sky, letting a ray of sunlight pierce through the hallway window. Stepping from its sudden brilliance, she blinked spots from her eyes. Before they had cleared, she noticed something perched on the eaves of the house. It stood about a foot high and, though it had no feathers, preened its right wing: a paper hawk.

Ceony gawked for a moment before stepping closer to the glass, making slow movements so as not to startle the lifelike spell. Dozens of papers comprised its body, each Folded so crisply into the next that Ceony could barely spy the seams. Brown paper, though a few off-white pieces formed the hawk's breast.

The creature couldn't have been Bennet's handiwork, which meant it had to be Mg. Bailey's creation. A cloud passed over the sun once more, allowing Ceony a better view of the bird. A fierce-looking spell, certainly, complete with tightly rolled paper talons and a sharp, cardstock beak hinged to open and close. Ceony hadn't seen a single spell adorning Mg. Bailey's estate besides the ones she and Emery passed back and forth. Had she missed this one, or was it new?

And why a hawk, of all things? Surely Mg. Bailey wasn't so sour as to want to scare away songbirds.

The hawk's wings spread, and it took off from the roof, flying out over the yard a ways before arching up and over the mansion, out of Ceony's line of sight.

"Hmm," she hummed, pulling away from the window.

Down the hall she spied Mg. Bailey speaking to one of the maids who came by thrice a week to clean the few lived-in portions of the house. Ceony hurried up to her bedroom before he had a chance to spot her.

———

Ceony drew her thumb across the crease of a dog-ear Fold, careful to ensure its edges lined up perfectly before inserting the newly formed triangle into a notch on the skeletal arm she was constructing on the breakfast table. Another hour or two and she'd have it finished and ready to test. If it didn't work, she'd have to go over each and every paper and Fold to find the mistake. If she couldn't find it, she'd have to start over. Fortunately, she was confident that she'd seen Jonto's arms enough times to get this spell right. The challenge was to make the arm act as its own whole, instead of a piece of a larger body.

#1. Something to open a door. Once she made the wrist fully functional, this contraption would do just that, and she could cross the first requirement for her magician's test off the list.

Fennel barked from his perch on the bed, his paper body barely heavy enough to dent the mattress. He hovered over Ceony's ledger and growled—which sounded more like a piece of paper flapping in the wind—then bit down on the mimic spell protruding from the ledger's cover. Two jerks of his head pulled it free.

Ceony bounced onto her feet and rushed over to the pup, tugging the spell from his mouth. As she watched, Mg. Aviosky's stiff penmanship scrawled across it in black ink, as though it were being written by a ghost:

I don't want you involving yourself in this, Miss Twill.

Biting her lip, Ceony took the spell to the breakfast table and wrote back, in pencil, *You promised you'd tell me. I need to know.*

A dot of black ink appeared below Ceony's words, growing larger with each passing second. Mg. Aviosky had set her pen down, likely debating her response, and the ink saturated the paper on her end. Finally she wrote, *He was spotted in Reading not long ago. Yes, he's still in England. Mg. Hughes believes he's trying to collect funds and false papers in order to escape through Europe unscathed.*

Again the pen soaked the paper. Mg. Aviosky's hesitant hand penned, *Mg. Juliet Cantrell has been murdered.*

Blood withdrew from Ceony's face and hands. Mg. Juliet Cantrell—Ceony knew her, though not personally. Criminal Affairs. A Smelter. She'd been involved in the hunt for Grath Cobalt. According to Emery, she was the one who had arrested Saraj in Saltdean.

Her eyes focused on Mg. Aviosky's last word: *murdered.*

Images of Delilah's wide, panicked eyes filled her vision. The way she'd struggled against her restraints in that chair as Grath grabbed her neck . . .

Ceony squeezed her eyes shut for several seconds, waiting out a chill that slid down her spine. Opening her eyes, she wrote, *He killed her?*

Ripped out her heart. Mg. Hughes isn't sure if he's used it yet.

Ceony pressed her hand to her chest, feeling her own heart-beat speed. Stolen her heart. Just as Lira had stolen Emery's. Just as Saraj had wanted to steal hers at the dock. Except Juliet didn't have anyone to steal it back for her. How much time had passed since Saraj . . . But would he have even left Mg. Cantrell's body whole enough to be revived?

Ceony shuddered. Her stomach twisted and knotted around itself, sending bile climbing up her throat. She swallowed hard.

Saraj had said he still needed a heart in Reading. He'd gone for Mg. Cantrell's. If Ceony had only stopped him then . . .

She paused, and for a moment her whole self felt empty. Had Saraj stolen Mg. Cantrell's heart because she had gotten too close to finding him, or had he stolen it because Mg. Cantrell had been one of two magicians responsible for his imprisonment?

Nausea replaced the emptiness. Emery had been the other.

Swallowing, she wrote, *Where?*

You are safe, Miss Twill, the Gaffer replied. *Mg. Hughes is on top of the case. I'll let you know—*

Ceony wrote in the space ahead of Mg. Aviosky's sentence. *Where?*

Several minutes passed before the spell read, *Do not be brash. I will let you know when Saraj is found.*

Ceony tried to goad Mg. Aviosky further, but the Gaffer refused to respond after that. The mimic spell had nearly run out of space in any event.

Crumpling into a chair, Ceony stared at the brief conversation in her hands. Saraj wouldn't have stayed in Reading, not after his run-in with Ceony, but Criminal Affairs would have started their search there after her anonymous tip. How far had Mg. Cantrell tracked Saraj before?

Ceony tapped her pencil against the tabletop, clenching her teeth to keep from sobbing. Deeper and deeper into England. Still not arrested. Mg. Cantrell was likely the reason Saraj hadn't tracked Ceony down yet—he hadn't had time, being on the run. Would he save the Smelter's heart for the spell he'd use on Ceony? On Emery? Ceony knew one thing: there was no limit to the number of people Saraj would kill to get his freedom and a little pocket change on the side. Was he headed toward London for her, in pursuit of Grath's secret, or had he given up that chase for the sake of escape?

She slammed her pencil tip onto the table, breaking it off. She'd beaten Lira. She'd beaten Grath. And yet still no one would confide in her! No one would let her *help*.

She couldn't go to Reading to try and track Saraj down, could she? Her magician's test was approaching rapidly. Could she scour an entire city searching for one elusive man? Her clues at Gosport had been found by luck alone. She hadn't even been able to deduce where Emery had gone off to.

But she had a better chance of beating him than anyone else. She could play both prey and predator. She could be Mg. Cantrell and Mg. Hughes and Mg. Aviosky and Emery all in one.

She scanned the mimic spell. Paused. Touched her necklace.

Whatever Mg. Aviosky knew, Mg. Hughes told her. And Ceony had a hunch as to how he'd conveyed the information.

She'd strike in the afternoon, when Mg. Aviosky would be away for her educational duties.

By this time tomorrow, Ceony would know, too.

CHAPTER 13

THERE WERE TWO nice things about mirror-transporting to the home of a Gaffer. First, there were dozens of available mirrors large enough for Ceony to fit through. Second, all the mirrors were crafted from Gaffer's glass, so they were free of impurities, which made the travel incredibly safe. Delilah had once told Ceony that one should *only* travel through Gaffer's glass to avoid becoming trapped, but so far Ceony hadn't afforded the caution.

Ceony's socked feet stepped soundlessly into Mg. Aviosky's mirror room on the third floor of her home. Ceony entered through a rectangular mirror taller than she was, and the swirling portal of its glass smoothed as soon as she made it through. She paused, holding her breath, listening to the creaks of the house. As far as her ears could tell, the house was empty.

She rubbed shivers from her neck. This mirror room was not the same as the one in which Delilah had died, but the mirrors were, and Mg. Aviosky had arranged them in the same way. Ceony hadn't been surrounded by these mirrors since the day Grath Cobalt had jerked her through the doorway and sliced open her skin with hundreds of window shards.

Ceony glanced to the corner, imagining Delilah strapped to a chair there. She felt hollow. Hollow, and an almost unbearable chill.

She shook her head, willing sad thoughts away. Mg. Aviosky herself had said it would do no good to dwell on the memories. Such an easy thing for the Gaffer to claim. If only Ceony's memories dulled as easily as others' did.

She searched for one mirror in particular—the one she'd used to contact Mg. Hughes as she lay bleeding on the floor beside Grath. Mg. Hughes had never asked her how she managed to contact him; he likely thought Delilah or Mg. Aviosky had performed the spell. And Mg. Aviosky . . . well, she had been unconscious at the time. She'd never questioned just how Mg. Hughes had come to the rescue.

Ceony turned around and spotted the mirror behind her. It had been moved. She approached its dark frame.

"Reflect, past," she said, fingers to the glass. Her image swirled. As in Gosport, Ceony rolled the images of the mirror backward, carefully watching them scroll. She saw sunlight fade and dim, saw Mg. Aviosky enter, use a different mirror, leave. The room darkened, lightened. Mg. Aviosky appeared again, standing right where Ceony now stood.

"Hold," Ceony commanded, and the image of the Gaffer froze. Ceony focused on Mg. Aviosky's spectacles, where she saw a reflection of Mg. Hughes in the lenses.

She scrolled back a little further and played out the conversation.

"—found her body near Waddesdon," Mg. Hughes said, his voice low and tired. Ceony couldn't see his reflection in the mirror, only his skewed face in Mg. Aviosky's glasses. "The heart was harvested, but no blood drained. I doubt he had time. I won't know the details for sure until the autopsy . . ."

Mg. Aviosky's face grew waxy and pale. Her lips quivered, but she said nothing.

"We're contacting her family tonight," Mg. Hughes continued. "In the meantime I'm sending patrol into Oxford and Aylesbury. We'll find him, Patrice."

Ceony froze the image. "He's heading back to London," she whispered. "He's coming for me."

She rolled her lips together—this was information Criminal Affairs didn't have. Closing her eyes, she pulled forward the memory of Mg. Bailey's map, traced her mind's eye over London, Waddesdon, Oxford, Aylesbury. If Saraj was going to pass through any of those cities, Ceony would bet a year's worth of stipends it was Aylesbury, which was closer to London. She had little time to prepare.

Breaking the spell, Ceony turned back for the mirror she had come through, using it to return to the lavatory on the third floor of Mg. Bailey's mansion. She gathered her things from the sink—toothbrush, comb, handkerchief—and brought them into her room, laying them out beside Fennel on the bed. She needed to pack light, but smart. Anything she could use. Plus anything she'd need for spells—

A shadow passed over the afternoon sunlight streaming into her room. Peering out the window, Ceony again spied the paper hawk from before, flying vulture-like circles beside the house. Such a peculiar pet for Mg. Bailey to keep around.

She checked the windowsill, but Emery had once again failed to contact her. She tapped her fingernails against the sill. Why had he stopped? It was starting to anger her. Emery Thane wasn't the passive-aggressive type. If he had an agenda, he would open his mouth and—

Her thoughts cut off. She looked again at the hawk. A strange choice of pet, indeed. That was the beneficial thing about paper animals—so long as they didn't get wet, they required less maintenance than real creatures. Take Fennel, for instance. Ceony never had to walk him, bathe him, clean up after him. Feed him.

And what do hawks eat? Ceony thought, retreating from the window. She pulled a square of paper off her breakfast table and Folded a songbird. Animating it, she opened her window and tossed it into the spring air. The small bird fluttered back and forth for a moment, then flew toward the tree line at the edge of Mg. Bailey's property.

And, like a real bird of prey, the hawk swooped down and intercepted it, snatching the bird in its long paper talons. Then it glided toward the mansion, where it perched near one of the windows of the first floor, the paper bird still in tow.

Mg. Bailey's office.

Ceony's hand rushed to her mouth. *He knows*, she thought, chills raining onto her from every direction. She hadn't seen the hawk in her first few days at the mansion because Mg. Bailey hadn't *built* it yet. He must have seen the birds leaving Ceony's window . . . or the creatures coming *to* her window. Messages from Emery. Messages he could break the confidentiality spells on. Messages that revealed her relationship with . . .

She stepped back from the pane. Emery hadn't stopped writing her; Mg. Bailey had intercepted his letters. Read them. He—

And like oil heating in a pan, something in Ceony *popped*. Searing heat evaporated any trace of fear. Reddened her face. Quickened her heart.

"How *dare* he!" she shouted. She stormed from her bedroom, unshod feet hammering into the floorboards of the hall, banging down two sets of stairs. Steaming, Ceony strode right to Mg. Bailey's office and threw open the door.

The room was unoccupied. The hawk remained perched outside the window.

Ceony rushed into the room, scanning the desktop, and pulled open one drawer after another. The bottom drawer on the right stuck—locked.

Her hand reached under her collar to her necklace. She murmured a few quick words and became a Smelter. She pressed her thumb to the lock, hoping it was made of an alloy, and commanded it, "Unlatch."

The lock clicked and Ceony yanked the drawer open. Inside was an assortment of skewed papers in various colors, once Folded, now just crinkled. They were covered in handwriting, both hers and Emery's.

She jerked out a violet sheet and smoothed it out in her hands.

I imagine you're swamped with preparations for your exam. Don't overexert yourself. You're bright; you'll win. Don't forget to relax once in a while; hopefully this will help, if this bat can even carry it that far!

Let me know how you're doing. I tend to worry, love.

Ceony's lips parted. She turned the paper over, then over again, noticing a smear of brown at its bottom. She smelled it. Chocolate. What had Emery sent her? And how long ago?

She smoothed out a teal paper.

I think I'm going to reorganize the library shelves by book thickness. What do you think? All the quick reads in one place, all the heavy tomes (your favorite) in another.

An orange paper that had once been a crane read, in her handwriting, *I'm worried about you. Why haven't you written? Has something come up? Do you need help?*

A gray paper that had been wadded into a ball read, in Emery's penmanship, *I hope I'm not bothering you, or that you've moved rooms. Remember to think outside the box. I believe in you, Ceony. Also, I'm either suddenly allergic to walnuts or whatever wool the grocery lad had on today.*

Another bat, white, reading, *Alfred confirmed Saraj's sighting. He has officers watching your family, and one who comes by the cottage a couple times a day. I'll keep you posted—*

"What are you doing?" Mg. Bailey's sharp voice cut from the doorway, jerking Ceony to her feet. His pale skin flushed, and his shoulders grew rigid. He stomped toward her, reaching for the note in her hand. "This is trespassing—"

"And this is stealing!" Ceony shouted back, loud enough that her voice echoed off the walls. She pulled her hand back, keeping the notes from Mg. Bailey's reach.

"Stealing!" the Folder repeated. "On my property? Perhaps you should have tried harder to hide your little secrets. You're lucky I haven't reported you, Ceony Twill!"

"Go ahead!" she said. "Report me! Read the rule book, *Prit*. I've done nothing wrong, and neither has he. Why do you think he'd send me here? Why do you think I'd *tolerate* being under the same roof with a man as intolerable and insufferable as you? It's in the interest of fairness! Not that you could understand that concept!"

She stooped and snatched up the remaining stolen letters. Again Mg. Bailey tried to grab for them, but she back-stepped before he could get a grip.

"It's not his fault, you know," she said, seething. "It's neither Magician Thane's fault nor mine that you're so depressed and angry all the time. You feed off your own sourness. You grow it like a vineyard!"

The Folder's eyes widened.

"You wonder why no one likes you," she spat, stepping around the desk. She charged for the door, escaped into the hallway. Mg. Bailey didn't follow.

She reached the staircase out of breath, fumbling with her mess of notes. At the top of the stairs she saw Bennet, searching the well with worry on his face. What had he heard? No details from such a distance, but certainly the shouting.

Ceony met his gaze. It bore into her like a cold spike. She glanced away, glanced back. Took a deep breath. Collecting the letters, she shoved them into her skirt pocket and returned to the office.

Mg. Bailey sat facing the window. His glasses rested on top of his head, and one hand massaged his right temple.

When Ceony spoke, he startled.

"I suppose . . . that was a bit harsh," she said, stiff-backed in her efforts to stay cool. "I apologize for that, though I in no way condone any of . . . this." She waved her hand before the desk.

Mg. Bailey merely eyed her, his expression unreadable. She wasn't sure he could even see her clearly without his glasses.

"You're smart, Magician Bailey," she said, "and obviously very successful. Bennet speaks well of you, and he's never given me reason to disbelieve him."

"Is there a point to this, Miss Twill?" Mg. Bailey asked.

"What I mean to say is that you have good traits. I just wish you'd *use* them for good. You can't be content meddling with other people's lives like this."

Mg. Bailey snorted.

"You think I've misjudged you," she said, folding her arms, "but you've misjudged me. You sized me up before you ever met me, Pritwin Bailey. I have no doubt about that. I can only hope we'll find a right foot somewhere on this bumpy road."

She turned to leave but hesitated. Glancing back, she added, "And if any of your personal feelings toward me alter the outcome of my magician's test, I'll know, and I *will* report you to the Cabinet."

She waited an extra second for a response, but when none came, she excused herself and tromped back to the stairs in a much slower, calmer fashion. She slipped a hand into her letter-filled pocket. She couldn't send a bird from the mansion, not with that hawk scouting the grounds. Instead she spied into the cottage lavatory with her makeup compact. No towels hung on the wall; no sounds pierced the lavatory walls.

"Cease," Ceony said, shutting her compact. She could send a bird after she left the estate. She had an Excisioner to find, and this time neither of them would leave the confrontation running.

CHAPTER 14

CEONY HAD NO giant paper gliders at her disposal and didn't want to involve Bennet any further in her dark-rooted hobby, so she set to work on getting to Aylesbury herself—work that would let her get *out* of Aylesbury quickly, without needing to find an untarnished mirror.

She recalled the spell being in *The Apprentice's Reference Guide to Siping*, a book that was now long overdue at the Maughan Library. Though this trip to Mg. Bailey's estate had been focused on Folding, Ceony had not possessed the heart to leave behind all her references and supplies for the other materials magics. In fact, she'd brought about two-thirds of them with her, all crammed into the bottom of her suitcase.

After scrolling through the table of contents, Ceony flipped to page 84, the header of which read "Speedy Footwork," under the chapter title "Travel."

She reviewed the spell carefully; she had never performed it before, and if she botched it, she'd have to travel through mirrors, assuming she could find a good one in Aylesbury, which would take time.

She counted out her round rubber buttons and came up two short for her shoe size, which meant she had to borrow two from Fennel's paws. Using a Siping lancet—the only Siping tool she owned—Ceony carved the buttons with a meticulous hand: a half circle here, a slit there. Mistakes forced her to borrow two more of Fennel's rubber paw pads. Finally, she laid the buttons out on the floor in the specific, zigzag pattern shown in the book, five for each shoe. Then she placed her most comfortable shoes over them and commanded them, "Merge."

The rubber made a sucking noise as it adhered to the soles of her shoes. Crossing her fingers, Ceony slipped the shoes on and said, "Quicken, times two."

She took one step, then another, a normal walking pace. However, she found herself on the other side of the room twice as quickly. She smiled, relieved. "Cease," she commanded the shoes, and she prepared the rest of her spells, stowing them away in her purse alongside her pistol. She had only one round left; if only she had access to a forge. Smelters had spells for making a bullet hit its intended target, but such spells had to be crafted from molten metal, and there was no time for her to achieve such a feat. Not today.

She slipped the rest of her materials and spells into her bag and took the servants' stairs down to the main floor, where she took the back exit out of the mansion. Enchanting her shoes to increase her speed tenfold, Ceony ran to the Central London Railway station in less than ten minutes, startling far more than ten passersby on her way.

———

Ceony stood outside a locked room in Aylesbury's council building, ear pressed to the door. The officer's words came through as only mumbles; no one was angry enough to shout bits of useful information to her. The clock on the wall across from her read 4:36.

She had sought out the council building second, after the sheriff's office, and had seen several police officers exiting an automobile across the street—more than she would consider necessary for a town of Aylesbury's size. The London police department patch on one man's uniform had tipped her off: these were Mg. Hughes's men, and now they sat behind this door discussing something important with an older man who Ceony could only assume was with Criminal Affairs.

She fished through her bag, pulling out a tiny, square mirror about twice the size of her thumbnail. Ensuring she had no witnesses, Ceony pinched her necklace, murmured her incantations, and became a Gaffer. She then slid the mirror under the door near the jamb, out of sight of those gathered in the room, and walked away.

Ceony didn't go far, just to the end of the hallway and around, where she found two chairs and a fern perched outside an office door paned with frosted glass. She sat and pulled out her ledger, trying her best to get some studying accomplished while the men in the room discussed affairs relating to her.

She noticed a newspaper, still rolled, nestled against the door beside her. Read "Education Board" on the front in large, blocked letters.

She eyed the door. There were no electric lights on inside, just the gleam of the sun from an open window. An office of some sort, perhaps.

Leaning over the armrest of the chair, Ceony grabbed the newspaper and unfolded it. The article in question read, "Mg. Cabinet Education Board Rules Against Opposite-Sex Apprenticeships." The subtitle: "Board estimates the disbanding of over 100 magician apprenticeships. New ruling to take effect 14 September."

Ceony blanched as she began to read the article. *Oh God, they've listed names.*

She skimmed first, searching the four-column article for any mention of "Thane" or "Twill," but she found none. Releasing only half a breath, she read the brief summary of a Mg. Blair Peters, a Gaffer, whose relationship with her apprentice had caused nationwide scandal in Scotland last year—

"*Her* apprentice?" Ceony whispered. She wondered at their ages, but the article didn't say, nor did it give the name of the apprentice. At least the newspaper had decided to only publicly humiliate one of the two.

The writer also mentioned a Mg. Jumaane Ibori, a Smelter, who had been accused of extramarital relations with his apprentice, though solid evidence had yet to be collected.

Were these two scandals what caused the change, or have there been others? She thought again about Emery, Zina.

She read the article in its entirety; the new rule was being put into effect in time for the new school year at Tagis Praff, which would allow most apprentices to transfer at or near a year mark, and would supposedly make their transitions easier.

September 14. Only three months away. If Ceony didn't pass her magician's test, she'd certainly be transferred. Only for a short time, but the thought didn't comfort her.

Shaking herself, Ceony rolled up the newspaper and dropped it in front of the door. She wondered if Emery had read today's paper yet. What he thought about the article.

Two minutes short of an hour later, she heard the door down the hall open. Rising from her seat, Ceony peeked around the corner and watched six policemen and the older gentleman exit the room and head toward the front of the building. None of them spoke, save for a whispered exchange between two of the London officers.

Ceony watched them go, counted to twenty, and then walked back down the hall. Checking for bystanders and finding none, she slipped into the room and found her mirror tile resting against the edge of a very old rug. She scooped it up and hurried outside, passing one of the officers on her way out, receiving nothing more than a glance. After all, there was more than one administrative office in the council building, and she could have come from any of them.

Ceony hurried to a church down the street and staked out a quiet spot on an outdoor bench before enchanting the mirror in her hands. "Reflect, past," she said. While the mirror's silvery surface showed her only the white ceiling, the officers' voices rang with adequate clarity.

She listened as one man recounted the demise of Mg. Cantrell—a story that made Ceony wince. She held on to every detail. She couldn't afford to miss anything.

Another voice spoke of an Indian man arrested in Aylesbury two days ago, who'd turned out to be a businessman with a mere resemblance to the infamous Excisioner. Then they brought up the story of a Mr. Cliff Prestonson, whose body had been found drained of blood in the passenger seat of his own automobile.

"His wallet and briefcase were missing," a bass voice explained. "As far as we can tell, none of the banknotes have been used in Aylesbury."

A tenor added, "But the witness claims the attacker—matching Prendi's description—abandoned Prestonson's vehicle and tried two more before starting the engine of a Ford Model A. I assume Prendi couldn't find Prestonson's keys on his person."

"Wait, a witness?" asked another tenor.

"It's in my report, sir," replied the man. "She asked not to have her name disclosed, but she saw an Indian man follow Prestonson out to his vehicle and then grab him by the back of the neck. Prestonson reacted as though he'd been stabbed, though the witness saw no knife. The attacker pulled Prestonson into the passenger seat of the car, then emerged about a quarter of an hour later. He proceeded to steal the Ford—it belongs to an Ernest Hutchings, whose statement I have here—and take the highway toward Brackley."

Brackley, Ceony thought with a shiver. Brackley sat northwest of London and Aylesbury.

"When?" asked the second tenor.

The bass replied, "Four o'clock this last night, sir."

Ceony palmed the mirror and rose from the bench. Changing her allegiance to rubber, she enchanted her shoes and took off for Brackley. At the pace the Siping spell carried her, she imagined she'd reach the town before the officers did.

Whether or not that was a good thing, she wasn't sure.

———

The spell was exhilarating.

Ceony's enchanted shoes turned the world into mosaics of color and sound as she whipped through it, taking the long way around towns to avoid running into anything substantial, though she did trip over a gopher hole near Stratton Audley. Each step made her skin pull tight and her skirt fly behind her; Ceony held it down with either fist for the sake of modesty.

Ceony wondered if such spells were the reason Mg. Hughes had become a Siper.

She arrived in good time. Brackley, northwest of Aylesbury, was a small town. As soon as Ceony arrived at the edge of a groomed park near a tree swing, she removed the spell from her shoes.

The sun, though it hadn't set yet, had grown orange with age, and made the town look more orange in turn. Beyond the park, Ceony passed a shop for bobbin lace and another for fabrics. A small grocery store and an inn sat on Bridge Street, where a few men in suspenders loaded some kind of animal feed onto a horse-drawn wagon.

She continued past Market Place, passing houses bricked in red and blue, an almshouse, and the Woodard Anglican School. Only one student graced its grounds at this hour. He sat on a bench reading a mathematics textbook.

Ceony asked him if he'd seen any Indian men, especially one driving a Model A, but he hadn't.

The sun drooped, encouraging Ceony to stick to the shadows. She wished she had brought a hat with her to hide her hair—surely its vibrant color would give her away to Saraj, though he wouldn't expect to see her in Brackley. The element of surprise was still hers.

Her hands danced over the charms of her necklace as she skirted by a small hospital. Scaffolding on its east side spoke of renovation. She peered down the next intersection, eyeing a row of apartments and a tall parish church the color of sandstone. A Ford Model A was parked across the street from it.

Ceony stiffened and stepped beneath a brick alcove overhanging the door of a single-story library. Could this be Saraj's vehicle? The policemen hadn't mentioned the automobile's number. Perhaps she should check again in the glass.

The sound of an engine caught her attention as a second Model A came around the corner—or perhaps a Model C. The driver wore a top hat and an auburn mustache. His passenger, a woman in a frilly pink dress, laughed at some joke as they passed.

Some clue you have, Ceony, she thought. *Half the people in this town probably own a Ford!*

She lingered in the alcove a moment longer, watching the first automobile, until a young man exited the library with two books under his arm. He tipped his hat at her as he went, and Ceony stepped into the library.

Passing a well-dressed gentleman reading the day's paper, she approached the librarian behind the desk and said, "Excuse me, I'm looking for someone. An Indian man, perhaps forty years old? Thin, tall—he dropped his wallet outside the hospital and I didn't see which way he went."

The librarian—an older woman with gray hair worn in Mg. Aviosky's favored tight bun—shook her head. "I think I'd remember . . . Sure he wasn't Spanish?"

"Spanish?"

"Mario lives on Bridge Street," she explained. "He's from Madrid, been here four years with his wife and little girl."

"I . . . Perhaps it was him," Ceony said, and tried to graciously accept the address the woman scribbled down on a scrap of paper. She tucked it under her collar and into her brassiere; her skirt pockets were full with spells.

As she walked through the streets of Brackley, Ceony's hand counted the spells in her bag and occasionally caressed the handle of her pistol. By the time she came full circle to the park, it was getting dark and her legs hurt. She chose a different route this time, one that took her by an old-looking spike. She saw some of the workhouse employees through lit windows, though none of them looked remotely like Saraj.

A Ford drove by without its lights on, startling her. The driver was a middle-aged Caucasian male.

She crossed the street and wound back through another residential street, stopping to ask a gardening woman about Saraj, but she had seen nothing, either. As the evening darkened, Ceony became a Pyre and held a match in her right hand, just in case. She searched the houses carefully, thinking that Saraj might avoid busy streets if he wanted to stay out of sight.

When the sun had sunk three-quarters of the way behind the horizon, she considered sending out birds to gather information for her but didn't dare risk it.

Crouching behind a whitewashed picket fence, Ceony pinched phosphorus and paper and became a Folder. She pulled a long sheet of paper and rolled it between her hands, commanding it, "Zoom."

Eye to the telescope, she searched the area with what little light was left, even spied through a few windows. A man out walking his dog a few doors down eyed her with suspicion. Flushing, Ceony lowered the telescope and continued down the street and around the corner, emerging near the school.

She searched with her telescope again, spying another empty Model T near the back of the school. She made a mental note of its location—

Ceony's breath caught in her throat as she angled the telescope up a centimeter, putting the back wall of the school in her scope. A sudden whirl of movement—a flash of black hair and the billowing of a dark cloak—caught her eye, but just as she registered what she was seeing, the man disappeared into one of the back doors.

Lowering the telescope, she let it unfurl in her hands, breaking the enchantment. Her heart raced in her chest. The familiar prickle of fear stippled her skin, but she ignored it. Lira. Grath. She had done this before; she could do it again. She was more prepared than anyone could be. One more Pyre spell and it would all be over.

She'd killed before. She could do it again, couldn't she?

Her pulse, still fast, seemed to change its rhythm. It sounded— *felt*—unfamiliar to her, like she had stepped into the body of another person, moving their flesh as her own.

"Material made by earth," she whispered, pinching the wooden staff of one of the matches on her necklace as she moved toward the school, "your handler summons you. Unlink to me as I link through you, unto this very day.

"Material made by man," she continued, pressing her hand to her breast, "I summon you. Link to me as I link to you, unto this very day."

She lit the match and said, "Material made by man, your creator summons you. Link to me as I link to you through my years, until the day I die and become earth."

She closed her hand around the flame as she stepped onto the grassy lawn of the school. Heat radiated through her palm and arm—tingling, though not burning. She let the match drop from her fingers but kept its tiny flame at her palm.

Saraj had left the door cracked open. She pulled its handle to open it wider, then stepped into a dark hallway lit in dim patches from shutterless windows. She stepped softly, balancing on the rubber pads still adhered to her soles. The narrow spaces between her fingers glowed red with the flame they concealed.

She heard a footstep around the corner, the faintest creak of a shoe as the other foot stopped short. He was listening. Waiting. He knew she was here.

Ceony stepped up to the corner. Pushed her shoulder into the brick. Brought her fist up to her mouth and whispered, "Flare."

The footsteps started again and sped up, louder, louder. Coming for her.

Her body surged around the corner, flames bursting from her hand now, sending their golden brilliance down the hallway. Illuminating her attacker and the burst spell flying from his hand.

And in that light she saw him, his dark hair cropped short, his charcoal-gray coat, the flames reflected in his green eyes.

Instead of yelling the "Combust" command lingering at the edge of her tongue, Ceony stopped short and croaked, "Emery?"

CHAPTER 15

EMERY'S EYES WIDENED. Stumbling, he shouted, "Cease!"

The vibrating burst spell dropped from the air and hit the floor, harmless.

Ceony felt a *thunk* as her body suddenly became hers again. The school walls seemed more solid, and her heartbeat, though frantic, was steady.

She flushed and grew gooseflesh at the same time. Her thoughts spun ovals in her mind. "Wh-What are you doing here?" she asked.

Emery's eyes remained large. He took a step forward. "Ceony—"

"You cut your hair!" she exclaimed.

He paused, eyebrows skewed. "And . . . your hand is on fire."

Ceony blinked and turned to the flames still burning in her palm. "Cease," she said, and the fire extinguished, leaving only the faintest trail of smoke behind.

Half a second after the flames dispersed, Emery grabbed Ceony's upper arm and pulled her into a nearby classroom, shutting the solid-wood door behind them. Three rectangular windows, one of which was unlocked, let in blue-hued twilight. Ceony's hip bumped against one of the many desks. The chalkboard at the front of the class still bore a half-erased reading assignment from Alfred Lord Tennyson.

"What," Emery began, but he shook his head and rubbed his

temples. Closed his eyes, opened them. "Heavens, I don't even know where to begin."

"Then let me," Ceony said. "What are you doing here?"

"I could ask you the same."

Ceony felt her forehead crease as she narrowed her eyes. "You're here for Saraj, aren't you? You tracked him down."

"A habit of mine," the paper magician replied, rolling back the sleeves of his coat. They fell back into place at his wrists mere moments later. "I severely doubt you're in Brackley for a shopping expedition, Ceony! You promised me you wouldn't—"

"*I* promised?" Ceony asked. "*You* promised!"

He opened his mouth to respond, closed it. Pushed fingers back through his short hair, then actually laughed. "I suppose we're both horrible people."

Ceony's shoulders slumped. "I suppose so."

His eyes met hers. "Is this why you've been avoiding my letters, then? To hide . . . this?" He gestured to the classroom.

"No! I haven't been . . ." she began, but changed to, "Magician Bailey's been intercepting our messages. I found them earlier today in his office. He had an animated hawk scouting the estate and attacking anything paper and mobile."

Again Emery raked his fingers back through his hair. A soft chuckle escaped his lips. "Well, that's a relief."

"A relief?" Ceony repeated, spine stiffening. "He read them, Emery! He knows about—"

"I hardly care. Prit's a nose and always has been. I just thought I was clever enough to stay over his head." Another chuckle. "And here I thought you were having second thoughts."

Ceony felt herself soften, even smile. "I worried the same."

Folding his arms, Emery leaned back against a navel-high bookshelf pressed against the wall. "Care to explain the pyrotechnics?"

Ceony blanched.

"I believe you told me you were not going to dabble in . . . this. After that day in hospital—"

"I know, but . . . how could I not do something with that information, Emery? How could I let a secret like that go to waste?"

"How could I think you wouldn't pursue it?" he asked, more to himself than to her. "A Pyre," he said, his voice light and incredulous. He rubbed his forehead. "And a Gaffer, too. Next thing I'll be living with a Polymaker."

Ceony bit her lip.

Emery straightened. "Polymaking? And . . . Siping? Smelting?"

Rubbing the back of her neck, Ceony said, "All of the above."

He stood still as a statue for a moment before his expression fell. "Ceony," he said, cool as a tombstone, "please tell me you haven't tried—"

"No!" she said, louder than necessary. "Not Excision, Emery. You know what I'd have to do to . . . You know how I feel about that."

"I know, I know," he said, hands raised in surrender. "I'm sorry. It's just . . . with Saraj, I don't know how far you'd go—"

"Not that far," she replied. "Never that far."

They were silent for a moment.

"He's here?" Ceony asked, dropping to a whisper.

Emery shook his head. "I'm not sure. I suspect he's in Brackley. After hours—the building is empty. A safe holdup, but I have no hard evidence."

"Magician Hughes sent you?"

"Ha . . . no. I assure you I broke my word entirely on my own." He sobered. "Ceony, I don't need to explain to you how much I *don't* want you to be here. I'd be furious if it didn't make me an utter hypocrite."

"Same," she said, though without malice. "But I think . . . I think the reason Saraj is in Brackley is that he's heading to London after his chase with Magician Cantrell."

Emery's face fell at the mention of the Smelter.

Ceony pushed forward. "You see . . . I may have broken my promise first. I . . . ran into him in Reading."

Color leached from Emery's countenance. He lunged forward, gripped Ceony's shoulders. "You *what*? Ceony—when—I—what happened? Did he—"

"He didn't touch me," she assured him, lifting one hand to his jaw. Despite the circumstances, it felt wonderful to be so near Emery again. It felt . . . safe. "I happened to be a Pyre at the time."

Taking a deep breath, he released her and attacked his hair again. "A Pyre. Right. Because you know how . . . God's mercy, Ceony."

"I think he's coming back for me, though," she confessed, averting her eyes so she would not have to see any fear or disapproval in Emery's face. "He thinks it's a game, Emery. And I may be his playmate. That, and he knows I can break bonds. I hit him hard, but not hard enough."

"We're leaving," he said, grasping her hand. "Please, Ceony. Come with me."

The bud of a protest rose in her throat. She'd come so far. Prepared so much. She could do this. For Delilah, for Anise. She had the power. Couldn't Emery see that?

She looked at his eyes, hard on the edges and glistening in the centers.

And she realized that no amount of power or preparation could put Emery's heart at ease. His broken, beaten heart. More than anything else, she wanted to calm its tremors. Make it whole again.

I broke my promise, she thought. *His actions aside, I broke my promise.*

She nodded, and Emery heaved a heavy sigh. He reached for the door handle.

"Where were you?" she asked before he turned the knob. He paused, and she clarified: "I came to the cottage last week to find you, to tell you about Reading, but you weren't there. Where were you?"

He glanced back at her. "You'll have to be more specific."

"Tuesday," she said. "I searched for a hint . . . waited, but you never came. I left the note on your windowsill."

A small smile touched his lips—almost a *sheepish* smile, of all things. Ceony had never before seen such an expression on his face. "Just out for a stroll."

"You don't stroll." *Why is he lying to me?*

"I've had a lot of free time on my hands."

"Emery Thane."

He rolled his eyes without quite rolling them, his own small show of exasperation. "I was with your parents, Ceony. Your father, specifically."

Ceony blinked, relaxed. "To warn them. They're safe?"

Emery hesitated for a moment, and Ceony thought she saw the slightest glimmer of confusion, but he only nodded. "They're well taken care of."

A comfortable, hot-cocoa kind of warmth spread through her. "Thank you, for seeing after them. It means a—"

The red, iron-scented smoke filling the room broke off Ceony's sentence. Emery stiffened and reached for her just as a sharp and resounding *thud* echoed through her skull, and the room went dark.

The first thing Ceony sensed was the smell of dust—metallic and rotten and dry. Then she registered the throbbing at the back of her head, the stiffness in her neck, the tight, bruise-like pain encircling her arms and torso. Dim light prodded at her eyelids, and she pulled them apart, blinking. A groan escaped her throat.

She was in a long rectangular room with tall windows draped in long, muslin cloths. Large brown tiles. Two folded hospital beds had been pushed into a corner near a door. Two rows of support pillars cut through the room, and it was to one of these that Ceony had been tied. On first glance, the room appeared to be empty apart from her.

She struggled against her slick bonds, realizing after a few futile attempts that the rotten scent came from them. She studied them in the dim light, their sackcloth-like color, flatness, translucency. Almost like sausage casing.

Bile rose up in Ceony's throat, and she barely managed to swallow it down. Her sinuses burned from the effort.

Intestines. And they couldn't be from a pig or cow. Only humans were man-made. Excisioners could do spells with only humans.

Saraj. Ceony lifted her head to search the room, spying the tiny, floating orbs that provided light. About the size of an infant's fist, each bore a ring that didn't glow: green, blue, brown. She bit her lip upon realizing they were eyeballs. It took all her willpower and a silent prayer to keep the contents of her stomach down.

The entrails bound her arms tightly to her sides, but Ceony could move her wrist just a little, back and forth. She clawed at her skirt pocket, slipped in a thumb and forefinger . . . but found it empty. The other, too. Her bag, missing.

And she realized one more thing, looking down at her rotting bonds. To tie her up . . . to bring her to the hospital . . . Saraj had *touched* her.

The thought sprung tears and turned her skeleton to ice. She shivered. Acid clawed at her throat. *Oh Lord in heaven, he touched me. I'm dead. I'm dead.*

Emery.

She pulled against her bonds. Her breathing quickened as she rescanned the room, searching for the paper magician. Two tears etched trails down her cheeks. Had Saraj killed him? Had he escaped? Emery . . . where was . . . ?

She spied him on the other row of columns kitty-corner to her. Saraj had bound him the same way, but he faced the windows.

Ceony could see only a sliver of his person. His head drooped forward. Unconscious. Saraj had taken his coat and turned out the pockets of his slacks.

"Emery!" Ceony cried, trying to keep her voice low. "Emery, please wake up!"

The paper magician stirred, and so did the Excisioner.

"The game isn't fun when you cheat, kitten." Saraj's accented voice sounded from Ceony's right. She strained against the entrails as she watched him enter the room through another door, one that led to a staircase. He'd changed his clothes since Reading; he wore a narrowly tailored gray suit without the jacket. A splatter of crimson stained his shirt where it tucked into his slacks, and another dark stain coated his left knee.

He muttered something under his breath, a spell, and the slick entrails binding Ceony to the pillar shifted, moving her to its right side so that she faced Saraj. He grinned at her and said, "There's no pleasure in the chase when you come to me."

Ceony swallowed, searching for the voice trapped somewhere in her shaking body. "I guess y-you're not used to p-people playing back," she said, but there was no confidence in it.

"Saraj," came Emery's voice—Ceony could see even less of him now—"your fight is with me."

Saraj laughed. "Oh, no it isn't. You'll be discarded in a moment, Thane."

Ceony writhed against her bonds, her heart hammering. "Saraj, no! Deal with me; leave him out of this!"

"Don't change the rules, kitten," Saraj said, holding up a scolding finger. "Now"—he reached into his pocket and pulled out Ceony's necklace—"tell me your little secret, hm?"

Ceony froze.

"Grath had been so . . . What is the word? Adamant? Adamant about breaking his bond to glass. Obsessed," Saraj said, strolling between the lines of pillars, fondling the charms on the necklace. "I didn't know he'd succeeded. Unless you figured out the secret on your own?"

He paused, held the necklace up to his face. "You have some strange things on here. Wood for paper, sand for glass. Oil . . . and a match? So the foundation of the material is part of it. But how?" He lowered the necklace and met Ceony's eyes. "Tell me how it works, kitten."

"Ceony!" Emery shouted, but with a wave of Saraj's hand, Emery's bonds tightened around him, choking out any ensuing words. Choking out his air.

"Stop it!" Ceony screamed.

Saraj smiled and lowered his hands. Emery's bonds loosened, barely. The paper magician's next breath came as a gasp.

He'll kill him. Ceony panicked. She breathed hard and fast. The ceiling started to spin above her. *He'll kill him. Oh, Emery. Not him.* She could not even bear to contemplate . . .

But she couldn't tell Saraj, either. She couldn't give him that power. How many more people would die once Saraj knew her secret?

Emery, or them?

She never should have come after Saraj. She never should have tested her knowledge in the first place. She never—

"Ticktock," Saraj said.

"Tell him nothing!" Emery shouted.

Ceony pressed her lips together. Tears trickled down her face.

Saraj chuckled and walked toward her, his gait unhurried. Once close enough, he placed a hand on the pillar beside her head.

Emery struggled against his bonds—Ceony could see his legs kicking. "Saraj!" he shouted, his voice filling the room. "Touch her and I'll have your head for a mantelpiece!"

"This is the strange thing about Englishmen," Saraj murmured to Ceony, his breath caressing her forehead. It smelled like cardamom and some kind of meat. "They make threats they cannot carry out."

He smiled without teeth and slid his fingers into the hair above Ceony's ear. She winced and pulled her head as far away from him as she could, but Saraj simply wound a lock of her hair around two fingers and, with a growl, yanked it from her head.

Ceony yelped.

Dangling the orange hair from his fingers the same way he did the necklace, Saraj ignored Emery's cursing. "I don't joke," he said. "I'm not a funny man."

"I think you're hilarious," Ceony spat.

He smiled. "Oh? Then you'll love this."

He strode away from Ceony. Toward Emery. The entrails holding the paper magician shifted and turned him about so that Saraj—and Ceony—could see his full person.

Ceony barely recognized him. He looked so pale, so wide- and white-eyed. There was a trail of blood on his neck, likely drizzled from where Saraj had hit him, too.

Saraj muttered under his breath for several seconds—Excision spells tended to be longer than other spells, unless pre-prepared—and the hair in his hands stiffened and straightened. It looked sharp as glass.

"How much blood must be spilled before the kitten sings?" Saraj asked, tracing Emery's jaw with the hair. It split the skin open, leaving an angry red trail. Saraj hesitated. "But kittens don't sing, do they?"

"Stop it! *Stop!*" Ceony cried.

Emery's eyes were locked with the Excisioner's, but he said, "Tell him nothing, Ceony."

"Don't hurt him!" she wailed, wrenching back and forth. The entrails didn't budge. Whatever enchantment Saraj had placed on them held tight.

Saraj jammed the hair-blade into Emery's shoulder. Blood welled around the wound, seeping through his shirt. Emery bit back a scream.

Ceony's eyes darted back and forth, scanning the room. Searching for her bag, her things, *anything* that might help her. She pressed her hands to the pillar, but she could do nothing with stone. Nothing with the entrails, with her clothing. The rubber was still on the bottom of her shoes! She felt a rush of hope for a moment, but she was a Pyre now, with no way of changing that. She feebly patted her pockets, studied her blouse buttons—

"Please!" Ceony begged, blinking through tears. She had to tell him—she couldn't live in a world without Emery. She couldn't!

Saraj retracted his hand and patted Emery twice on the cheek as though he were a dog. Emery scowled at him.

"Did you know, kitten, that Excisioners can break a man's fingers, one at a time, without even touching him?" Saraj asked, glancing at Ceony over his shoulder. He reached into his pocket and drew out a pair of rusted pliers. "All I need is one nail. I don't even have to be in the same room to make the bones bend."

He opened and closed the pliers in his hand, returning his focus to Emery. "I like the thumbnail, myself. Call it a . . . what's the word? Quirk."

Ceony wrenched herself back and forth, squirmed, loosening pieces of hair from the twist at the back of her head. The locks stuck to her tear-moistened skin. Not Emery. Emery wasn't supposed to be here! He wasn't supposed to be part of this!

Saraj turned to her one more time. "I might be willing to kill him mercifully with, say, a piece of glass instead of bone by bone, but of course, you'll need to tell me what you know."

Her body trembled against the entrails. Visions of Anise lying in a pool of bloody water and Delilah hanging white and limp against her own bonds flooded Ceony's mind. Drowned her.

"I—"

"Ceony," Emery warned.

But I'm here, she thought, another tear cascading down her cheek. *I'm here this time. I can't watch you die. I'm* here.

Shrugging, Saraj reached for Emery's hand.

"I'll tell you!" she blurted, stopping the Indian man's hand. Tears trickled down her throat, making her voice husky. "I'll tell you, but only if you let him go!"

"Ceony!" Emery shouted.

Saraj grinned and retracted the pliers. "A fair bargain. I'm listening."

"Let him go first," Ceony pleaded.

"You English and your bartering," Saraj quipped. He folded his arms, took a few steps away from Emery. "You don't have leverage, kitten. But I'm in a pleasant enough mood. I already have one magician's heart; I don't need another yet. I might let him go. You, on the other hand—"

"Ceony, don't you dare say another word!" Emery yelled. "It's not worth it!"

"But you're worth it," she cried, though the words came out so quietly she didn't think he heard them. Swallowing, she said, "The secret is yourself."

Emery wilted against the entrails holding him.

Saraj raised an eyebrow. "You'll need to be specific."

"That's what Grath discovered," Ceony said, feeling her body hollow out with each confessed word. She'd be little more than a bag of skin in a moment. "You bond to your material's natural substance, then to yourself, then to the new material. That's how it's done."

The Excisioner smiled. "Interesting. The words?"

Ceony swallowed against a dry throat. "Material made by earth, your handler summons you. Unlink to me as I link through you, unto this very day. It starts with that."

Saraj lifted the charm necklace, his eyes glancing over each charm. Then he studied them with his hand, pinching and turning. He frowned. "And what, pray tell, do I bond to?"

Ceony paused, looking at her necklace. Glanced at Emery. Refocused on Saraj. She had never considered that question, since she had never dreamed of dabbling in Excision.

Excisioners became Excisioners by bonding to a person—Ceony had seen Grath do it to Delilah. But what was the natural material of a person? People made people. They were one and the same. Unless Excisioners bonded to their original victims' parents?

But that didn't make sense. Even if an Excisioner managed to track down both parents of the person he murdered to gain his magic, he couldn't bond with *both* of them.

Ceony blinked and licked her lips. "You . . . can't."

Saraj's countenance darkened. "What?"

She shook her head. "You can't. By definition humans are manmade, but they don't have a natural substance. They merely . . . are." A smile spread on her lips, and she added, more to herself than to Saraj, "Once a person becomes an Excisioner, they're stuck. They can't change.

"Excisioners can't use the other magics."

Emery lifted his head, his eyes reflecting the unnatural light hovering overhead. He actually smiled.

Ceony laughed. "You can't use it, Saraj. You can't, and neither can the others. No Excisioner can have those powers. You're *stuck*. Forever."

Saraj's face darkened and contorted until he hardly looked a man anymore. His brow crinkled, his lip lifted, and his cheeks sunk into the spaces between his teeth.

"Well, then," he said, his voice dark and thick. He shoved the necklace into one pocket and pulled the pliers from the other. He turned back to Emery.

All smugness drained from Ceony, leaving her cold and empty. "No, no!" she cried, but the words didn't slow Saraj in the slightest. She had no leverage. Not anymore.

Her eyes did another sweep of the room, scanning the walls, the floor—

Her eyes stopped at her collar, and she spied the tip of the piece of paper the librarian had given her with the Spaniard's address on it. Saraj hadn't taken it. But she couldn't cast paper spells without changing her material.

She couldn't, but Emery could.

She couldn't Fold a spell for him, and his arms were bound just as surely as her own. He hadn't touched the paper, so he couldn't call it to him with a sorting spell. Ceony sagged against her bonds— useless. Her one hope, and she couldn't even—

Saraj crouched, reaching for Emery's hand.

Yet again she searched for something she could use—a flame, a spark, *anything*. But Saraj had thought of that—the only light came from those eerie, glowing eyes. No lanterns, no candles. Nothing that could make fire, save for the match on her necklace—

Her necklace. It was in Saraj's pocket. It had a paper charm on it—a charm she'd made from her history paper. Emery had *touched* it when he graded it.

Her memory transported her to the day she'd crafted the charm at her desk in her room. The scrap of paper had been torn from her homework. The date 1744.

"Sort it, Emery!" she cried. "Sort with the date 1744!"

Saraj turned around, perturbed. Emery didn't question Ceony's plea. He called out, "Sort: 1744!"

The necklace flew out of Saraj's pocket and into Emery's left hand. Saraj spun back to Emery, but not before Emery tossed the necklace to Ceony, using as much force as his restrained wrist would allow.

The glass perfume vial carrying the oil and the bottle containing the liquid latex shattered the moment the necklace hit the floor. The necklace skidded across the tiles toward Ceony's pillar, slowing down before it reached her. Saraj hadn't bound her below the hip, so she reached out a foot and pulled the necklace toward her with her toe.

Saraj spun back toward Ceony.

Sweating, heart racing, Ceony pulled the necklace between her feet. The entrails encircled her tightly enough to hold her in place as she pinched the necklace between her shoes and, bending her knees, lifted it up until her right hand could reach the cord.

Saraj sprinted for her, pulling a bloodstained handkerchief from his pocket.

Ceony's fingers hunted over the necklace until she found the match tied there. She pressed her thumbnail into its tip, scraped in and up.

Lit it.

"Flare!" she yelled just as Saraj reached for her, his handkerchief glowing a ruddy sheen. The fire in her hand grew a thousand times its former size, licking out and causing Saraj to stumble. Whatever spell Saraj had been about to cast nullified itself.

"Burn!" Ceony commanded, and the fire chewed away at the entrails holding her. She stumbled from the pillar, her ribs aching as they expanded back into place. With the command "Split," she divided her fireball into two. She sent one flying toward Saraj, forcing him to retreat. Running to Emery's side, she used the other to incinerate his bonds.

Emery gasped for air as the entrails broke apart. His hand flew to his shoulder to rip out the hair-blade there; he groaned and pressed his palm into the wound, which began bleeding with renewed vigor.

"I need . . . my coat," he wheezed, gawking at the fire in Ceony's hands. "Spells."

"The stairs," she guessed. "He came from the stairs—"

Emery's eyes widened and he grabbed her fireless hand, yanking her behind the pillar just as red throwing stars soared past where they had been standing. The stars bounced off the stone pillar and reverted to liquid blood upon hitting the floor.

"Split! Flare! Combust!" Ceony cried, dividing her flames once more. She kept one fireball in reserve and threw the other at Saraj. He leapt from its path; the flames sailed toward the hospital beds, charring their metal rods as it went.

"Go!" Ceony shouted. "Find the spells. I'll hold him off!"

"Ceony—"

"Go!"

Still clutching his shoulder, Emery ran to the door to the stairwell. Ceony cast a pinwheel spell on her fireball and tossed it toward the pillar behind which Saraj had barricaded himself—the fire bloomed into a four-petal flower and spun back and forth across the tiles, forcing Saraj to withdraw farther. The spilled oil on the ground ignited into a puddle of flames.

Gripping her necklace, Ceony recited the words for bond breaking so quickly she nearly tongue-tied herself. She became a Gaffer and ran to the window, yanking down the muslin sheet covering it. If nothing else, perhaps someone would see the flames before they went out and would send for help.

Making contact with the glass, Ceony commanded, "Leftward, Shatter!" The window fragmented into hundreds of pieces and, with a swipe of Ceony's hand, flew toward Saraj. The glassy darts broke into even smaller shards as they collided with walls, pillars, and the floor. One slid between Saraj's ribs before he could take cover.

"*Kutiyaa!*" Saraj shouted. Ceony moved for the next window, but her legs suddenly gave out under her. She dropped to the floor, catching herself on her hands.

She tried to get up but couldn't move her legs.

She couldn't *feel* her legs.

"You forget, kitten," Saraj said between heavy breaths, "that I've touched your skin. I *own* you!"

He stepped out from behind a pillar, holding his bloodied side. The first two fingers of his right hand were crossed—perhaps a method of holding the numbing spell over her.

Ceony pushed herself backward with her arm. Glimpsed the oil puddle, still burning, barely. If she could get that fire—

Clutching her necklace, she moved her hand to the pouch of sand, only to have her tongue and lips go numb as well. The spell turned to mush in her mouth.

"No more of that," Saraj said. He took a deep breath and started chanting. The hand holding his wound began to glimmer with gold, and within moments his breathing evened. He pulled his hand away, the wound healed.

He managed to take one step toward Ceony before a gunshot rang out through the room. Saraj stumbled and gasped, his hands flying to his chest, cupping the bullet hole there. As soon as he uncrossed his fingers, Ceony's numbness vanished.

Ceony scrambled to her feet as Saraj fell from his.

Whipping around, Ceony spotted Emery in the doorway, her pistol clutched in his hands. He wore his charcoal coat and Ceony's bag slung over his shoulder.

Saraj lay lifeless on the floor.

"Emery," she breathed. She inched closer to Saraj, watching his chest, waiting for it to rise with air . . . but it remained still. The Excisioner's eyes stared up at the ceiling, half-closed.

She hurried to Emery and threw her arms around his waist. He dropped the pistol and embraced her in turn.

She pulled back, glancing toward Saraj. "I didn't know you were such a good shot."

"I'm not," he said, wincing as he moved to hand her the bag.

Ceony returned the charm necklace to her neck and grabbed Emery's hand. "We need to go. The police are searching for him; if they haven't seen commotion through the window, they'll be here when—"

"Wait," Emery said, jerking back.

Ceony paused.

"The lights," he said, glancing to the floating eyes. "When an Excisioner dies, his spells become void."

Ceony stopped breathing. She turned back to Saraj's prone form, which began to shake with convulsive laughter.

"Too true, too true," his accented voice said. He rose from the floor, each wheezing breath wet and heavy. He moved like a rag doll in a child's hands, hunched and loose.

He turned toward them and, with glowing fingers, plunged his hand into his own chest, removing a beatless heart.

Bile returned to Ceony's mouth.

"A benefit of having two hearts, Thane," he gurgled with a laugh, dropping the organ at his feet as the cavity in his chest stitched itself together. "My regards to Magician Cantrell."

Emery growled and ran from Ceony's side, his coat flying behind him like a cape. The burst spell from the school flung out from his hands and began vibrating wildly in the space between himself and Saraj.

Ceony ran back toward the windows, shattering one just as the burst spell exploded. She caught sight of Saraj in the corner of her eye and sent the shards raining toward him. She had to keep him busy, keep him moving, or he would cast another spell on her body. On Emery's. The moment the Excisioner had time to think, she and Emery would be dead.

She ran back for the stairs, hand flying over her necklace as she uttered the words to become a Smelter. She reached for the pistol Emery had dropped on the floor—

The room warped around her, dizzying her, causing her to stumble. Not the result of an Excision spell—this was Emery's doing. A distortion spell. The jellyfish-like paper bobbed in his hand.

She took two more steps before falling onto her hip. The floor rippled like an angry ocean. Her pistol wavered like oil on water.

She reached for it, clasped it. The room froze back into place, a thin mist of blood spraying over Ceony—remnants from a spell aimed at Emery.

Shaking off the effects of the distortion spell with only moderate success, Ceony stood and, holding out her pistol, called, "Attract!"

The spell radiated out from the metal of the pistol, calling forward anything and everything made of metal alloys. Buttons from Saraj's shirt cuffs ripped from their stitches; needles lost between floor tiles rose into the air. Even the charred hospital beds zoomed across the room, hitting Saraj in the back of the knees and forcing Emery to duck behind a pillar to keep from being run over. At the last second Ceony dropped the pistol and darted for the corner, narrowly missing being hit by the hospital beds herself. The needles and buttons rained onto the pistol, clinging to it.

Saraj vanished in a swirl of red smoke and reappeared behind Emery.

"Behind you!" Ceony cried.

Emery spun and dropped to the floor, missing Saraj's outstretched arm by inches. Saraj's hand hit the pillar instead, leaving a bloody print, and Emery slammed his foot into the other man's shin, knocking him over.

Grabbing one of the hospital beds, Ceony dragged it across the room with her. Emery got to his feet; Saraj clawed at his pant leg, murmuring under his breath. His hands began glowing red.

Ceony didn't need to call out for Emery to see the spell. The paper magician grabbed Saraj by the hair and slammed his fist into the Excisioner's cheek.

"Throw him against the pillar!" Ceony shouted.

Emery hit Saraj again and grabbed the man's collar, heaving him against one of the stone pillars. The instant he was in place, Ceony shoved the hospital bed against him and shouted, "Bend, circular!"

The charred bones of the bed creaked as they wrapped around Saraj and the pillar, pinning him in place.

Saraj began to laugh.

Emery grabbed Ceony and pulled her back, then reached into his coat, bringing out handfuls of paper spells. To Ceony's surprise, he commanded them, "Shred!"

The spells tore into hundreds of pieces, ruined.

"Gather, forward!" Emery commanded, and the pieces of paper collected into a cloud and stormed toward Saraj, floating about him and clinging to him like leeches.

"Lacerate!" Emery shouted. A command Ceony had never before heard.

The paper cloud pulled apart, half the pieces soaring one way, half the other, their edges slicing through Saraj's skin.

Paper cuts. Hundreds and hundreds of deep, slender paper cuts.

The papers drifted to the ground, lined with red.

Saraj drooped in his metal-barred prison, and the glowing eyes turned black.

CHAPTER 16

SILVER-GLEAMING GAFFER torches lined the walkway to the half-renovated hospital, pierced into the soil by both London and Brackley policemen. Two police automobiles blocked the road, and three horses grazed lazily at the hospital lawn while their riders investigated inside. Ceony shivered despite Emery's coat draped over her shoulders. Emery himself sat on a bench near the walk, where a medic was checking the wound on the back of his head. He had already handed the paper magician a wet rag to press against his shoulder. He'd been hurt, yes, but he was alive. They both were. And Saraj wasn't coming back—even the most experienced Excisioner couldn't resurrect himself, no matter how many stolen hearts he'd cached inside his body.

Ceony thought of Anise, not lying prone in her bathtub, but with her pencil clenched between her teeth as she tried to solve a math problem far too complex for Ceony to ever comprehend. Ceony thought of Delilah, not with Grath's hand clasped around her neck, but smiling at her from across the table at St. Alban's Salmon Bistro.

Finally, it was finished.

"I have a hard time believing you were simply in the right place at the right time, Thane," Mg. Hughes said, approaching the bench. Ceony hadn't seen him arrive. "If you insist on going through all the trouble, you might as well join our ranks. It pays well, as I've told you before."

Emery managed to smile—a weary gesture—at the Siper's chiding. "Too much paperwork. You know that, Alfred."

Alfred snorted. "Paperwork. A Folder of all people, complaining about paperwork."

Mg. Hughes scratched his white mustache and glanced over to Ceony. "Ah, Miss Twill," he said. "Why am I not surprised to see you here? Third strike, eh? Maybe you'd like to be recruited instead? When is this blasted apprenticeship of yours over?"

Ceony tried to smile as well, but her nerves may have made it into more of a grimace. "Just under two weeks, with luck."

Mg. Hughes brightened. "Oh? Well, there's some good news. My well-wishes, of course."

He turned back to Emery and bent over to get a better look at his wounds. "Once Magician Kilmer gets his hands on you, you'll be good as new."

"Magician Kilmer?" Ceony asked.

"A Binder," Mg. Hughes said. "I normally wouldn't say, but you've met him already."

Ceony scrunched her eyebrows together. A Binder? "I would remember . . ."

"You'd be dead if you hadn't," Mg. Hughes clarified. "He's one of few, but he happened to be in London the day of the incident with Grath, if you recall."

Ceony took a moment to process the information, which sent an icy shock down her spine. "You mean . . . the Excisioner, at the hospital?"

"Binder, my dear," Mg. Hughes corrected her. "There's a difference."

Ceony shook her head. "What difference? He may heal instead of hurt, but explain that to the person he killed to earn his magic."

"He volunteered, actually."

Ceony spun around to see a tall man standing behind her, his shoulder-length black hair unbound and glimmering in the Gaffer light. He wore a dark suit with a dark shirt underneath, no tie. His was a long face with high cheekbones and deep-set, almond eyes that spoke of Asian lineage.

Mg. Hughes cleared his throat. "Miss Twill, Magician Kilmer. I did mention he was here, didn't I?"

A flush crept up Ceony's chest and neck, banishing her chills.

Mg. Kilmer gave her a somber smile, one that moved the lips just enough to be noticeable. Stepping past her, he said, "He suffered from cancer of the bones, and everyone in his family had already passed on before him save for one son. He would have died within days regardless, if it helps your conscience."

What could Ceony say to that? It didn't seem right to apologize . . . or to thank him for healing her, for healing Emery now. Despite the man's judicially anointed abilities, Ceony's stomach still tightened as he stood over Emery, uttering the same old tongue Saraj had used. His hands glowed with a familiar gold light, and he touched Emery's shoulder, head, and jaw, erasing his wounds as if they had never existed.

"I need to speak with Magician Aviosky," Ceony said.

Mg. Hughes leaned toward her. "Hm?"

"I've given my statement," she said. "Could we leave? It's important."

Mg. Hughes shrugged. "Be my guest. That's in Magician Thane's jurisdiction now."

She nodded once, then moved to Emery as Mg. Kilmer left. She knelt before him, hands on his knees, not really caring who saw.

"You lied to me," she whispered.

He met her eyes. "Which time?"

"About my being ready to test for magicianship," she said. "Lacerate—I don't know that one. How many more spells do I not know?"

"Not even Prit knows that spell, Ceony," Emery said. He rested his hands on her shoulders, lifted a lock of her hair to see the place where Saraj had ripped out another. Ceony hoped it didn't look too obvious. "That is a Magician Thane original."

Ceony's fatigue subsided at those words. "You discovered a Folding spell? How?"

"It's an intense version of 'Shred,' really," he said. "And yes, when Lira was still a threat. I'm a Folder, Ceony. I needed to find something besides 'Burst' spells that could incapacitate a person."

She nodded, slowly, digesting the news. "Are there any others I don't know?"

"No."

Another nod. A pause. "Emery," she said, enunciating each syllable of his name. Proceeding with caution. "How many people have . . . have you—"

"Killed?" he finished for her.

She bit her lip.

"You and I are one for one, love," he answered.

"Oh, Emery—"

"I'll be fine," he said. Ran a thumb over her cheek. "I hardly feel remorse over the loss of Saraj Prendi. By all means, I killed him twice. I guess that puts me one ahead, hm?"

Silence fell between them for several seconds.

"I need to tell Magician Aviosky," Ceony whispered. "Knowing what we know about bonding Excisioners . . . I think I should tell her."

"I would do the same."

"Did you arrive by buggy? Is it still here?"

Emery stood and pulled up Ceony with him. He rolled his head and stretched out his shoulder, testing it. Glancing behind him, he nodded once to Mg. Kilmer.

"Let's go," he murmured, hand pressed to Ceony's back. "I do hope Patrice likes early-morning visitors."

Ceony walked close to him, leaving the hospital—and the Excisioners—behind.

———————

Mg. Aviosky opened the front door on the ninth knock, already groomed and powdered, though the hair pulled into its habitual tight bun at her crown looked wet. She didn't mask her surprise at seeing Emery Thane and Ceony Twill on her doorstep a quarter after seven in the morning. Adjusting her glasses on her nose, she asked, "To what do I owe this visit? I'm afraid I have an appointment with the Cabinet in an hour."

Taking a deep breath, Ceony said, "Saraj Prendi is dead."

She stiffened. "What, how? Are you sure?"

"Alfred will likely fill you in soon enough," Emery said. He stifled a yawn.

Mg. Aviosky blanched. Her gaze fixed on Ceony. "Don't tell me you were invol—"

"Saraj isn't why I'm here," she interjected. Glanced at Emery. After another deep breath, she added, "There's something I didn't tell you about Grath. What he did the day in the mirror room—how Delilah really died."

Mg. Aviosky stilled until even her chest failed to rise, her lips limp.

"I didn't tell you what he discovered," Ceony continued, "but I need to tell you now, if you can find the time."

The Gaffer nodded mutely and stepped back from the door, clearing a path into her home. Ceony slipped off her shoes at the door, as was Mg. Aviosky's preference, though she noted Emery did not. The Gaffer made no comment and simply led the two of them into the front room. Ceony sat on the couch, Emery beside her. To her surprise he took her hand in his in plain sight of Mg. Aviosky. Still, the Gaffer didn't comment.

Nerves prickling the lining of her stomach, Ceony said, "Delilah died because Grath bonded to her. He became an Excisioner, Magician Aviosky. He was about to steal your heart when I . . . stopped him."

Mg. Aviosky's eyebrows sailed nearly to her hairline, then dropped down close to her eyes. "Miss Twill, Grath Cobalt was a Gaffer. A man cannot bond to more than one material."

"Not at the same time, no," Ceony said. She glanced to Emery before adding, "What if I told you that, at this moment, I was a Smelter?"

Mg. Aviosky rubbed her chin. "Miss Twill—"

"Bring me a coin," Ceony said. "I'll prove it."

CHAPTER 17

DURING THE DRIVE to Poplar, Ceony thought of Mg. Aviosky. Yesterday's meeting had gone just about as well as could be expected, but Mg. Aviosky didn't know what to do with the discovery. Neither did Ceony.

"I'll think on it." Mg. Aviosky's departing words. She hadn't even said good-bye as Ceony and Emery walked back to their buggy.

Today's buggy pulled up alongside the curve outside the new Twill house. Ceony shook thoughts of magic and bonding from her mind and focused on the task at hand. She had one more item of personal business to take care of before returning to Mg. Bailey's abode, and her studies.

Tracking Zina down proved to be a more complicated task than Ceony had imagined. Being unmarried and having chosen not to further her education outside of secondary school, Zina still lived at home, but she had gone out. No one knew where.

"I don't know what to do with her, Ceony," her mother groaned as she poured Ceony a cup of weak tea. "She rarely alerts me when she goes out, and only God knows what she does. Your father is losing hair over it. I'm ready to kick her out!"

Rhonda Twill would never force one of her daughters out of the home, of course, but Ceony understood her mother's sentiment.

Birds would do no good in locating Zina in such a highly populated area. Instead, Ceony stopped next door to inquire of Mrs. Hemmings, whose daughter was a new friend of Zina's. Mrs. Hemmings suggested a few places to look, including the Carraways' residence back in the Mill Squats.

The sun had risen to noon by the time Ceony arrived in her old neighborhood. Fortunately Megrinda Carraway, Zina's on-and-off friend and two years Ceony's junior, happened to be home.

"She's probably out with Carl and Sam," Megrinda said, leaning against the door frame of the squat house as she twisted a lock of umber hair around her finger. It didn't look as though she'd bothered to get ready for the day, save for changing from a sleeping gown to a faded yellow sundress.

"A tall fellow with sandy-colored hair and a cleft in his chin?" Ceony asked.

Megrinda nodded. "That's Carl. Sam's his little brother. He's a real bugger, if you don't mind me saying."

Ceony did mind but saw no use in mentioning it.

"They usually hang out by the theatre in Parliament Square or the Maple By."

Ceony furrowed her brow. "The saloon?"

Megrinda smiled. "Yeah." She eyed Ceony, head to foot to head. "Even you'd get some attention there."

Inhaling deeply to prevent a huff, Ceony thanked Megrinda for her help and had her buggy drive her to Parliament Square.

She first checked the small road where she'd run into Zina before, but there was no sign of her sister. She walked around the theatre, even going so far as to ask a man at the ticket counter if he'd seen anyone meeting Zina's description, but he hadn't. Ceony walked by the rows of shops near the Parliament building, peeking into their windows, before finally giving up and making her way to the saloon. Despite having come to terms with her hair color years ago, she found herself wishing it were a less noticeable shade. She didn't need rumors of intemperance to be added to the chatter about her relationship with Emery. Maybe she should just hug a "Conceal" spell about her person and walk invisibly through the streets. If only she had brought a sheet of paper large enough.

God had mercy on her, for when she stepped into the saloon, too dimly lit to encourage good behavior, she spied Zina only moments after being assaulted with the smell of cigar smoke. Someone whistled; Ceony didn't look to see if it had been directed at her. She trudged up to the high table where Zina stood with a cigarette perched in her fingers. Carl sat next to her, turning an empty glass over in his hands. There was no sign of Sam.

"Hello, sister."

Zina looked up at her, and for a moment her face flashed pale, but she hid her reaction so swiftly Ceony wondered if she'd imagined it. Her sister's eyes darkened and her brows tightened. "What the hell are you doing here?"

Ceony sighed. "Spoken like a true lady. I need to speak to you, and I'd like to do it outside of this . . . establishment. Preferably before I start to smell like the fag in your hand."

Carl stood. "I know you. Older sister?" He didn't ask it in a friendly tone.

Keeping calm, as Delilah had always complimented her for doing, Ceony pulled a sheet of paper and her Smelted scissors from her purse and set the supplies on the table, focusing on them and not Carl. "I believe my use of the term *sister* would say that much. Elder sister, which is why I don't want Zina in a place like this with a man like you. If you'll excuse us."

Carl snorted. "Shove off."

Ceony had expected he'd say something of the like. Without so much as glancing at him, she cut her squares and, after pulling out a pencil, quickly doodled on their corners before returning the pencil and scissors to her bag. She whispered "Adhere" to one of her squares.

"Send me a letter if you want to talk," Zina said, puffing around the fag. She didn't seem to be enjoying it much, stupid girl. "Your fancy mail birds. Or have your blighter make one for you."

Carl grabbed Ceony's upper arm. "Time to go, sweets."

Ceony turned to face him, their chests only inches apart, and tucked one of her squares into the front pocket of his trousers. "I am not your 'sweets,' Carl," she said, shaking off his hand and simultaneously throwing the other square with a flick of her wrist. The "Adhere" spell she'd placed on it made it suction tightly to the floor. "And if you touch me again, I'll have you tossed out. Or, better yet, I'll do it myself. Affix!"

The bearing square in Carl's pocket leapt to connect with its partner on the floor, regardless of what—or who—stood in the way. The force of the magic knocked Carl onto the ground and slid him several feet to meet the other paper square.

Zina gaped. "Ceony!"

"Come with me, or I'll do the same to you," she snapped, snatching the fag from Zina's lips. With an uttered "Shred," the cigarette's paper tore itself to pieces, leaving a barely smoldering mess on the tabletop.

Having grabbed Zina by the elbow, Ceony dragged her out of the saloon and into the blessedly fresh-smelling sunlight. Fortunately, her sister didn't resist until they were several paces from the dreaded place's front doors.

"You've got some nerve!" Zina shot.

Ceony brushed her hands over her blouse as though the action could scare away the smell of cigars. "Apparently not as much as you. My affair with an established magician hardly seems notable compared to whatever rubbish you're up to."

Zina deflated, leaned against the outside wall of Maple By. "Don't act like you understand me."

"Why would I pretend to when I don't?" she countered. "What has gotten into you? Mother is worried about you, and so am I. Talk to me."

Zina frowned.

"I don't see Carl coming to your rescue."

Rolling her eyes, Zina folded her arms, then unfolded them to flick her black hair behind her shoulders. It fell forward again. She ignored it.

Ceony frowned. "We used to be close, you know."

Her sister continued to fuss with her hair, eyes averted. "Before you took off and became the apple of Mum and Dad's eye, maybe."

Ceony raised an eyebrow.

"I'm sick of being second-rate, Ceony!" Zina said, loud enough to earn a few glances from passersby. Apparently, without Carl and Sam as her shield, the looks bothered her. Lowering her voice, she continued. "Compared, overlooked. If one daughter can become a magician, then certainly another can do something equally great."

"You can, if you want to," she offered quietly. "And I'm not a magician yet."

"Easy for you to say. We don't all have rich men paying for our schooling."

"You hate school."

"I wish I didn't."

That took Ceony aback. She felt herself soften, inside and out. "Oh, Zina."

Zina folded her arms tightly over her chest. "I hate being poor."

"Is that the appeal to this Carl? Money?"

She guffawed. "He's a street sweeper, so no."

But he pays attention to you, Ceony thought, though she knew better than to voice the words. Instead, she said, "Come," and gently took Zina's elbow. Zina, eyes fixed on the walk, came without protest.

"What do you want to do?" Ceony asked after a minute of silence.

"I don't know."

"Well, we can't do anything until we figure that out. What about your art?"

She snorted. "Can't afford the equipment."

Ceony paused, looked at her. "Oh, Zina, I can help you out with that. You just have to ask."

"I don't need any debts to you."

Ceony resisted rolling her own eyes and continued walking. "We all need help once in a while. And if I pass my magician's test, I will have the means to help you financially. The rest is up to you."

"I don't want handouts."

"Then sell something and pay me back. Accept a little help from your family, Zina. I doubt you want to spend the rest of your life inside a saloon next to someone who manhandles women."

Zina sighed. "Carl is an idiot."

"See? We're already becoming more agreeable with each other."

Despite the tension, Zina laughed, though it was a somewhat bitter sound. They walked in silence for a moment longer before Zina said, "I just need to find some old rich man to marry."

"And that's not a handout?"

Her sister smirked. "To suffer through a marriage like that? I'd be earning my allowance."

That made Ceony pause again. "I know someone who might appreciate you. Your art, at least."

Another eye roll. "Got another Folder up your sleeve?"

Ceony thought of Emery's first apprentice, Langston. "Well, yes, actually. But I won't introduce him to someone who smells like a saloon and who doesn't respect herself."

Zina pulled away from her, brows drawn together again. "I respect myself just fine."

"Then act like it, Zina."

Her sister opened her mouth to retort, but Ceony pulled her into a hug before she could speak. "I believe in you," she said into Zina's tobacco-scented hair. "Believe in yourself. I'll see you at my announcement?"

Pulling back, Zina studied Ceony's eyes. "So sure you'll pass, eh?"

Ceony smiled. "When one believes in oneself, even the extraordinary is possible."

CHAPTER 18

THIRTEEN DAYS AFTER her battle with Saraj and twelve days after her confession to Mg. Aviosky, Ceony stood in a short corridor in the Ministry of Licensing, in the wing devoted to the use of magic. She had at her side a giant tweed bag purchased to hold all fifty-eight of her handcrafted spells based off the list Mg. Bailey had given her. She had received no further instructions save that she was to bring the spells with her to the ministry. She wondered if they would be examined by a group of Folders for skill, or perhaps by other magicians who would judge her creativity. Perhaps it was merely a test of whether or not she had been able to complete the list. She might have to debate her reasoning for each spell. Emery had never encouraged her to study debate.

She squeezed the handle of the bag, trying to ignore the moistness of her hands.

A small, golden bell hanging over an unmarked door in the hallway rang—her signal that it was time to begin. With a deep breath, Ceony hefted her tweed bag and approached the door, turned the handle, and—

She paused when the doorknob stuck. She twisted it again, back and forth, but it didn't budge. The door was locked.

She glanced up at the bell and felt a flush creep up her neck. Swallowing against a dry throat, she lifted her hand and gently rapped on the door.

Nothing happened. No voices or noises of any sort came from within, though Ceony knew both Mg. Aviosky and Mg. Bailey were inside. She'd seen them enter herself. She rapped again, only to be met with silence. She twisted the doorknob. Locked.

Then it dawned on her. Though Mg. Bailey's list was stowed in her skirt pocket, she easily remembered the first item on it: *Something to open a door.* Was this part of the test, then?

Ceony fished through her bag for the skeletal arm she'd crafted and held it to the doorknob, only to freeze when the paper fingers were a centimeter away.

"Something to open a *locked* door, Mg. Bailey?" she asked, blood draining from her face. Despite her flawless memory, Ceony dug the list out of her pocket and reread the first task: *#1. Something to open a door.* It said nothing about it being locked. Had the Folder purposely left off such a critical element for the sake of revenge on Emery?

Her breath quickened. She stared at the doorknob. Surely she wouldn't fail her test before it even started!

"Breathe," she told the arm, and she held it to the doorknob, but the lock was nothing magical and her spell couldn't open it. She pulled the arm away, the fingers of its hands wriggling like an overturned beetle's legs.

Tears welled in her eyes. Surely if she showed them the list . . . but they wouldn't even talk to her through the door. Would she really have to walk back down the corridor in shame, her bag of paper spells in tow? She had no other spells to Fold . . . nothing that would open this bloody door!

Ceony grit her teeth. No, she wouldn't fail, not after everything she'd been through. She would pass her magician's test. She would be a Folder. She would see that smug look wiped off Mg. Bailey's face when she opened this door if she had to break it down herself—

She paused, studying the door. It had no locks besides the one in the knob. For a moment she was tempted to become a Smelter so she could use an unlocking spell, but she'd left her necklace with Mg. Aviosky. And it would be cheating anyway. Ceony Twill was no cheat.

A simple lock. She could get past a simple lock; her old friend Anise Hatter had done it once at their junior academy when the principal ordered no desserts were to be served at lunch after discovering graffiti on his office window. Anise had broken into the cafeteria, and she and Ceony had eaten two pieces of cake each.

Stepping back, Ceony began dismantling her enchanted arm, which broke the animation spell on its bones. She pulled a thin, rectangular piece of paper from below the wrist and, with a "Stiffen" command, wedged it between the door and the doorjamb. She shimmied the paper down until it hit the knob's latch. Sawing the paper back and forth, she wriggled it under the latch and, with a clipped sigh of relief, pushed the door open.

Bright afternoon sunlight poured through window blinds, illuminating the rectangular room, which measured smaller than Ceony had imagined. It had unpolished wooden floorboards and sand-colored walls, undecorated save for a large, clean chalkboard on the wall with the door. The only furniture in the room was the long table across from the chalkboard, behind which sat Mg. Bailey, Mg. Aviosky, and two men Ceony didn't know.

Mg. Aviosky stood and gestured to the two men. "Miss Twill, this is Magician Reed, the headmaster of the Tagis Praff School for the Magically Inclined. He is a Polymaker."

The man, who was gravely overweight and wore a thick, white mustache, nodded his head. So this was Mg. Aviosky's replacement at the school.

"And this is Magician Praff, nephew of Tagis Praff," she said, gesturing to the second, younger man. He looked to be about Emery's age and had a very straight nose and kind eyes. "He too is a Polymaker, and is attending this testing as a witness."

Ceony offered a small curtsy and a nod, since it didn't seem appropriate to march over and shake their hands. "The pleasure is mine," she said.

Mg. Aviosky sat down and read a paper set before her, pursing her lips. After a few seconds, she said, "A . . . creative way to complete your first task, Miss Twill, but I'm not entirely sure it counts."

Ceony stared at Mg. Bailey and said, "I believe the request was for *something*, not a spell specifically. Correct?" *Fight this and I'll show the others your lack of specifics on the paper you gave me*, she thought. She prayed none of the other tasks had been similarly abridged.

The slightest twinge touched the corner of Mg. Bailey's mouth. The inkling of a smile, perhaps? "Correct," the Folder agreed. "If you'll continue to item number two, Miss Twill, we will proceed."

Ceony nodded and tugged her large bag into the room, letting the door close behind her. She moved to the center of the room, backdropped by the chalkboard, and pulled a paper crane from the top of her pile of spells. *#2. Something that breathes.* The first Folding spell she had ever learned.

She passed that task easily. Her spell for the third item, *Something to tell a tale*, also dated back to her first days as an apprentice. After her visit with Mg. Aviosky two weeks ago, Ceony had returned to the cottage with Emery to collect the children's book *Pip's Daring Escape*. She now read the story in its entirety, and the four magicians across from her watched the ghostly images of a gray mouse dance before them. Mg. Reed seemed especially entertained, which bolstered Ceony's confidence in her solution to item number four: *Something that sticks.*

Ceony laid out four bearing squares on the floor, the same she had used when decorating Mrs. Holloway's living room for her husband's celebration party. While she had been tempted to use the squares to hang a dunce sign on the back of Mg. Bailey's shirt, something as critical as her magician's test required a certain level of politeness. Instead, she used the squares to stick a paper doll of herself to the chalkboard, which also completed task number five: *Something that copies.*

The magicians remained silent save for the occasional "Please continue" or "Go on" from Mg. Bailey, though after the first dozen spells, he merely nodded or gestured with a hand for her to continue. It seemed Mg. Bailey had also determined the test required a certain level of politeness.

On Ceony worked.

She displayed her blind box for item fourteen, *Something to hide the truth,* and a "Conceal" spell for item fifteen, *Something to hide yourself,* to which Mg. Reed commented, "Good show." To Ceony's relief, she did not have to make item twenty-four, *Something to cross a river,* actually cross a river. Mg. Bailey simply stood from his chair, walked over to her Folded boat, and inspected it. A simple "hmm" from his lips indicated it passed inspection, and she moved on.

Despite having her spells premade, Ceony found the time dragging. The room bore no clock, but she checked the windows after every spell to see how the sunlight had moved behind the blinds. She shook out the front of her blouse as she reached for her thirty-seventh spell, *Something to defend against a tramp,* in an attempt to cool her skin. She didn't dare break the silence of her test to request that the magicians open a window.

After encircling her "Enlarge" chain spell around her torso, Ceony retrieved a "Ripple" spell from her tweed bag. The commands "Enlarge" and "Ripple" grew her to ten feet and distorted the room enough that Mg. Praff cried out for Ceony to stop, which she did immediately.

A nod from Mg. Bailey allowed her to bring forth her next spell.

Her forty-fourth spell, the flying starlights, managed to impress the impermeable Mg. Aviosky, whose eyes widened in childlike delight once Mg. Bailey closed the blinds and the starlights began to glow. For item forty-five, *A way to be in two places at once*, Ceony defaulted to her paper doll.

Mg. Bailey frowned and folded his arms. "You cannot use the same spell for two different tasks, Miss Twill."

Ceony's heart missed a beat. Her tongue went dry, and she had to swish it around in her mouth before croaking, "Wh-What?"

The Folder leaned forward. "You cannot use the same spell. You've already showcased the paper doll. If you do not have an alternative solution, I will end the examination."

Taking a deep breath and trying to keep her voice level, Ceony said, "I don't recall that requirement being in the rules, Magician Bailey."

The Folder's face remained unchanged. "It's there, Miss Twill."

"Is it?" Mg. Praff asked. The two, simple words sparked some hope within Ceony. She was so close to finishing. She couldn't flunk now!

Ceony glanced at Mg. Aviosky, meeting her eyes. *If I were a Gaffer, I could be in two places at once*, she thought. She wondered if Mg. Aviosky could read her thoughts, for a knowing smile touched her lips.

It vanished quickly. Mg. Aviosky pulled out a briefcase hidden behind her chair and opened it. She filed through the papers within until she pulled forth a booklet, which she then thumbed through without comment. The silence of the room pressed on Ceony from all sides. She reminisced traveling through the tight, hot valves of Emery's heart. This felt very much the same.

Mg. Aviosky's voice severed the quiet. She read from the booklet: "An apprentice cannot use the same prepared spell for two consecutive tasks. The perpetration of this will terminate the test."

"I'm sorry, Miss Twill," Mg. Bailey said.

Ceony's heart splattered onto the floor.

"Don't be, Magician Bailey," Mg. Aviosky said. "The rule book says 'consecutive.' These two tasks are more than a dozen list numbers apart. Therefore, the paper doll is eligible."

Ceony's eyes widened and her hands flew to her heart. She bit down a loud *Thank you!* that threatened to break her teeth.

Mg. Bailey frowned all the deeper. "You realize that a simple reordering of the list would make the doll unusable, yes?"

"One does not simply 'reorder' the test list, Magician Bailey," Mg. Aviosky said, placing the booklet back in her briefcase. "It has a set order determined by the Supreme Council of Magic. If you truly believe Miss Twill deserves to fail, you'll have to send your request for reversal to them."

Ceony felt a drop of sweat trace a path down her backbone.

The frown engraved itself onto Mg. Bailey's features, but he nodded for Ceony to continue.

Ceony moved through her last spells with renewed energy, sprinting at the end of the marathon in a desperate attempt to reach the finish line before Mg. Bailey could cut the ribbon ahead of her. She demonstrated a vitality chain, the "Shred" spell, the illusion spell she had created of the night sky, even a cardboard box used to keep food from spoiling. For *#53. A means of escape*, she threw down two handfuls of navy-blue concealing confetti. She felt her body warp before it reappeared behind the judging table.

Finally, after what felt like hours, Ceony reached for the final spell in her bag, one that took up barely more space than her fist.

She imagined task number fifty-eight had been meant as the most challenging, one intended to make the apprentice reflect on her years of training and ponder her future years as a magician. *A means of living.* Unspecific, yet inspiring. As a paper magician, she could easily have written an inspiring essay on how Folding had changed her life, how it would shape her career as a magician. She could have orchestrated an army of animated spells, creating a room full of magic-induced life. She could have created a wall-to-wall illusion grander than the junglescape in Mrs. Holloway's mansion, displaying an abundance of wild, perceived life.

But she hadn't.

She'd used the first idea to bloom in her mind upon reading the last task. She'd set it aside at first and pondered on more clever and striking things, but her thoughts always returned to this one, simple spell. She could defend it with pretty words and tear-filled emotions if need be, but with Mg. Aviosky on her panel of magicians, she doubted she'd need to utter a single syllable.

Her fingers wrapped around the paper heart sitting in the corner of the tweed bag. She straightened and held it before her, cradled in both hands, and whispered, "Breathe."

The heart pumped softly in her hands, it's *PUM-Pom-poom* rattling gently against her skin.

A means of living. The greatest spell she had ever crafted.

She said nothing. Even Mg. Aviosky didn't offer an explanation, which made Ceony wonder how far word of Emery's near demise had reached.

Mg. Bailey stared at the beating heart in Ceony's grasp.

And smiled.

CHAPTER 19

"MAGICIAN ERNEST JOHNSON, Siper, District Four."

Ceony's hands sweated beneath her white gloves. She wrung them together as she watched the newly appointed Siper, garbed in a black magician's uniform, rise from two seats to her left and approach the podium on the other end of the stage, where Tagis Praff himself shook his hand and handed him a framed magician's certificate. The audience that filled the Royal Albert Hall applauded, the noise sounding like crashing ocean waves in Ceony's ears. She could feel the stage shake with it.

"Magician John Frederick Cobble, Smelter, District Three."

The words summoned the man sitting beside Ceony, dressed in the light-gray uniform of a metals magician. He left Ceony alone in a row of four chairs.

She felt eyes on her but couldn't see into the audience for the bright Pyre lights lining the stage. She knew where the watchers sat, though, having spied them from behind the red velvet curtains before the ceremony. Her mother, father, sisters, and brother occupied the second row in the middle set of seats. Emery sat beside Mg. Aviosky in the first row in the leftmost seats. She wondered what they thought of her, sitting up here.

"Magician Ceony Maya Twill, Folder, District Fourteen."

Magician. The word expanded inside her, spreading a sugary warmth to her fingers and feet. Her legs, half-numb, managed to pick her up off her chair. Her white skirt fluttered about her ankles, and the silver buttons of her blazer glimmered in the enchanted light. She moved across the stage toward the podium that bore the magician's seal on its face.

Tagis Praff extended his hand. Ceony didn't remember lifting hers to meet it, but suddenly the man's fingers were clasped around hers. In his other hand he held a crisp white certificate, lined with gold leaf and signed in dark ink.

Its printed letters read her name.

Magician. She had finally made it.

The applause sounded louder than before, as though it came from all sides. As though it poured from the ceiling and bubbled up from the floor. Ceony's hand closed on the black frame embellishing her certificate. *Magician Ceony Maya Twill, Folder, District Fourteen.*

She shook Tagis Praff's hand with renewed vigor, blinking tears from her eyes.

A few choice words from Tagis Praff closed the ceremony. The Pyre lights dimmed, and folk began to rise from their seats. Ceony hurried down the stage stairs. Her foot had not firmly touched the carpet before her father's broad arms clasped about her. He swung her in a circle, laughing heartily in her ear.

"That's my girl!" he chortled. "A real magician. A Folder!" He set her down and plopped heavy hands on her shoulders. "Look at her, Rhonda, all grown up and working magic."

Ceony's mother dabbed her eyes with a handkerchief and tugged Ceony from her father's grip, then kissed her on the cheek. "I'm so, so proud of you," she croaked. "You're really making something of yourself."

"She's *made* something," her father corrected.

Ceony grinned until her cheeks hurt and puffed her chest with the praise.

"Ceony!" Margo, Ceony's youngest sibling, called, tugging at the fine white wool of Ceony's skirt. "This means you'll make us a paper house!"

Ceony laughed. "Why would anyone want to live in a paper house?"

Margo crossed her eyebrows, off-put by the question.

"Nice work, sis," Zina said from behind Margo. She clutched a sketchbook to her chest and eyed Emery warily, tracing his person from foot to head. Ceony didn't know what to make of that, but she was relieved Zina had come. "Not that I'm going to *love* trying to live up to this."

"Oh, Zina," Ceony's mother sighed.

"What?" Zina asked. "I'm congratulating her. It's called satire, Mom."

"Can we get cake now?" Marshall, Ceony's brother, asked, his eyes following the lines of people exiting the hall. "You said we'd get cake, right? I'm hungry."

Ceony didn't hear her father's reply; a warm hand on her shoulder drew her attention away from her family and to Emery. He wore a pale button-up shirt and well-ironed slacks instead of his magician's uniform, and had forgone the usual long coat.

He cupped her face, said, "You are magnificent," and kissed her on the forehead. She felt herself flush under the crystal light of his gaze . . . and under the gaze of her parents. She glanced to them, but her mother appeared unsurprised and her father had busied himself with negotiating desserts with Marshall. Zina had already headed for the exit.

Don't worry about what they think anyway, she thought to herself, allowing her smile to fully encompass her mouth. *What any of them think. This is right. This is where I'm meant to be.*

Emery entwined the fingers of one hand with hers and pulled her close so he could whisper in her ear, "No need to be bashful. You're not my apprentice anymore."

Ceony laughed softly, trying to rub pink from her cheeks. "I'm almost disappointed," she murmured back.

Her father refocused on her and said, "All right, Ruffio's Bakery it is, unless you'd like something different?"

Ceony shook her head. "Sounds wonderful." She turned to Emery, hopeful, and said, "Will you come? It can't be *too* crowded."

"I can bear it," he replied, a smile dancing across his lips. He lifted Ceony's knuckles to his mouth and kissed them.

Ceony beamed. From the corner of her vision she spied Mg. Aviosky speaking to an unfamiliar man. The conversation ended and the man walked away, leaving the Gaffer free.

"One moment, please," Ceony said to both Emery and her parents. "I'll meet you in the hallway."

Releasing Emery's hand, Ceony walked toward Mg. Aviosky. As her family shifted toward the exit behind her, she heard Emery say, "Mr. Twill, I have a favor to ask of you—"

"Magician Aviosky!" Ceony called before the glass magician could get away. Mg. Aviosky turned her attention on Ceony, her expression soft but unsure.

Glancing about to be sure they stood alone, Ceony asked, "Have you thought about what I told you? What we should do?"

The Gaffer sighed and removed her glasses from her prominent nose. She rubbed the faint red mark they'd left on the bridge. "It's all I've thought about, Ceony. There are times when I think we should take an oath to never repeat the information, and there are times I think we should offer a multiple-material magics course at Tagis Praff."

Ceony nodded slowly. "What are you thinking now?"

Another sigh. "I may tell Magician Hughes, but I'm still unde-cided. Something like this can't be handled rashly. It could change the fundamentals of magic as we know it—the entire governing structure." She replaced her glasses. "And if the information leaked out to unsanctioned magicians, we could have real problems on our hands. Magic, even easily obtainable as it is, isn't meant to be in the hands of everyone. Imagine what would happen to the crime rate if every John and Jane in this city knew how to break through locks and conjure fireballs with a snap of their fingers. There would be no limits."

"I suppose I shouldn't mention it if I apply for Criminal Affairs, then."

Mg. Aviosky smiled, but it didn't feel genuine. "No, not now. Though I recommend building some experience before you apply for such a position. And I would urge you to also consider the con-sequences."

"What consequences?"

"You are a woman, Miss Twill," Mg. Aviosky pointed out. She glanced toward the farthest exit door, where Ceony's family was stepping out into the hallway. Ceony knew the magician's focus was on Emery. "We are beginning to have more leverage in today's society, especially as magicians. There are dozens of promising career choices for you, but Criminal Affairs is no place for a mother."

That made Ceony pause. "I . . . don't know what you mean."

The Gaffer sniffed. "I am not naïve, Ceony, though I congratu-late you on your modesty. Needless to say I'll be surprised if you're still 'Miss Twill' by Christmas. I merely wanted to present it as something to consider. Decide where you want your life to go before you set it rolling."

Ceony's cheeks tingled at the words, but she realized something. "You never call me by my first name."

Mg. Aviosky smiled. "We're equals now. It seems appropriate. As for the bonding . . . I'll keep in touch to let you know what I decide."

"Thank you."

Mg. Aviosky walked up the aisle.

"Ceony?" asked a familiar voice from behind her.

She turned around and spied Bennet approaching from a nearby aisle.

"Bennet! You came."

"Yeah," he answered, rubbing the back of his neck. He stuffed his other hand in his pocket. "Congratulations. I knew you'd pass."

"Thank you. Send my regards to Magician Bailey, if you would."

"Oh, he's here . . ." Bennet searched the auditorium. Ceony followed his gaze to Mg. Bailey, who stood near the back with his arms folded. He looked a little less sour, at least.

"But you probably need to go," Bennet added. "I'll tell him."

She smiled. "Thank you."

"So . . ." he dropped the hand from his neck. "You and Magician Thane are . . ."

The flush returned, but not strongly. "I . . . yes. That's why Magician Bailey tested me. To avoid favoritism."

"I had wondered."

"Bennet—"

"I'm a bit surprised," he confessed. "I admit I was a little jealous of you when you came to stay with us. You and Magician Thane seemed close. I envied your relationship. But I didn't think you . . ." He shrugged. "I guess I didn't think you were that kind of woman."

Ceony's muscles went rigid. "And *what* kind of woman would that be, Bennet Cooper?"

Bennet shook his head. "I shouldn't have said anything."

"No, you shouldn't have," Ceony retorted. Clasping her framed certificate to her chest, she said, "You'd better take the test soon, before Magician Bailey rubs off on you."

Bennet took a step back as though the words had physically moved him, but Ceony didn't stay to argue. She had only fondness for Bennet, and she didn't want thoughtless words to change that. She'd lost enough friends.

Ceony hurried up the aisle to catch her family. However, upon exiting the auditorium, she found only Emery waiting for her.

He extended his hand. "Shall we?"

She took his hand and let him lead her outside. "We're going to Ruffio's, aren't we?"

"Mm hm," the paper magician replied. "Just in a different buggy."

Ceony smiled—what a wonderful day this was turning out to be!—and reached up with her free hand, running it along the side of Emery's head. "I still can't get used to how short it is. Why did you cut it?"

"So I'd look more gentlemanly."

Ceony snorted, but the mischievous glint in Emery's eyes made her wonder if his statement was, perhaps, not a joke.

Emery didn't call a buggy; he already had one parked outside the hall and just down the street. The driver waited by the engine and opened the door for them when they arrived, and he smiled when he saw Ceony's uniform. *All of England will know I'm a Folder when I wear this*, she thought, leaning against the back of the seat. *No more aprons. I'm legitimate now. This time next year I might even have an apprentice of my own!*

That boggled her mind. Would more Folders be assigned at the end of the school year? Was she even ready to train an apprentice?

"Maybe I'll start volunteering at the school," Ceony said. "Tagis Praff, I mean. Perhaps I can do a guest lecture or become a teaching assistant. There aren't any Folders employed there, and more students might sign up for Folding if they understood it better."

"Not a bad idea," Emery said with a smile. "I'd comment on the commute, but I suppose your glassiness would get you there quickly."

She nodded. "I'll order a Gaffer's mirror to minimize any accidents."

"Only now does she think about minimizing accidents," Emery murmured. He laughed. "You are an enigma, Ceony. To think how dull my life would have been over the last two years had I not been forced to tutor you . . ."

"*You*, forced?" Ceony scoffed. "Pardon me, Magician Thane, but I wanted to be a Smelter."

"You want to be everything," he countered.

"Well, if the option exists . . ." She grinned and turned in her seat, watching the late-afternoon sunlight whip through the buggy windows, dancing about Emery like fairies.

"Hmm?" he asked.

She exhaled slowly through her nose. "Just thinking."

"About how much you adore me?"

"About how skinny you are," she teased. "I leave for three weeks and you can't even feed yourself properly."

"I'll amend it soon enough."

Ceony began to speak, but spotted the post office outside Emery's window. She turned about and looked out her own.

"We missed the turn," she said. "Ruffio's is down Steel Drive."

"Oh, we're not going to Ruffio's just yet," he explained. "We have a quick stop to make first. Your family knows."

"I take it this is the 'favor' you asked my father about?"

"Mm."

Ceony relaxed in her seat and pulled off her white gloves as she watched buildings and people zoom past her window. The stop was apparently not at all close to the bakery where she was to meet her family—the buggy continued down the road, pulling farther and farther away from Steel Drive. The buildings outside her window grew less commercial and shrank in size until they turned to houses, and then the spaces between houses stretched wider and wider. The buggy eventually turned off the paved street and took a narrow dirt road that cut between two grassy knolls.

She turned back to Emery. "Where are we going?"

Rather than meeting her eyes, Emery looked ahead, watching the scenery unfurl through the windshield. "You'll recognize it."

Ceony, lip pinched between her teeth, twisted back for her window and leaned closer to it, fingers resting on the buggy door. Wind tousled her hair, but the clip holding it back remained firm.

The knolls grew in number as the buggy continued onward. Their grassy faces became wilder, more unkempt, and some began to sport trees. Wildflowers in shades of fuchsia, marigold, and amethyst coated an especially large hill just off the bumpy road, and the tips of grass were beginning to turn golden under the late-spring sun.

The buggy slowed, and Ceony stared at that flowery hill. She *did* recognize it, though she had never stepped foot on it, not in reality. No—this was a place cherished in Emery's heart, one she had seen embedded in his hopes. One she had seen in the vision given to her by a fortuity box two years ago.

Her heart raced. It hammered against her ribs and the base of her throat. A cool sensation like falling water cascaded over her. She didn't even notice that Emery had left the buggy until he came around to her door and opened it.

He took her hand. Leaving her framed certificate on the seat, Ceony stepped out of the buggy and followed Emery wordlessly up the hillside. Her heart pounded harder with each step, and not because of the exercise.

They reached the top of the hill, upon which grew a familiar maroon-leafed plum tree, its fruit only days from being ripe.

Emery paused, studying the plum tree and the view before turning to Ceony, who could read everything in his vivid, bright eyes. Her pulse beat with knowing.

She squeezed Emery's hand and he leaned in to kiss her. A breeze laden with the scent of wildflowers danced around them.

He pulled back. Rested his forehead against hers. Looked into her eyes.

"I love you," she whispered.

His eyes smiled. "I believe I'm supposed to do the talking, Miss Twill."

She gazed at him, silent.

He released her hand and ran his fingertips along the sides of her neck, their noses a breath apart. "You are the kind of woman who makes me believe in God, Ceony," he murmured. "I don't know how else it could be possible to find you. For heaven's sake, you even delivered yourself to my front door."

She smiled. Her heartbeat steadied.

"How many men can honestly say a woman has walked their heart?" he asked. "But I can. And if you'll have me, I'd like you to stay there."

Tears welled in Ceony's eyes. She didn't blink them away.

Emery reached into his pocket and pulled from it a loop of white and violet paper about the width of his fist, made of dozens of tiny, crisscrossing links. Not a spell, just something crafted to be beautiful. From it hung a gold ring that glimmered rose in the sunlight. A diamond carved in the shape of a raindrop sat at its center, flanked on either side by a small emerald.

The paper magician slipped the ring off the paper loop and turned it in his hands. Dropping to one knee, he said, "Ceony Maya Twill, will you marry me?"

THE END

AN EXCERPT FROM
CHARLIE N. HOLMBERG'S

FOLLOWED BY FROST

Editor's Note: This is an uncorrected excerpt and may not reflect the final book.

PROLOGUE

I HAVE KNOWN COLD.

I have known the cold that freezes to the bones, to the spirit itself. The cold that stills the heart and crystallizes the blood. The kind of cold that even fire fears, that can turn a woman to glass.

I have seen Death.

The cold lured him to me. I saw him near my home, his dark hair rippling over one shoulder like thick forest smoke as he stooped over the bed of the quarryman's only son. I saw his amber eyes as he tilted the rim of his wide-brimmed hat to greet me. I saw him kneel in the snow before me with his arms wide and heard him whisper, *Come with me.*

I have known cold, the chills with which even the deepest winters cannot compare. I have lived it, breathed it, and lost by it. I have known cold, for it dwelled in the deepest hollows of my soul.

And the day I broke Mordan's heart, it devoured me.

CHAPTER 1

THE FIRST BITE OF HONEY taffy melted in my mouth. I savored its sweetness, spiced lightly with cinnamon imported from the Southlands beyond Zareed—strange, savage lands with strange people and stranger customs, but nothing in the Northlands could compare to their intense, exotic spices. Merchants only delivered the candies in the early spring, and their first shipment had arrived that morning. Together, Ashlen and I had bought nearly half a case. My satchel bulged with paper-wrapped taffies to the point where I had to switch the strap from shoulder to shoulder every quarter mile, the bag weighed on me so.

"My pa will be so angry if he finds out!" Ashlen laughed, covering her mouth to hide half-chewed taffy. Her plain, mouse-brown hair bobbed about her shoulders as she spoke. "I'm supposed to be saving for that writing desk."

"This is a once, maybe twice-a-year opportunity," I insisted, resting my hand on the satchel. "We could hardly let it pass us by." I didn't tell her that I had more than enough in my allowance to cover her share. If Ashlen needed a writing desk, her father could put in more hours at the mill.

Ashlen unwrapped another candy. "I could die eating these."

I poked her in the stomach. "And you would die fat, too!"

We laughed, and I hooked my arm through hers as we followed the dirt path ahead of us. It wound from the mercantile on the west edge of Euwan, past the mill and my father's turnery, clear to Heaven's Tear—the great, crystal lake that hugged the town's east side, and the only thing that put us on Iyoden's map.

My world was so small, then. Euwan was an ordinary town full of ordinary people, and I believed myself an oyster pearl among them. But I was about to spark a chain of events that would shatter the perfectly ordinary shell I lived in—events that would undoubtedly change my life, in its entirety, forever.

My father's turnery came into view, the tar between its shingles glimmering in the afternoon sun. At two stories, it was the second largest building in Euwan, though still the most impressive, in my opinion. The sounds of saws and sandpaper echoed from beyond its door, left open to encourage a breeze. My father had been a wainwright for some twenty years, and his wagons were the sturdiest and most reliable that could be found anywhere within two days' distance, and likely even farther. For a moment I considered saying hello, but spying my father's single employee outside, I instantly thought better of it.

Mordan was bent over a barrel of water, washing sawdust from his face and hands. Unlike most, Mordan hadn't been raised in Euwan—he had merely walked in during fall harvest, on foot, carrying a filthy cloth bag of his immediate necessities. His sudden appearance had been the talk of the town for weeks, making him something of an outcast. Much to my dismay, my father was a charitable sort, and he hadn't hesitated to hire the newcomer. The community mostly accepted him after that.

Mordan, twenty-five years in age, was a slender man, though broad in the shoulders, with sandy hair that wavered somewhere between chestnut and wheat. He had a narrow, almost feminine face, with a long nose and pale blue eyes. I didn't notice much about him beyond that. At that time I only noticed that he existed and that he was a problem. I quickly stepped to Ashlen's other side, using her body as a shield.

"What?" she asked.

"Shh! Talk to me," I said, quickening my pace. I kept my head down, letting my blonde hair act as a curtain between myself and the turnery. It was natural for a man to take an interest in his employer's family, perhaps, but Mordan's interest in me had grown more ardent over the last year, to the point where I could hardly stand on the same side of town as him without some attempt at conversation on his part. Even my blatant regard for other boys while in his presence—whether real or feigned—hadn't discouraged him.

I thought I had escaped unseen when he called out my name, his chin still dripping with water. "Smitha!"

My stomach soured. I pretended not to hear and jerked Ashlen forward when she started to turn her head, but Mordan persisted in his calls. Begrudgingly I slowed my walk and glanced back at him, but I didn't offer a smile.

He wiped himself with a towel, which he tucked into the back pocket of his slacks, and jogged toward us.

"I'm surprised to see you out so late," he said, nodding to Ashlen. "I thought school ended at the fifteenth hour."

"Yes, but lessons cease at age sixteen," I said. Only a dunce wouldn't know that. "I finished last year. I only go now to pursue my personal endeavors and to tutor Ashlen." My personal endeavors included theatre and the study of language, the latter of which I found fascinating, especially older tongues. I planned to use my knowledge to become a playwright, translating ancient tales and peculiar Southlander fables into performances that would charm the most elite of audiences. My tutoring of Ashlen was more a chance for chatter and games than actual studying, but so long as she pulled passing grades, none would be the wiser.

"Of course," Mordan nodded with a smile. "You're at that age, now."

There was a glint in his eye that made me recoil. *That* age? I struggled to mask my reaction. Surely he didn't mean engagement. As far as Mordan was concerned, I would never be *that* age.

Glancing nervously at Ashlen, Mordan continued, "I've been meaning to talk—"

"In fact," I blurted out, "Ashlen is being tested on geography tomorrow morning, and I promised I'd help her study before dinner. Her family eats especially early, so if you'll excuse us . . ."

Ashlen had a dumbfounded look on her face, but I tugged her along before she could question me in front of him. "Good evening to you," I called. Mordan quickly returned the sentiment, and he may have even waved, but I didn't look back over my shoulder until the next bend in the road hid the turnery from sight.

"You're loony!" Ashlen exclaimed, pulling her arm free from mine. A grin spread on her face before her mouth formed a large O. "Goodness, Smitha, don't tell me Mordan is *still* at it."

"Absurd, isn't it?" I rolled my eyes and switched my candy-laden bag to my other shoulder. "He has to be the most stubborn man I've ever met."

"Maybe you should give him a chance, if he's trying so hard."

"Absolutely not. He's too ridiculous."

She merely shrugged. "People can change for those they care about."

"Ha!" I snorted. "People don't change; they are what they are. Did you know he actually pressed the first blooms of spring and left them on my doorstep? He would have given them to me in person, but I didn't answer the door when I saw it was him. No one else was home."

"How do you know they were the first blooms?"

"Because he *told* me. In a *poem*. And Ashlen, the man is as slow as he looks. It was the most wretched thing I've ever read in my life, and that includes Mrs. Thornes' lecture notes on the water cycle!"

"Oh, Smitha," she said, touching her lips. "How harsh. He seems nice enough."

"But not so nice to *look* at," I quipped before glancing at the sun. "I'd best head home before mother throws a fit. I'll see you tomorrow. Don't eat all your candies tonight; I won't share mine!"

Ashlen stuck out her tongue at me and trotted off the road into the wild grass. Her home lay over the hill, and that was the fastest way to reach it.

She grinned back at me as she went and waved a hand, her fingers fluttering the words *"Don't get fat"* over her shoulder. The signs were part of the hand talk I had invented at fourteen, when I first learned of a silent language that had once been spoken in the Aluna Islands in the far north, beyond the lands where wizards were said to dwell. That would not be the last time Ashlen spoke to me in our secret signs, but it would be the last time she looked at me with any semblance of a smile.

My family lived in a modest home, though large by Euwan standards. My little sister Marrine and I had our own bedrooms. After bidding Ashlen farewell, I retired to my room and stashed my share of the honey taffies in the back of my bottom dresser drawer, where I hoped Marrine wouldn't find them if she came snooping, which she often did. My sister begged for punishment, and I had a variety of penalties waiting for her if she crossed me.

A small oval mirror sat atop my dresser, and I studied myself in it, appreciating the rosiness my walk had put in my cheeks. Retrieving my boar-bristle hair brush, I ran it through my waist-long hair several times from root to tip. I knew I was pretty, with a heart-shaped face free of blemishes, small nose, and big green eyes. The doctor himself had told me they were big, and I had learned that batting them just so often helped persuade the boys—and often grown men—in town to see things my way.

At seventy-six of one hundred strokes I heard my mother's voice in the hallway.

"Smitha! Could you fetch some firewood?"

I groaned in my throat. I wasn't the one who had diminished the supply, and the last thing I wanted to do was dirty my dress gathering firewood. I cringe to remember my behavior then, but it is part of the story, and so I will tell it honestly.

Hearing Mother's steps, I set down my brush and crouched against the side of my dresser. The door opened. I held my breath. Mother sighed before closing it and retreating.

I smiled to myself and picked up my hairbrush to finish my one hundred strokes. After taking a moment to admire my reflection, I braided my hair loosely over my shoulder, savored one more honey taffy, and quietly stepped into the hall.

My mother didn't notice me until I reached our kitchen, large given that we were a family of only four. My mother, still in good years, spooned drippings over the large breast of a pheasant in the oven. It was from her that I got my blonde hair, though I hoped my hips wouldn't grow so wide. Across the room, a pot boiled on the hearth. Someone else had fetched the firewood, I noticed.

Straightening, Mother wiped her forehead and glanced at me. "I called for you."

"Oh," I said, fingering my braid, "I was at the latrine. Sorry."

Mother rolled her eyes and turned to a bowl of cornbread batter on the counter. "Well, you're here now, so would you wash and butter that pan for me?" She jerked her head toward a square pan resting beside the washbasin.

Frowning, and knowing I didn't have an excuse, I dragged my feet to the ice box for the butter.

After the cornbread baked, the pheasant browned, and I had grudgingly mashed the potatoes from the cook pot, I stepped out of the kitchen to cool off. I had not yet reached my room when I heard the front door open and my father exclaim, "Smells good! Room for one more?"

"Always." I could hear my mother's smile. "It's good to see you, Mordan. How was work?"

Cursing to myself, I hurried down the hall, almost crashing into Marrine. With her plain brown hair pulled into a messy ponytail, her narrow-set eyes, and a cleft to her chin, I was obviously the better looking sister, so much so that a stranger would never guess that Marrine and I were related.

"Where are you going?" she asked. "Is Pa home?"

"Shh!" I hissed at her, but rather than explain, I ducked into my room and shut the door. I rushed to my window and opened the pane, wincing at how boldly it creaked. Ashlen would be more than happy to have me for dinner, and with an extra mouth in the kitchen, surely my parents wouldn't miss me.

This was not the first time Mordan had come to eat, of course, but I had a bad feeling about it. He was getting bolder in his attentions. Besides, the best way to tell a man he had less chance with you than a fair hog was to ignore him so completely that even *he* forgot he existed.

Balling my skirt between my legs, I lifted myself over the sill and dropped a few feet to the ground below. I had only made it halfway across the yard when I heard my name called out from behind me. Mordan's voice raked over my bones like the teeth of a dull plow.

He walked toward me, waving a hand. Why had he stepped outside *now*? Perhaps he needed to use the latrine, or he might have spied me in my escape. Regardless, I had been caught, and no amount of talking would see me to Ashlen's house now without sure embarrassment.

I released my hair. "Oh, Mordan, I didn't notice you."

He stopped about four paces ahead of me. "Your father graciously invited me over to dinner."

"Is it time already?"

He nodded, then suddenly became bashful, staring at the ground and slouching in the shoulders. "I've actually been meaning to talk to you, but I haven't gotten the chance."

My belly clenched. "Oh?"

"But . . ." he hesitated, scanning the yard. "Not here. And I've got a delivery in about an hour . . . Smitha, would you mind meeting me? The dock, around sunset?"

His eyes, hopeful as a child's, finally found mine.

At that moment I truly appreciated my study of theatre, for I know I masked my horror perfectly. For Mordan to want to speak to me alone—and at so intimate a spot!—could only mean one thing: his interest in me had come to a head, and no amount of feigned ignorance would dissuade him.

Mordan wanted to marry me. I almost retched on his shoes at the prospect.

"All right," I lied, and a mixture of relief and warmth spread over his delicate features.

Before he could say more, I touched his arm and added, "We'd best hurry, or dinner will be served cold!"

I walked past him, but he caught up quickly, staying by my side until we sat at the table, where I had the forethought to wedge Marrine between us. I remained silent as my father told our family, in great detail, of the work he had done that day. While not one for exaggeration, my father always told every last corner of a story, explaining even mundane things so accurately that I often felt I wore his eyes. Tonight, though, halfway through his tale of broken spokes, he interrupted himself for gossip—something for which he rarely spared a moment's thought.

"Magler said there's a fire up north, near Trent," he said, carefully wiping gravy from his lips before it could drizzle into his thick, brown beard. "Already burned through two silos and a horse run."

"A fire?" asked Mother. "It's too early in the year for that. Did they have a dry winter?"

"Rumor says it was the craft."

That interested me. "Wizards? Really?"

"Chard, Smitha, I'll not take that talk in here," Mother said.

Let me take a moment to say that wizards were unseen in these parts, and supposedly rare even in the unclaimed lands far north, where they trained in magicks beyond even my imagination, and none of them for good. A traveling bard once whispered that they have an academy there, though to this day I'm not sure where. I certainly never thought I'd one day search for it, myself.

Mordan's eyes left me to meet my father's. "What's the rumor?"

"Some political war or some such, which led to two of them fighting one another. Perhaps even a chase. I have a hard time believing any man could throw fire, but that's what Magler claimed. He heard it from a foods merchant passing by this morning."

Marrine, mouth half full of cornbread, said, "I'd like to meet a wizard."

Mordan smiled. "They can be a dangerous sort. Tales often fantasize them, for better or for worse."

"So long as they don't come down here," Mother said, roughly heaping a second helping of potatoes onto her plate, spoon clinking against the china. I hoped she wouldn't butter them. Mother gained weight in the most unsightly of places. "Mordan, how is your sister? I recall you mentioning her a little while ago."

Mordan's blue eyes glanced back to me, as they had already done several times during the meal, smiling even when his mouth was not. I did not smile back. Returning his focus to Mother, he described a sister of his who lived somewhere in the west, but I paid little attention to what he said. Instead I wolfed down my food and excused myself to my room. If either parent disapproved, they did not voice it in front of a guest.

Inside my little sanctuary, I stretched out on my bed and selected one of three books I had borrowed from Mrs. Thornes, my teacher, which she had borrowed from a scholar in a neighboring village. To me old tongues seemed like secrets—secrets very few people in the world knew, let alone knew well. The book in my hands was written in Hraric, the language of Zareed and the Southlands, where I believed the sun never set, men built their homes on heaps of golden sand, and children ran about naked to escape the heat—with their parents hardly clothed more than that. I had studied some Hraric two years ago. I didn't consider myself fluent, but as I browsed through this particular book of plays, I could understand the main points of the stories. Southlander tales were far darker and more grotesque than the ones we studied in school, and I soon found myself so absorbed that I hardly heard the scooting of chairs in the kitchen and Mordan's good-byes as he went to complete his deliveries. However, I did take special note of the time, and as the sun sank lower and lower in the sky, casting violet and carmine light over Euwan, I smiled smartly to myself, imagining Mordan standing alone on that dock long into the night, his only company the proposal I would never allow him to utter.

While I wish I could say otherwise, my conscience did not bother me that night, and I had no trouble sleeping. Had I known the consequence of my actions, I would never have closed my eyes. I slept late, as there were no requests upon my responsibility on sixth-days. I woke to bright morning sun, dressed, and brushed one hundred strokes into my hair before deciding I ought to have a bath. Spying Marrine in the front room, I asked her to fill the tub for me.

She looked up from her sketch paper and frowned. "No!"

"Why not?"

"I don't want to carry the water."

"I'll give you a taffy. Honey taffy, with cinnamon."

She considered this for a moment, but ultimately shook her head and returned to refining her mediocre talents as an artist. With a sigh I stepped outside into the warming spring air and trudged to the barn to retrieve the washbasin myself. On the far end of the barn where we took our baths, there was an empty stall, which was mostly free of horse-smell. Despite my best efforts, I could not convince my father to let me bathe in my room, so it was an inconvenience I had learned to endure.

I set the tub in the stall and retrieved the pail for carrying water. As I turned to exit the barn, I shrieked and dropped the bucket, my heart lodging in the base of my throat. Mordan watched me from the open door. I had hoped his shame would keep him at bay for at least a month. Why couldn't he tuck his tail like any other dog and leave me be?

"Mordan!" I exclaimed, seizing the pail from the hay-littered floor. I gritted my teeth to still my face. "What are you doing here? And with me about to bathe!"

"I apologize," he said, somewhat genuinely, but there was an unusual hardness to his eyes and his voice. "I need to speak with you."

"I'm a little—"

"Please," he said, firm.

I let out a loud sigh for his benefit, letting him know my displeasure at his interruption, but I hung up the pail and followed him out into the yard. I folded my arms tightly to show my disapproval, all while hiding my surprise that he had come to see me so soon after my blatant disregard for him and his intentions. He had not been the first man I had left waiting for me—I suppose it gave me a sense of power, even amusement, to push would-be lovers about as though they were nothing more than checkers on a board. But Mordan *was* the first who had dared confront me afterward. Still, his backbone shocked me.

He didn't stop in the yard, but rather led me across a back road and into the sparse willow-wacks behind my house, on the other side of which sat the Hutches' home. He stopped somewhere in the center, where there were enough trees that I couldn't quite see my house or the Hutches'.

He eyed me sternly, though a glint of hope still lingered in his gaze. "I waited for you at the dock until midnight, Smitha," he said. "What happened?"

I kept my arms firmly folded. I preferred subtlety when breaking people, but if this was what it took to sever whatever obligation Mordan thought I had to him, then so be it. "Nothing happened," I said. "I didn't want to go."

He jerked back, a wounded animal, but then his expression darkened. "Then why agree? I don't understand. I had—"

"You're dense as unbaked bread, Mordan!" I exclaimed, flinging my hands into the air. "Do you think me stupid enough not to read your intentions? Not to notice that pathetic way you look at me when you think my back is turned?"

His eyes widened, and his face flushed, though from anger or embarrassment, I couldn't be sure.

"I don't know if my father has given you the wrong impression," I continued, the words spilling from my lips, "but I do not give you the slightest thought."

Mordan turned from red to white, and his eyebrows shifted in such a way that he resembled a starving hound. I should have left it at that, but my knack for the dramatic and my fury at the situation fueled me.

"Surely a toad could hold my interest longer, and be more pleasant to look at!" My cheeks burned. "We live on different levels of life, Mordan Alteraz, mine far higher than yours. The sooner you realize that, the better off you will be. I do not care one ounce for you, and I never will. *That* is why I didn't go to the dock, and why no sensible woman ever would!"

I found myself oddly breathless. Mordan had gone to stone before me, and I admit that a twinge of fear vibrated through me, rather than the sense of sweet victory I had expected. Never had someone looked at me so grimly.

He laughed—no, growled. The noise that escaped his lips sounded more animal than human. He stepped forward, and I stepped back, my back hitting the trunk of a green-needle pine.

"And to think I felt anything for a woman like you," he whispered, his face contorting into a snarl. "How blind I have been. Your heart is ice."

I opened my mouth for a retort, but his hand came down hard on the trunk beside my head. I winced. He leaned in close, a malicious smile on his face.

"If only you knew who I was," he said, even quieter now. Gooseflesh rose unbidden on my arms. "Now I can see the soul that lies hidden behind your beauty. You are a horrid, selfish woman, Smitha."

I slapped him hard across his cheek, putting my full weight into the blow. It turned his head, but his hand did not budge from its place on the tree beside me.

He licked his lips, smearing blood along the corner of his mouth. Straightening, he studied me up and down, his expression covered in shadow.

"I came here to get away from it, to leave it all behind," he growled. "But I have enough left for you."

"Enough *wha*—" I asked, but his other hand came down on my throat, cutting off my last word. I clung to his wrist and dug my nails into his skin, but he didn't so much as flinch. He stared hard into my eyes, and my fear ignited so abruptly I felt I would turn to ash in his hold.

"*Vladanium curso, en nadia tren'al,*" he murmured. "I curse you, Smitha Ronson, to be as cold as your heart."

His fingers turned to ice around my neck, and I shivered as the cold traced its way down my skin and beneath my clothes, branching out to my arms and legs, my fingers and the tip of each toe. It rushed up my neck and over my head. The chill gushed into my mouth and nostrils, washed down my throat, and crept into my stomach and bowels. It opened my insides like a newly sharpened knife, cutting down to my very bones.

"May winter follow you wherever you go," he said, "and with the cold, death."

Mordan did not move, but some force punched me, and my entire body caved in on itself. The breath left my lungs, and a chill colder than any I had ever experienced filled my core and shot through my veins. My arms and legs went rigid, and every hair on my body stood on end. My very heart slowed. The sun vanished from my face, hidden by a thick, white sheet of clouds. A bitter wind blew over me, tousling my hair.

Mordan released me with a sneer and vanished, the air behind him swallowing him whole.

Charlie N. Holmberg's FOLLOWED BY FROST
is available Fall 2015 from 47North.

ACKNOWLEDGMENTS

Dear God/the Big Man/Heavenly Father/Creator of All:

Seriously, this has been awesome. I am utterly floored that I've been able to make it to a third book, that people are reading this third book (though likely skipping the acknowledgments), and that the road hasn't ended yet. I can never thank You enough for the outpouring of blessings I've received.

I should let You know that my alpha readers did a great job in helping me get this story in shape, namely Andrew, Hayley, Laura, and Juliana. On the other side of the fence, as always, are Marlene, Jason, Angela, and the 47North team. Slip them a little something special if You get a chance, please.

Thank You so much for my sweet baby girl, whose birth somehow got me to finish this book faster.

Thank You for my dear husband, who continues to read all my crappy writing and manages not to entirely glaze over when I need help brainstorming.

Really, You've been great. Not that I expected You not to be. Just . . . thanks. A lot.

Best wishes,
Charlie N. Holmberg

ABOUT THE AUTHOR

Homegrown in Salt Lake City, Charlie N. Holmberg was raised a Trekkie with three sisters who also have boy names. She's a proud BYU alumna, plays the ukulele, and owns too many pairs of glasses. Charlie currently resides in Utah with her family.